FATED SOULS

SHADOW CITY: DEMON WOLF

JEN L. GREY

CHAPTER ONE

THE ANGEL'S arms were wrapped around my waist, his hold ironclad. The night sky held a chill of early September, but that could've been from my nerves. My chest was tight, and I could barely breathe as fear roiled inside me.

His tawny brown wings flapped, raising us higher than the house's roof.

Cyrus's howl promised vengeance. *Annie, I'm coming,* he vowed through our mate bond. *We won't get separated again.*

In the three weeks since Cyrus and I had completed our fated mate bond, we'd been attacked nonstop. A few days ago, we'd rescued Cyrus and four other wolf shifters from the demon wolf pack. My entire life, I'd been hidden from the supernatural world and my wolf because the demon wolf pack alpha had promised me to an actual demon. When my wolf began breaking through the spell

Eliza had placed on me—because I'd found my fated mate, Cyrus—the demon wolves were able to locate me. They'd taken Cyrus and several other wolf shifters to force me to go *home*, but what the pack failed to understand was that Cyrus and the silver wolves were my true home.

My throat dried, and as the mossy-green-eyed angel smirked at me, my blood boiled.

The higher he took me, the harder it would be for me to get away. My wolf surged forward, and I let her take over my instincts. She was my best bet to get out of this situation.

I bit the angel's shoulder, tasting the cotton of his shirt, and his daisy scent filled my nose. Keeping my teeth clenched, I reached up and fisted his ginger-blond hair, then yanked as hard as possible.

He hissed and jerked away. "Quit it."

Yeah, like I would listen to him. My jaw clenched harder, and pain seared through my muscles.

My brown hair blew into my eyes, so I closed them. I didn't need anything distracting me from determining a way out of this.

"I said *quit it*," he rasped. He placed a hand against my forehead and pushed my head back.

The only way I'd move was if I took a chunk of his skin with me.

The sound of flapping wings came from behind us, and my lungs froze. *There's another angel*, I linked to the entire pack. From my vantage point, I couldn't tell if it was friend or foe.

Rosemary left shortly after us. I called her, and she's coming to help, Sterlyn replied. *Alex and Ronnie are with Griffin and me, and we're about to pull into the pack neighborhood. Killian and some of his pack are coming, too.*

I should've known that my sister, Ronnie, and her vampire king husband, Alex, would be with Griffin and Sterlyn. Our friends had become a family, some bonded by blood, others by friendship. Sterlyn was Cyrus's twin and the alpha of the silver wolf pack.

A rose scent swirled around me, confirming the angel behind us was Rosemary. She said, "Ingram, put her down."

The angel growled and pushed my head harder. My jaw screamed, and I couldn't hold on any longer. My head snapped back, and I yanked harder on his hair.

"Rosemary, this doesn't concern you," he replied as Cyrus snarled below us.

Ingram grabbed my hands, which were still clinging to his hair, and squeezed. Pressure exploded, and my grip gave out. I glanced down at my mate, who was in his wolf form. The two bear shifters who had handed me off to Ingram lay dead on the back porch, their throats ripped out.

Cyrus leaped, trying to reach us. His silver fur shone in the moonlight, and his silver eyes glowed as brightly as the moon. Blood covered his snout.

Ingram had us hovering ten feet above the roof, too high for Cyrus to catch.

"Like hell it doesn't," she snapped. "She's one of my

best friends. I won't tell you again. Put her down, or be prepared to fight me."

"Don't you find it odd that your best friends are shifters, vampires, or have demon ties?" he spat. His ivory skin looked sinister in the moonlight. "You weren't partial to other supernatural races until I discarded you."

Her laughter held an edge. "Is that the story you tell yourself? Because if memory serves me right, I ended things because you were subpar in bed."

His chest heaved, and his nostrils flared.

Something slammed into us, and we dropped toward the backyard.

My stomach jumped into my throat, and when I opened my eyes, I almost peed myself. We were spiraling toward the tree line that separated our backyard from the woods. The tall cypresses, redbuds, and oak trees rushed toward us, eager to greet us.

Chad's golden-wheat hair caught my eye. He reached Cyrus on the back porch of the one-story house we called home and lifted a gun at the angel, squinting his smoky topaz eyes to aim. He'd been on his way to help us when the four bear shifters had dragged me through the kitchen and out of the house while another five had attacked Cyrus in the living room, preventing him from reaching me.

Don't shoot, Cyrus commanded, but it was too late.

Gunfire exploded, and Ingram flapped his wings, spinning us continuously. The world blurred, and my stomach roiled. I couldn't make sense of anything; it was like I was in a black hole. Pressure built in my ears, and I gagged.

Just when I couldn't take it any longer, Ingram jerked us upright and jolted toward the clouds.

"No more shooting," Rosemary commanded, and flapped hard, chasing us.

The world continued to spin, and the pizza Cyrus and I had eaten moments before the five Suburbans full of men had arrived to attack us threatened to expel itself. I was not made for the air and preferred my feet and paws firmly on the ground.

The arm around my waist loosened, and I wrapped my arms and legs around Ingram's body, gluing myself to him. Moments ago, I'd bitten him to get him to release his hold, but I was way past that point. If he dropped me, I would splatter on the grass. Even though I didn't want to be taken captive, I wanted to live.

Black wings flashed beside me, and Rosemary punched the asswipe in the nose. Her long, straight mahogany hair snapped from the movement, and her piercing stardust-purple eyes tightened. In the moonlight, her fair skin glowed just like Sterlyn's. Her movements were graceful, as if she'd been practicing the punch like a dance.

His head jerked backward, and his hold on me loosened. Warm liquid hit my chest as a metallic stench assaulted me. I didn't have to look to know it was blood.

I clung tighter to him, afraid that he'd release me if Rosemary punched him again. I both wanted and dreaded her doing that very thing.

"Let her go," Rosemary commanded.

"Fine." He released his hold.

My grasp on his body was tight, and I didn't fall.

"There." He snickered. "I let her go."

Rosemary's hands touched my waist, and I let go of him. As she was securing me, Ingram kicked her in the face. She flipped backward, and I fell through her hands. My shriek would be embarrassing later if I lived.

When I was little, I'd always wanted to go skydiving. Now I had no desire, yet here I was.

Eliza had always told me to be careful what I wished for.

I'd never truly understood the meaning of those words until that moment as I plummeted to my death. I spread out my arms and legs, hoping I could channel a flying squirrel and somehow control the speed. My strategy didn't change my rate of acceleration.

The grass was getting closer, and my wolf howled in my head.

Cyrus ran underneath me and linked, *I'll catch you.*

"Move!" I yelled, not bothering to use our mate connection. He was a huge-ass wolf, almost the size of a horse since the moon was three quarters full, but I had velocity working against me. Yet, he wasn't as large as he would be when the moon was full. *I don't want to hurt you.*

I closed my eyes, not wanting to see my end. I could only hope that if I didn't survive, I'd die on impact. *I love you, Cyrus.*

My body tensed, and my chest burned as I braced for

the pain, but then strong arms wrapped around me, and my fall stopped.

"I've got you," Rosemary gritted out, her hands digging into my sides hard enough to bruise.

Oh, thank God. I opened my eyes to find myself only inches away from landing on Cyrus. I linked, *You dumbass. I could've killed you.*

But you would've survived, and that's all that matters. His irises matched granite as I stared into them.

Rosemary had set my feet on the grass and moved several yards away when Ingram slammed into her. She hit the ground, sending grass and dirt exploding everywhere, the sound deafening.

"Rosemary!" I screamed and charged toward her. No! This couldn't be happening.

Dirt burned my eyes as I tried to reach my friend, Cyrus and Chad flanking me.

Be ready to shoot Ingram, Cyrus linked to Chad.

The dust settled, and the two angels came into view. Ingram straddled Rosemary's back, pinning her to the ground. He had his arms around her neck, strangling her.

Rosemary bucked like a bronco.

"I'll let you up if you calm your fine ass down," Ingram sneered, and continued to choke the angel.

Oh, hell, no. I snatched the gun from Chad, since the prick wasn't using it, and aimed at the angel's chest. This twatwaffle was going *down*. But when I fired, Ingram's wings surrounded his body, and the bullet bounced off the feathers like they were a shield.

Of course it did. Nothing about this world or super-naturals surprised me anymore.

Rosemary jumped to her feet, and Ingram fell on his back. As his wings pulled in, she spun around and kicked him in the stomach. He lurched up, then groaned and went back down.

She flashed up to his head and kicked at his face, but he caught her foot.

I'm going to help her. Cyrus sped toward the angel.

Ingram jerked Rosemary's foot upward, but she flapped her wings, countering the movement. She lifted into the sky as Cyrus lunged toward Ingram. The angel punched Cyrus in the snout, and my mate flipped back-ward and landed with a *thud*.

I grabbed the gun, tired of the drama, but I didn't want to risk injuring Cyrus. I put the safety on and thrust the gun into my waistband, determined to kick Ingram's ass with my bare hands. *Chad, let's help Cyrus.*

Howls filled the air as paws padded toward us.

We're on our way, Sterlyn linked. *The Suburbans are leaving.*

Someone needs to follow the shifters to see if they moved locations, Cyrus instructed as his pain flowed into me. He got back on all four legs and shook out his coat.

Some of the tightness in my chest vanished.

Chad reached the enemy angel and lifted his foot to kick him in the stomach. As with Rosemary, Ingram caught his foot, then punched Chad in the jaw. My stomach dropped at the *crack* of Chad's bones breaking.

This kept getting worse.

As I reached Ingram, Rosemary appeared in front of me, shielding me from him. She told him, "You've pissed me off now," and tried to punch him, but Ingram blocked it.

When he countered her move and struck, she kneed him in the stomach. He groaned and leaned over to stop her next kick, but she followed it with a punch to his face.

More blood trickled from his nose as she reinjured it.

A shadow rushed toward us. My sister had arrived. Her emerald eyes locked on Ingram, and she lifted her hand. I could see the outline of her demon dagger in its shadow form. The dagger had triggered her demon side, almost resulting in her death. If Alex, her soulmate, hadn't been there to change her into a vampire, we would have lost her.

"Stop," Ingram rasped as he blocked the next hit. "You have no clue what you're up against."

"Like hell I don't," she said, and kicked him in the chest. "You don't get to come here and try to abduct someone—especially someone I love."

Cyrus growled and lunged at the angel. He linked, *Your sister's here.*

Any angel descendant could see demons, even in their shadow form. *I see her.*

The enemy angel took flight, and Rosemary followed. She clutched one of his wings and dragged him backward. "Don't you dare fly away." She grunted and slung him downward, her hands raking down his wing, dislodging some feathers.

"That was a low blow," he growled and fluffed out his wings, reminding me of a bird grooming itself.

"Why are you trying to take Annie?" Rosemary asked, ignoring the jab. "Why are you working with those shifters?"

He laughed and shook his head. "I'm not working with *them*. Don't insult me."

Ronnie floated behind him, but he seemed focused on Rosemary. My sister wrapped her arm around his neck and placed the dagger against his throat.

Nightmares swirled inside my brain as bile filled my mouth. That was exactly what I'd done to Ronnie a few months ago when a rogue vampire had brainwashed me. He'd commanded me to kill her, and I'd nearly done it. I'd held a knife to her neck. Alex had tried to make me forget what I'd done under that vampire's influence, but even after Alex had manipulated my mind to erase the memory, I'd had nightmares about it—right up until my wolf had emerged and I'd remembered everything.

Even though I hadn't been in my right mind, it was still me who'd threatened my sister, one of the few people I loved in this world.

Annie, Cyrus linked as he brushed against my leg. *What's wrong?*

This was insane. We were in a life-and-death situation, and I was almost having a meltdown. I had to get my shit together. *It's the way Ronnie is holding Ingram. It reminds me of my past, but I'll be fine. We need to end this.* He knew my story; I didn't need to explain it.

Ingram went limp, forcing Ronnie to lose her grip. He sped toward me, and before I could move, he had me back in his arms.

Not again!

CHAPTER TWO

THE WIND BLEW through my hair as Ingram lifted me into the sky. Cyrus growled and lunged for the angel's legs, but Ingram flew so fast, he was already out of range, causing my mate to miss him by mere inches.

A figure blurred toward us, and as it slowed, Alex's form appeared. His sun-kissed brown hair was disheveled, and his normally soft blue eyes had darkened to navy. He glanced at the air, searching for my sister. As a vampire, he couldn't actually see her, but they could still speak through their soulmate link.

A huge silver wolf with lavender-silver eyes appeared beside the house with a sandy-blond wolf running right behind her. Sterlyn and Griffin had arrived as well.

The sound of paws running through the woods alerted me that Darrell, Cyrus's beta, was heading our way, too. He'd sounded the alarm when the enemy shifters and this damn angel had come for us.

All these people had arrived moments too late to keep me from being taken again.

I pounded against Ingram's chest as my breath caught. I couldn't believe this was happening again so soon. I'd never flown before in my life, and I realized I never wanted to. "Put me *down*." Normally, I'd have said let me go, but I'd already gone skydiving without a parachute, and it was completely overrated.

"Ingram!" Rosemary shouted as she flew toward us. "You aren't getting away, and I know where to find you!"

My throat tightened. She was right—all angels lived in Shadow City. What was he hoping to accomplish since Rosemary knew he was involved?

And how had he gotten out of Shadow City? Although Griffin and Sterlyn were working on permanently opening the city borders, people needed permission to come and go. Was he a university student like Rosemary?

A shot fired, and like last time, the enemy angel swirled us around. The world spun, and I closed my eyes, hoping for a reprieve, but my stomach revolted harder.

Hold your fire, Cyrus commanded. *It's not helping.* He then linked to only me, *Hold on. Rosemary is gaining on you.*

It's not like I have much of a choice. I was the angel's prisoner, and he was stronger than me.

Chad linked to Cyrus and me, *You have the gun, remember?*

Damn, he was right. I wasn't thinking clearly. If I could grab the gun from my waistband, maybe I'd have a chance. To keep Ingram distracted, I increased my thrashing and kicked out.

Why does she have a gun? Cyrus asked, his fear making it hard for me to swallow.

Chad replied, *She took it from me.*

The enemy angel crossed his legs to protect his family jewels as he stopped spinning.

Good. He was more worried about his junk than what I was doing. If I could keep him focused there, I might have a shot at getting the gun out undetected. I continued to knee him, pretending to be desperate enough to fight dirty. Hell, I wasn't above that, anyway, so it wasn't hard to fake.

"Stop it," he growled, and dug his fingers into my waist. His face twisted in pain, and I slipped a hand under my shirt.

My hand brushed the metal, but I missed the handle, my head still spinning from the tornado-like circling he'd been doing. I inhaled deeply, needing oxygen to fuel my brain, but my frantic movements made it hard. My heart raced, my lungs hurt, and I had to pee.

Really badly.

This asshole had literally scared the pee out of me, and he might receive a golden shower very soon.

Don't do anything stupid, Cyrus linked, beside himself with worry. *Rosemary will be there soon.* He howled loudly, the sound echoing around me, tugging at my heart. I hated that he felt so worried, and I'd be damned if I let this angel hurt any of us.

"Keep still!" Ingram yelled, and I stupidly opened my

eyes and glanced down. We were rising higher and higher, Cyrus and the others growing smaller by the second. Soon, they'd be as small as ants.

My only solace was that Rosemary was twenty yards below, her eyes tense with concentration as she raced toward me. All my life, I'd distanced myself from people, afraid to trust and get hurt, but Rosemary was one of many people who had wiggled into my heart. I had no doubt that she would ensure nothing bad happened to me, and I trusted her with my life. That had never been clearer than in this moment; otherwise, I wouldn't have been brave enough to pull this off.

I had to time things perfectly. *I'm going to shoot him.*

Wait until she reaches you, Cyrus replied. *If you do it too soon, she might not be able to catch you.*

The urge to get away from Ingram overwhelmed me, but Cyrus was right. I couldn't be stupid. I glanced over my shoulder and saw that Rosemary was about ten yards away. She was gaining on us, but I didn't want to be arrogant. The enemy angel could take her and Ronnie on, so he was smart, but he was carrying me, and I was fighting him. I was distracting him enough for Rosemary to catch up to us.

My ears popped as thick pain pulsated in my temples. Wind rushed over my face and filled my nostrils until I couldn't breathe. I grew lightheaded, and puffy clouds weren't far away. He was flying faster than I'd realized. If he went any higher, I might pass out from the altitude.

It was now or never. I needed to make sure Rosemary

was on the same page. Not only that, but the longer I took to get the gun, the likelier it was that Ingram would realize what I was attempting. My pulse pounded in my head as I continued my assault.

This time, when I touched the cool metal, I clutched the handle. The chill penetrated my palm. With my thumb, I inched my shirt up, the wind catching underneath, causing it to flap. I unclasped the safety and held the weapon beside my leg.

I jerked to the right, where the gun was, and got a good glimpse of Rosemary. Her gaze landed on the gun, and she nodded slightly.

Black spots appeared at the edge of my vision as unconsciousness loomed. I inhaled deeply, needing oxygen before I couldn't help Rosemary. *We have a plan.*

What do you mean, 'we have a plan'? Cyrus's panic mixed with mine, adding to my angst. Using every bit of energy I had left, I increased my thrashing.

"Stay still, or I'll knock you out," Ingram grunted as he removed an arm from my waist and yanked me upright.

I placed the barrel against his side.

"What the—" Ingram gasped as I pulled the trigger.

The bullet lodged in his side, and the angel snarled. He released me to clutch the wound, and we both dropped.

Warm air rushed against my body, and the pressure grew.

Smaller arms wrapped around my waist. My descent stopped, and the black wings I could see now eased the lump in my throat. My head settled against Rosemary's chest, and I breathed in her rose scent—my current second-favorite smell in the entire world.

Cyrus's panic gripped me. *Are you hurt? Ingram is falling, and I heard a gunshot.*

Eyes fluttering, I watched as Ingram sailed toward the ground. *You'd feel it if I were.* I knew all about that. When the demon wolves had kidnapped Cyrus and beaten him, I had felt his pain. The sensation wasn't the same as if I'd experienced it myself, but emotionally, it had been brutal. Since I hadn't been there with Cyrus and couldn't help him, it had been worse than any pain they could've inflicted on me. *Rosemary has me.*

My stomach sank. "Did I kill him?" I asked, my voice barely audible. I'd killed before, but that didn't mean I enjoyed it. In fact, each kill seemed worse than the last. If it hadn't been for Cyrus, I wasn't sure I would've survived the aftermath the previous time.

Rosemary's hair blew across my face, and she answered, "No, but he'll wish you had. We have to get to him before he heals himself." Her wings shifted, and we were speeding toward the ground.

The air assaulted me like before, so I turned my face into Rosemary's chest. The position didn't give me much of a reprieve, but I could somewhat fill my lungs. I wanted to ask her to slow down, but I didn't have enough air. Besides, she was trying to reach Ingram, and I didn't want to interfere with that plan. Lord knew, with my luck, I was in for another capture and flight if we didn't incapacitate him.

Wings fluttered nearby, and I peeked to see Ingram. He was much lower than us and moving slowly, about fifty yards above the ground. Blood trickled onto the grass, leaving a trail behind him.

More of our pack had arrived. Theo, Martha, and Rudie were in human form, while Darrell's silver wolf stood next to Cyrus.

Something bright glowed in Ingram's hand, almost as bright as the sun.

"Somebody stop him!" Rosemary yelled. "He's trying to heal himself."

Ronnie chased after Ingram, dagger raised over her head. Even in her shadow state, I could see her chest heaving.

When my feet touched something solid, I almost cried in relief. Cyrus brushed against my side, lending me strength, but we hadn't eliminated the threat.

"Stay here," Rosemary said as she released me and raced toward Ingram and Ronnie.

Theo had lifted a gun and was aiming it at Ingram when Alex rasped, "If you fire and it hits my mate, I'll rip your head off. I don't give a shit if you're part of the silver wolf pack."

"I can see her," Theo said, but his voice wavered.

The silver wolves weren't very comfortable with guns, and even in shadow form, Ronnie could still get hurt. We couldn't take the risk.

"Stand down," I commanded Theo, wanting to ease some of Alex's worry.

He lowered the gun and jerked his head to get his

shaggy, dark brown hair out of his honey-colored eyes. "Yeah, okay."

"Before doing something like that again, make sure no one—especially my mate—is next to your target," Alex growled. Then he blurred toward Ronnie as she swung her dagger at Ingram's shoulder.

Ingram spun around and caught Ronnie's wrist. He grimaced as he used his left hand to hold her off. His right side was injured, and he had his hand clasped over the bullet wound as blood leaked between his fingers.

"I'm going to kill you," Alex vowed, glaring up at the angel and Ronnie. His hands clenched into fists as he stood there, helplessly watching his mate fight.

Ingram chuckled. "You can't do a damn thing to me."

Using the enemy angel's arrogance to her advantage, Ronnie pulled the dagger back, and he surged toward her. She easily stabbed his left shoulder since she used his forward motion.

A guttural groan escaped him as his bloody right hand grasped her wrist. He jerked it forward and flew lower, dislodging the dagger from his shoulder.

Blood saturated his shirt.

The guy should've known there was no way he was getting out of this, but he swung at Ronnie, not giving up.

Before he could make contact, Rosemary slammed into his stomach, and he fell backward onto the ground between Darrell's house and ours.

Alex blurred, and when Rosemary climbed off the enemy, he kicked the angel right in his bullet wound. Ingram moved quicker than I expected, trying to catch

Alex's foot like he'd done earlier, but Rosemary punched him in the face. The two of them danced around Ingram, landing one blow after another.

Tires squealed, and my breathing turned ragged. The last thing we needed was more enemies to fight. *Guys, we have a problem—they may have backup.*

It's Killian, Sterlyn reassured me as she ran up to join us. I was flanked, and the wolves crouched, ready to fight. Sterlyn continued, *And this jerk won't get you a third time.*

Damn straight, Cyrus growled. *If you go up again, I'm going with you, even if it's by biting into the dickwad's leg.*

I'd make sure that didn't happen. If I'd struggled while Ingram had held me securely, I didn't want to imagine the suffering Cyrus would go through hanging on by his teeth. Ingram would only need to kick my mate hard enough to send him spiraling to his death. No one needed to go through that trauma. I'd done it enough times for all of us.

Ronnie stood to the side, dagger lifted, as she watched Alex and Rosemary fight Ingram.

If the enemy angel gets away, fire unless I say otherwise, I linked to the group near me. I didn't want to use Ingram's name because that would make him more of a person. That was a trick I'd learned from the kids at the group home—they used nicknames to prevent themselves from growing more attached. When we started to personify someone, they could hurt us, not only physically but emotionally, too.

Martha nodded as the darkening sky emphasized the brown in her auburn hair and her light aqua eyes.

Understood, Rudie answered, her sapphire eyes glowing. She tucked her long dark chocolate bangs behind her ears to see clearly and lifted the gun in preparation. Ever since we'd saved her, she'd been determined to train and become stronger, despite not having power from the moon.

Even though Ronnie hadn't been shot, I had no doubt that a gun could injure her. A demon wolf had bitten her, and vampires had knocked her around, so it only made sense that she wasn't immune to a bullet. I'd do anything to protect my sister.

Focusing on Ingram, I almost felt bad for him. His face was bloody. His once white shirt was crimson except for a few splotches, and he moved his hands as if he wasn't sure what to protect. He had to be in pain, but he had come here with bad intentions.

That was the craziness of the entire situation. He didn't emanate evilness or maliciousness like my father, Tate, and the other demon wolves did. He also didn't radiate goodness like our group did, especially Sterlyn. But he wasn't *evil*. Whatever he was doing wasn't out of impure intentions. Kidnapping someone wasn't nice or normal, but normal was relative, especially in this world.

Griffin ran to Sterlyn's side as Killian and Sierra appeared between our house and Darrell and Martha's. Killian's chiseled face held a scowl as his deep chocolate eyes locked on Ingram. His cappuccino hair, normally perfectly styled, hung in his eyes as he raced toward Rosemary.

Not missing a beat, Sierra's gray eyes locked on me and the others. She hurried toward us, evident by her sandy hair bouncing in its usual ponytail. She stood in front of me, knowing what was going on. Sterlyn must have been linking with Killian the entire time.

Face pink, Rosemary flared her nostrils as she lifted a finger at Alex, gesturing for him to stop. She stared the angel down. "Why are you here?"

"Ha!" Ingram snorted, but it quickly turned into a cough. He winced and took a moment to compose himself. "You think I'll just tell you after this?"

"If you aren't injured enough, I'd be glad to continue," Alex sneered. "Please refuse to tell us anything. My anger hasn't eased."

Slowly standing, the angel glared at us. "I'm not telling you a damn thing."

I was done. This asshole had tried to take me twice. He was going to tell me *everything*. I marched over to him, ready to make him bleed even more.

CHAPTER THREE

AS I STEPPED between Rosemary and Alex, I clenched my hand. Ingram's mossy eyes sparkled, and even in his beat-up state, he looked attractive. Another benefit of being supernatural, I guessed.

Cyrus snarled as he stepped between Alex and me, baring his teeth at the angel. He wanted to hurt the enemy more than I did, and I understood that sentiment well. I'd wanted to kill the demon wolves with my bare hands when they'd injured Cyrus.

We all need to stay rational, even though it's hard, Sterlyn linked with the pack. *Our anger will encourage him to act more belligerently and reinforce that he has control over the situation.*

Damn her and her sanity. I wanted to inflict more pain on the turd. Biting and shooting him hadn't been enough. What disturbed me more was that those dark thoughts didn't bother me.

Refusing to let him continue enjoying the moment, I

paused and forced my body to...become less tense. Relaxing was completely out of the question, so that was the best I could do. "Alex, don't compliment him."

Alex's brows furrowed, and his head snapped in my direction. "What are you talking about? That wasn't a compliment."

I forced a laugh, which grated against my throat. This was not a funny situation, but I trusted Sterlyn. And she was right. He relished our anger—being laughed at would infuriate him, and that was *my* goal. "But you are. You're acting like he actually *knows* something. Obviously, he doesn't. No lackey knows the objective."

"Lackey?" Ingram tilted his head and examined me. "What is that?"

Oh, dear God. I forgot that some supernaturals weren't up to date on the modern world. That could work to my advantage if I swung it as even more of an insult. "It's the people who the leaders find unworthy. Kind of like what Rosemary thinks of your manhood?"

"My...manhood?" The angel blinked and stared at me as if I had two heads. "I'm strong and—"

Sierra snorted. "She means penis size."

"You could understand why he'd be confused." I winked at my dirty-blond friend. "His must be small."

Will you stop talking about his... Cyrus trailed off. The fur rose on the back of his neck, conveying his message perfectly even if we hadn't had the link between us.

I'm trying to upset him. I slipped my fingers into his fur, hoping to comfort him.

His fur smoothed out, but his displeasure still flowed into my chest.

"I'm *not* small." Ingram's wings fluttered, and he grimaced. "Tell them, Rosemary. You know."

Rosemary closed her eyes. "Then you'd be able to smell that I was lying."

His mouth dropped open, and Killian laughed as he sauntered up beside Rosemary. His eyes lightened back to the warm chocolate I was used to.

The enemy angel's face turned scarlet, but he couldn't say anything else without making the situation worse since there was no signature sulfuric stench of a lie swirling in the air. Rosemary had confirmed his size was below average.

Keep going, Sterlyn encouraged. *It's working.*

"Back to my original point. In those types of organizations, they don't value the underlings and send them out to do the grunt work." I waved my hand at the group around me. "Unlike how we operate, where we're all treated equally. Everyone goes into battle, and we leave no one behind."

"I'm *not* a lackey," he scoffed, but the last word rose as if in question. "I came here to—" He stopped, realizing he'd been about to say something he shouldn't.

Maybe he wasn't as stupid as I'd hoped.

The angel slowly moved his wings as if preparing to fly off. That was enough for Cyrus to lunge at him.

Cyrus's large front paws slammed into Ingram's chest, and the angel stumbled before falling onto his back. He grunted as Cyrus's snout got close to his neck.

Stop it, Sterlyn linked. *All angels live inside Shadow City. If you hurt him, that will give Azbogah more ammunition against us.*

He tried to take my mate. Cyrus opened his mouth as he stared the angel in the eyes. *He should die.*

I don't disagree, but that will make the silver wolves and Annie more of a target. Sterlyn ran over to stand behind the angel's head so she could see her brother. Her lavender-silver eyes glowed as her wolf surged forward. *All the wolves will be targeted in Azbogah's retribution. He's been trying to discredit us however he can. I can't allow our anger to overcome us.*

She's right, I added. We had enough stacked against us without willingly adding to the pile. Killing Ingram might satisfy us, but we had to get answers and continue playing whatever political game we were in. *Killing him won't solve the problem.*

Cyrus closed his mouth, and Ingram attempted to shove him away. The angel only managed to move my mate lower on his stomach. The blood loss and pain had to be catching up to him.

My sister's shadowy figure floated toward us, and her body became lighter and more transparent. The dark outline faded as her beautiful copper hair bled through, finally revealing her vampire-muted rosy complexion. Before long, her sugar-cookie smell filled my nose as she reappeared in human form behind Ingram and sneered, "Move one more time, and I'll gut you like a fish."

"Oh, my gods," Sierra moaned. "I'm so flipping jealous. I've always wanted to say that line!"

Leave it to her to lighten the mood. That was one attribute I loved most about Sierra, but it drove Alex insane. The two of them had an interesting relationship, and even though Sierra purposely pestered the hell out of the three-hundred-year-old vampire, they cared about each other.

"You have weird friends, Rosemary." Ingram lowered his hands to his sides and emphasized that he was no longer touching Cyrus.

Rosemary glowered. "At least they're loyal to me."

There had to be a huge story here, but I wasn't sure I wanted to hear it. They'd had a relationship at some point, and that was gross enough.

Theo, Rudie, Martha, and Darrell inched closer behind us as we formed a circle around Ingram. If he tried to fly, Rosemary and Ronnie could easily catch him, and if he tried to run, we would all pounce.

Cyrus backed off the angel and crouched, ready to attack if needed.

"So what's the plan?" Ingram arched an eyebrow and smiled. The smile fell flat, probably because he was in intense pain. He reached for his bullet wound again, and Rosemary smacked his hand.

She pushed her finger into his chest. "No healing yourself, or I'll beat you even more. Do you understand?"

"Fine." He rolled his eyes, appearing almost human. He stood slowly, putting everyone on edge. "What are you going to do?"

Rosemary's eyes turned charcoal, matching the color of her wings. "Where were you going to take her?"

He shrugged and smirked. "You never know, she could've wanted to fly."

We don't have time for this, Sterlyn linked. *The Suburbans left because Ronnie attacked them, and they didn't know what was going on. They could return with backup. We need to get out of here.*

I hadn't considered that. Of course, Ronnie would scare anyone who couldn't see her.

Not everyone could hear, so I needed to relay the message. "Look, he doesn't know anything, and we need to get moving. I'd ask him if the bear shifters were coming back, but he probably doesn't even know who's really in charge."

"You're right." Rosemary nodded, her eyes tightening. "We should take him back to Shadow City and inform the council what went on here."

Everything in these parts revolved around the Shadow City council, which Sterlyn, Griffin, Alex, and Ronnie were part of. The council consisted of twelve representatives, three from each of the supernatural races —shifters, angels, vampires, and witches. Ronnie had taken Alex's brother's spot after he'd passed.

The odd part was that even though there were dozens of shifter races, including bears, birds, cats, and foxes, the three shifter representatives were wolves.

That decision to only have wolves as representatives could be found in the hidden room in Sterlyn and Cyrus's parents' house, which we'd been staying in for the past week. The room held a large statue of the angel Ophaniel, the moon guardian angel who'd procreated with a Shadow City wolf shifter. The silver wolves were meant to protect all supernaturals and were the reason the shifters had decided on wolf representation. However, no one had known about the silver wolf persecutions that would shortly follow.

Because the silver wolves were hybrids, their magic was tied to the moon. Unlike normal wolves, who came in a variety of coat colors, the fur of all silver wolves was the same gorgeous silver shade, and their strength and size were magnified based on the phase of the moon. During a full moon, they were at their strongest and easily the size of a small horse, and during a new moon, they were like any ordinary wolf shifter someone would come across.

The demon wolves were the opposite of the silver wolves. They were strongest during a new moon. The two races balanced each other out like good and evil, and from my limited experience with my biological father and the other demon wolves, they really were evil and abusive.

"For once, it would be nice if we could handle things fairly." Sierra wielded her finger like a weapon. "That asshole deserves a beating."

"I agree." Killian crossed his arms and glared at Ingram with hatred.

I'm going to shift. Sterlyn took off toward the house. *I'll be right back.* She ran in the back door, not even flinching as she hurried past the dead bear shifters.

She had a few pieces of clothing in her room from when she used to live there.

Knowing we could be attacked again at any second

made dread pit in my stomach. I'd been hoping we'd be safe here, but in some ways, we were a bigger target. The enemy that had hunted us here had attacked Sterlyn and slaughtered her pack months ago, and the demon wolves who were hunting me had invaded the silver wolves' previous pack location. We had nowhere safe to go. "We'll need to coordinate watches with more people involved." I hated to put Killian on the spot, but I couldn't pack link with him. "Is there any way your wolves could help? I understand if they—"

Killian rubbed his hands. "Twenty are on their way now, and they'll stay long enough for you all to pack up and move out."

"Move out?" Martha asked, her eyes narrowing. "We don't have anywhere else to go."

"How sad." Ingram chuckled.

Prick.

Ronnie pretended to stumble and poked Ingram in the back with the dagger.

"Hey," he growled, spinning toward her.

She lifted her hands as blood dripped from the tip of the dagger. "Oops. I guess karma is real."

My sister's dagger was amazing. The demon blade was an oblong triangle with a small dip that blended in with the black leather handle. At the bottom of the handle sat a dark purple stone, and above it was a silver pentagram inside a circle with sun rays radiating outward. The dagger appeared in Ronnie's palm whenever she needed it.

The same pentagram etching on the handle was

tattooed on Ronnie's inner right wrist, and I figured the mark cemented their bond.

Ingram had taken one step toward her when Alex materialized in front of him. The vampire king placed a hand on the angel's chest and jeered, "You touch her, and I'll kill you. I don't care if it causes a war with the angels." His words were a promise, not a threat. Everyone here understood that, including Ingram, who took a step back.

Sterlyn rushed outside, her long silver hair blowing behind her. Her olive skin glowed under the moonlight as her alpha power wafted from her. "Let's get him in Griffin's Navigator. We'll take him back to Shadow City."

"What?" Sierra gasped. "You can't be serious. He hasn't said a damn thing."

Narrowing her eyes, Rosemary tilted her head like she was trying to figure out a puzzle.

Alex's soft blue eyes lit as if he understood what Sterlyn was doing. "The longer we keep him here, the more upset the angels will become."

"That's my—" Ronnie started, then stopped. Her eyes widened slightly, the only hint that Alex had used their connection to tell her something. She exhaled and glanced at Rosemary. "Come on. Alex and I will go with you to make sure he doesn't do something stupid and escape." She tossed her dagger in the air and caught it, then shook it in front of Ingram's face. "Or rather, let's hope he does something stupid so we have to stop him again."

Ingram frowned. Rosemary grabbed the arm of his injured shoulder and yanked.

He almost stumbled, confirming he was weaker than he was letting on. We watched the three of them walk away with Sierra, Griffin, and Killian following. Killian held a gun, ready to shoot, while Griffin remained in animal form.

Sterlyn linked with the entire pack, *Killian has a good suggestion. Since this location is compromised and people know about the silver wolves again, keeping you separate from everyone else makes us more of a target.*

What did he suggest? Cyrus asked as he scooted closer to me, his side brushing my leg.

The familiar buzz of our mate bond sprang between us, easing the edge in my chest.

He has ten available houses in his pack neighborhood in Shadow Ridge. They're at the front of the development, where we can help watch who comes and goes. She looked at Cyrus the longest before glancing at the rest of the silver wolves. *It's time to integrate back into the society we never should've left. We can unite with a much larger pack and help train them for when we attack the demon wolves.*

Wait. Darrell's shock rang through the bond. *Are you saying they'll help us fight the demon wolves?*

Unfortunately, my presence had brought the demon wolves to the silver wolves, and now these packs were at odds.

Of course. Sterlyn smiled at us. *Killian is one of my best friends, and his pack wants to do the right thing. The demon wolves are a threat to everyone. It makes sense for us to work together.*

Unless anyone has a valid reason we shouldn't go, I think it's the best plan, Cyrus agreed, and turned to look his pack members in the eye. *We aren't safe here, and Killian's pack can't leave Shadow Ridge unattended to protect us.*

The pack link remained silent.

Knowing that it usually took someone speaking up first for others to follow suit, I cleared my throat. *I hate moving again, as I'm sure you all do, but this could be what we need to finally find a permanent home.* I opened myself up to the others, wanting them to know I believed every word. I wasn't saying it for propaganda but because this decision felt right.

I agree, Rudie interjected.

Her timidness was slowly fading away, and the strong wolf shifter that had always been inside her was beginning to show. Any mate to a silver wolf had to be strong. Fate wouldn't have it any other way.

One by one, the others murmured their agreement, and Sterlyn winked at me and linked between the two of us, *Thank you.*

For what?

For standing by Cyrus and me. She walked over and hugged me. *These wolves think of you as an alpha, and not just because you're Cyrus's mate, but because you are in your own right.*

My cheeks flamed. Her praise made my eyes burn with unshed tears.

We're heading to the city, and Killian says his men are pulling into the neighborhood now. Gather what you need and move out. She gave us a quick wave. *Griffin and I will be there to check on you later.*

With that, our group dispersed, rushing to get things settled so we could leave.

PACKING DIDN'T TAKE LONG. The fact that the entire pack had moved so many times over the past year had yielded a very efficient process.

Luckily, the attackers didn't come back, and we were soon on the road, heading toward Shadow Ridge.

Guys, Sterlyn linked to Cyrus and me, an edge in her tone. *We have a problem.*

My stomach dropped. What was wrong now?

CHAPTER FOUR

DID THE ANGEL GET AWAY? Cyrus's grip tightened on the steering wheel, turning his knuckles white. He scanned the area for any threats.

No, he's at the capitol building with the rest of the councilmembers, including Ronnie, Alex, and Rosemary, she replied.

Why aren't you there with them? My heart pounded in my ears. I wanted to cover them, but it wouldn't have done any good.

She hesitated, and my lungs stopped working.

The council wants Annie to come before them, she finally responded. *We're getting in the Navigator and heading to the Shadow Ridge side gate to meet you.*

Cyrus shook his head, and though she couldn't see him, his feelings were very clear through the link. *Hell, no. She's not going in there.*

I agree. I had no interest in visiting Shadow City. I

was curious about how it looked inside because of Ronnie's descriptions, but not enough to step foot in there. *Remember what happened when Ronnie went before the council with Alex? They held her captive, and people tried to force her to turn.*

That was Matthew's doing. Sterlyn's displeasure wafted through the bond. *And he's dead.*

A low growl emanated from Cyrus's chest as we turned onto the road that led to Shadow Ridge. He linked, *Not good enough. Azbogah is still alive. He'll be gunning for anyone who's outside the norm. He gives you, Ronnie, and Griffin enough hell as it is.*

Usually, we would've passed a few vehicles by now, but this close to midnight, the roads were empty. Within seconds, we reached a sign that said *Welcome to Shadow Ridge.*

My leg bounced as my stomach churned. Cyrus was right. That angel probably wanted to make an example of me.

I swear to you, if I thought what happened to Ronnie would happen to you. I wouldn't be asking this. Sterlyn's sincerity was palpable. *He wants to meet the wolf that Ingram tried to capture, and he wants to know the reason supernaturals of so many different races got involved. I truly believe this is the best way to prevent him from escalating the situation.*

Oh, yes. The concept that only members of the same supernatural race could kill, fight, and punish one another was an archaic rule Azbogah clung to. From what Ronnie and the others had told me, the council enforced that each race should handle its own issues without interference.

If she goes, I do too. Cyrus put his foot down. *There's no way I'm willing to be separated from her after the hell we've been through tonight.*

I loved this man so much. I wanted to be glued to his side for eternity.

We followed Killian's truck through the quaint downtown area. Shadow Ridge had easily become my favorite place in the world, and now I understood why. This was where we belonged. This place cured the restlessness inside me, and my anxiety eased among the members of our own pack.

One thing I appreciated about this town over Shadow Terrace was the variety among the buildings, giving it a relaxed feel. Though most were made of brick, they were painted a variety of colors and designed differently. The original structures from when the town was founded had a traditional vibe, with the more modern styles scattered throughout as the town grew.

I'm glad you feel that way, Sterlyn responded. *They want you to come, too. They've learned that you're my twin brother and the acting alpha of the silver wolf pack. Not to mention you also attacked Ingram and are mated to the wolf the angel tried to take.*

But we can't abandon our pack. We haven't even reached our new location.

Since it was night, few people walked the streets

under the lights. Those who did were dressed in party clothes and out having fun. From the car, I couldn't tell which were human visitors and which were supernaturals, which bode well for us. The supernatural community was to remain secret, so the fact that everyone blended together showed that the supernaturals were comfortable with the humans and that side of themselves.

Darrell joined the link via Sterlyn, and she continued, *I know it's not ideal, but most of the shifters know Killian. He and Darrell can get the pack settled while you head to Shadow City with us. The silver wolf pack will be safe with Killian's pack. Besides, even if the enemy plans on attacking again, they'll need time to strategize for the new location.*

Great. I'd hoped we'd be safe here for more than a night, but we were with a much larger pack that could offer more protection, and we wouldn't have to run our own pack down with our limited resources while trying to guard the area twenty-four-seven.

Yes, I can help, Darrell agreed. *We're all exhausted. I have a feeling we'll make pallets on the ground and sleep there tonight.*

That thought hadn't crossed my mind, but now that he'd mentioned it, I could probably sleep on the floor tonight, too. My eyes were growing heavy now that the adrenaline had worn off.

You know I wouldn't ask if it wasn't important, Sterlyn added. *If you don't see them now, things will be worse for everyone, especially since they know the silver wolves are moving into Shadow Ridge.*

Why did we have to tell them? Cyrus asked, his jaw tensing.

We all knew why. *They'd have found out eventually, and it's better coming from the shifter council representatives and our alphas.* The politics in this place were worse than human politics because, unlike humans, supernaturals had no qualms about killing and torturing those they deemed unfit.

Exactly. Sterlyn sneered. *And we must play the game.*

This was one reason I'd wanted to go into law: to fight the injustices the system allowed. Even though the courtroom was no longer my goal, saving the women of the demon wolf pack from the archaic male-dominated hierarchy they'd established thousands of years ago was the battle I'd fight. Not every woman I'd met while staying there was a demon wolf, but it didn't matter. They were mistreated with no rights or respect given. They were objects for the men to control, just like I was supposed to be my father's bargaining chip for some demon he'd promised me to in exchange for more power. The demon wolves acted as if the women were disposable and valuable based on what we could gain for them, which was stupid and untrue.

I planned on saving every woman when we went back to fight Tate and the others.

Cyrus took the turn that led away from Killian's pack neighborhood. His shoulders sagged. *Can we do it tomorrow? It's been a long night, and Annie needs her rest.*

No, I'm sorry. Her reply was firm. *The council called*

an emergency hearing once they were alerted to Ingram attempting to take Annie.

We'll meet you there. Cyrus's words were simple, but his nostrils flared. His jaw ticked like a bomb.

Relief washed over us as Sterlyn replied, *If you're good with it, I was hoping you and Annie would stay with Griffin and me. I wanted to bring that up before they divided the available houses among the pack members.*

Cyrus glanced at me. "You would be safer with Sterlyn and me there together. Tonight, those bears focused more on me because I'm silver. If Sterlyn had been there, too, they might not have gotten you outside."

"You don't have to convince me. I like staying at their house." I'd stayed there and in Shadow Terrace while we'd planned Ronnie's wedding, and in some ways, Shadow Ridge was my second home.

That works for us, I replied, not wanting Sterlyn to think we were trying to find a way out of it.

Sounds great. We'll see you soon.

The pack link disconnected as we passed by the cypress and pine trees that announced we'd arrived.

Cyrus took my hand and squeezed it as he connected with the entire pack. *Unfortunately, Annie and I must meet with the Shadow City council to discuss what happened tonight. Darrell and Killian will oversee setting everyone up in their new homes. With ten houses, each family can have their own place, and the single men can share one house.*

We had twenty-six pack members. Two—Mila's daughter, Jewel, and Darrell and Martha's daughter,

Emmy—were still out of town, staying with Mila's father's pack.

Seventeen were the silver wolves who had broken off from Sterlyn's pack a few years before her and Cyrus's births to follow their uncle Bart. Along the way, five of them had found their fated mates, and two couples had one child each, giving us a total count of twenty-one silver wolves which included Sterlyn and Cyrus. Apparently, silver wolves usually only conceived one child, two at most, and that was rare. From what I could tell, the alpha line of the pack often had two children—probably nature's way of ensuring there was a spare if something happened to the elder.

Wait, Theo linked, his frustration bleeding through. *Why are we telling the council? Didn't they get us into this mess?*

Oh, great. I didn't need Theo confirming what Cyrus was already upset over. I got that the silver wolves wanted to remain hidden; that had been ingrained in them their entire lives. *Did keeping our location secret help?*

Exactly! Imagine if they'd known. We'd all be dead, Theo argued back. *Look at the damage they inflicted once they learned where the hell we were.*

I inhaled deeply, trying to remember strategies I'd learned from the law dramas I'd watched. Arguing with an irrational person took a different skill set.

Listen here, Cyrus warned. *You're going—*

"Stop it," I growled at Cyrus. This was the exact route one shouldn't take when handling them. Before long, those two would be out there challenging each other again, and we didn't have the time or headspace for drama. I linked with the pack, *The fact that we were hiding made them feel as if they were in control. Assholes get off on that, so attacking us when we thought we were safe made them feel powerful. By taking away that control, we'll level the playing field, at least mentally. Not only that, but we'll have Killian and his pack to help protect us.*

I waited for Theo to fight back, but Rudie responded instead. *I agree with you, Annie. I think this is our best route.*

Me, too, linked Martha.

Those two ladies were great allies to have—Martha because so many pack members respected her, and Rudie because she'd calm Theo.

Cyrus glanced at me, a proud smile on his face. *And my mate is right, as always. We have to do this. It's time for the silver wolves to show that we aren't scared and take our rightful place in this society.*

I can get behind that, Chad linked.

I'll take it from here until you two get back, Darrell replied. *We'll let you know if we need anything.*

"You are amazing," Cyrus sighed as he glanced at me, adoration on his face. "I could've had a handle on this pack much sooner if you'd been by my side from the very beginning."

Oh, to have more time with each other. "At least we're together now."

"Yeah, and I'm driving you straight into our enemies' home." Cyrus focused on the road, the little bit of happiness replaced by a scowl. "I'm supposed to protect you, not deliver you to evil."

"Your sister wouldn't—" I tried to reason, but he winced.

"I know. We're going," he confirmed. "But you're not leaving my side for anything."

"I never want to." I leaned my head against his shoulder, hoping my nearness would calm him as we drove deeper into downtown Shadow Ridge.

Suddenly, an enormous bridge over the Tennessee River came into view. I lifted my head, and my jaw dropped.

I'd been through this town several times on the way to Shadow Ridge University, but I'd never seen the bridge before. Even though I understood that the coven of witches in Shadow City spell the bridge to hide it from humans, I didn't see how that was possible now, looking at its size.

The river was ten times wider than it had appeared to be when my supernatural side had been suppressed, and the bridge connected this riverbank to a large, domelike structure. Towers jutted toward the sky, evenly spaced across the bridge, and just like Ronnie and Sterlyn had said, it reminded me of the Golden Gate Bridge, even in the moonlight. About a hundred yards from the city's main entrance was a section that reminded me of an old castle with a massive wooden door that could be raised to let people in and out of the city.

I gasped, not able to believe my eyes, and blinked a few times. "It's amazing."

Not sure if that's the right word for it. Cyrus fidgeted, and his anxiety flowed into me, tightening my chest. He drove onto the bridge, and there wasn't even a bump as we transitioned from the road.

The walls grew more massive as we drove closer; they stood over one hundred stories high. Carved into them was a skyline view of a city with a huge paw print hovering between the two tallest skyscrapers. The emblem was simple but gorgeous. "Is that the city? And why is there a wolf print on top?" I asked.

He frowned. "From what I've been told, yeah, it's the city. I guess we're about to find out for ourselves. Yelahiah —Rosemary's mom—demanded the paw print as a symbol of her brother and the silver wolves."

A glass dome covered the top of the city. I assumed it guaranteed that no one could fly in without approval. "They keep the place locked up tight."

"Lord forbid someone they don't like gets in," Cyrus rasped as the vein in his neck grew visible. "Only the worthy are allowed inside."

"What does that say about us?" I tried to tease, but grimaced when the joke fell flat.

Cyrus clamped my hand tighter. "That's what I'm worried about, because I know damn well they don't think I'm worthy."

As we approached the gigantic wooden door, gears ground, and it began to lift.

He linked with Sterlyn and me, *I take it you're the reason we're being let in?*

Yes, she answered. *Griffin and I are on the other side.*

The process was slow and loud. Inch by inch, the city came into view...and it was breathtaking. I could only imagine what it would look like in daylight.

The buildings were modern, with straight, precise lines. A huge, round, purple stained-glass roof highlighted a stucco-like building directly in front of us. Other structures were made of golden glass. Faint whispers of color streaked the air, and it seemed as if we were entering a different realm.

"This is so beautiful," I breathed as I scanned the city, wanting to take it all in.

Cyrus pulled into the city and growled, "It has to be pretty to hide all the corruption."

That was probably true.

Griffin's Navigator waited ahead, and when Cyrus pulled behind him, he drove deeper into the city.

Though it was midnight, the streets brimmed with people. I never would've guessed this place had been closed off for thousands of years. People wore jeans and tank tops. A few even wore skintight leather that didn't leave much to the imagination. I didn't know why, but I'd figured they'd be wearing long dresses and pants like in the eighteen hundreds.

The only light came from the sky and buildings, but since everyone here had supernatural sight, no one needed streetlights. The only two vehicles I saw were ours and Griffin's. All that was missing were horse-drawn carriages.

Hmm. Did they have horses here? And if they did, were they shifters? A question for a less serious time.

A few hairy men stood outside a bar holding beers, and several women were gathered around a store that sold herbs and plants. Everywhere I looked, there were groups of beings made up of similar people. I realized they were keeping to their own kind. Even though I'd heard that message several times from Ronnie and the others, I was still shocked to see it because of the dynamics of our own group.

Sterlyn linked with us, *We're almost there. It's the large white building ahead.*

My gaze landed on the capitol building. *Large* had been an understatement; it was colossal. The white rectangular building with a cathedral-like roof occupied an entire block. "Damn! That's bigger than the government building in Lexington."

Griffin turned into an uncovered parking lot on the right side of the building, and Cyrus pulled into the spot beside him.

When I moved to open the door, Cyrus tugged me back.

His face was a shade paler, and my stomach jumped into my throat.

"What's wrong?" I asked, scared of the answer.

"I don't know what will happen in there, but I need you to know how much I love you." He placed a hand on the base of my neck and pulled me toward him. When he kissed me, I closed my eyes, savoring the moment.

Even though we'd spent the last several nights in each other's arms, it would never be enough. I kissed him back, wanting him to know I felt the same way. *I kinda love you, too.*

He chuckled, and the knot in my chest eased. His laugh always had that effect on me.

Guys! Sterlyn warned a second before something loud banged against the window.

CHAPTER FIVE

I STARTED, and my heart pounded as I jerked my head toward my window.

Rosemary stood there, a frown marring her face. "We need you inside. Azbogah is making things worse."

Even though I'd never met the man, I believed her. The knot in my chest doubled in size.

I really hate this place. Cyrus turned rigid as he opened the door. *I can't even have a damn second with you without someone interrupting.*

That wasn't true, and we both knew it. Our wolves were on edge, and we hadn't been able to relax together since my attempted capture. He wouldn't calm down until we had alone time in each other's arms, and I had big plans that involved a lot more than cuddling when we got into bed. *We* will *have uninterrupted time after this meeting. I don't care if they attempt to beat the door down.*

His eyes almost lightened to the gray color I loved.

That color was reserved for me, and it had better stay that way.

Don't make promises you can't keep. He arched a brow and climbed out of the car, staring at me the entire time.

I licked my lips, my body warming. *Oh, I intend on keeping them...multiple times.* My wolf howled desperately, needing time with her mate.

"Dear gods," Rosemary scoffed and waved a hand in front of her nose. "Now is definitely not the time for foreplay."

Griffin chuckled. "They're newly mated, and she was almost kidnapped twice. Be thankful they aren't having sex right in front of us."

"We don't have time for this." Rosemary clutched my arm and dragged me out of the vehicle. Her fingers dug into my skin, and my arm throbbed. I'd have bruises there, but with my wolf healing, they'd be gone by morning.

Cyrus growled, his irises darkening. "Rosemary, don't push me."

"I don't understand why we're still out here," she huffed. "We need to get inside."

Sterlyn hurried over and placed a hand on Rosemary's shoulder. "We were giving them a moment because of what Griffin said. Their wolves are on edge, and they needed to connect before staring down the council."

"Wolves and their mates," Rosemary complained. She released my arm and turned her attention back to me, sighing. "I'm sorry. I'm not trying to be a jerk—I'm just trying to protect everyone."

The anger flowing from Cyrus calmed slightly, and my heart warmed. Rosemary was a good friend, and she didn't understand because she didn't have a connection like Cyrus and I had.

"Thank you for caring." I hugged her, but her words had sunk in, working better than a cold shower.

We needed to get inside.

Do you still need a minute? Sterlyn asked, tilting her head. *I understand—*

No, it'll drag out the inevitable. Cyrus moved to my side and held my hand. *Let's get this over with and get us the hell out of this city.*

She nodded and turned to the building, and she and Griffin hurried down the walkway to the front entrance.

Rosemary waved a hand. "After you two."

My lungs moved more freely at the thought of her having our backs, both literally and figuratively. I hurried after Sterlyn and Griffin.

Griffin reached the tall hunter-green front door and held it open for us.

I walked past him into a massive and mostly bare entry hall. Golden spiral chandeliers hung from the ceiling, spaced out every ten feet, lighting once-white walls stained dingy yellow from time and wear.

The faint scent of coffee hung in the air, and I glanced at a small coffee stand in a far corner of the mammoth room.

Sterlyn headed to another hunter-green door in the

middle of the gigantic back wall and paused, standing there for a second. *Every councilmember, as well as Ingram, is in there. Azbogah will continue to attempt to make us look bad. Please try your best to keep your anger in check because it will be hard.* She glanced at Cyrus.

He averted his eyes to the marble floor and stepped closer to me, and I stepped slightly in front of him.

That's not fair. This was the first time Sterlyn had done something that bothered me. Usually, she was empathetic and understanding, but she'd made Cyrus feel like the man I'd first met—ashamed—and I refused to stand for it. *He's changed a lot in the time I've known him, and he doesn't get angry like that anymore.*

When I'd met Cyrus, he'd been broken. We both had been. I'd been weak and childlike because Eliza and Ronnie had always taken care of me and protected me. I'd been suffering after the vampire Eilam had made me his own blood bag, manipulating me and making me forget who Ronnie was.

Cyrus had been kidnapped at birth by Eliza and handed to the enemy. He'd grown up unloved, and he'd been forced to train the people who were now our enemy —the very enemy that had killed his parents and slaughtered Sterlyn's pack. He'd been taught to view himself as a hindrance and to do whatever he could to survive, and he'd carried so much pain and resentment.

I believed that was one reason fate had put us together. We needed each other to get through our feelings of being tainted and unworthy and realize we didn't need to prove anything to anyone but ourselves.

I didn't mean that. Sterlyn's shoulders sagged. *What I mean is that you were just taken, and Cyrus hasn't had time to calm down. Azbogah will use his angst and turmoil against you because of your fated-mate connection.*

That sounded more in line with the Sterlyn I knew. *Okay, that I agree with.*

Cyrus squeezed my hand lovingly and stepped beside me as he linked to only me, *I love you.* His warmth flowed into me, and he didn't have to say more. My standing up for him meant everything to him.

Rosemary huffed loudly.

"Angels aren't known for their patience," Griffin murmured. He brushed past his mate and opened the door. "But she's right. We do need to get in there."

The five of us entered a room that contained a long U-shaped table that opened toward us. Six people sat at the table, while Ingram stood uninjured in the middle of the room.

Cyrus growled, and I looped my arm through his, standing close. Some tension eased from his body.

Rosemary stayed behind us, and I remembered that she wasn't officially part of the council. Her parents were, and she usually attended as an observer.

"As promised, we brought them," Sterlyn said as she walked to the left side of the table and took a seat at the far end of the back section.

A gorgeous woman with massive black wings sat beside her on the left side of the table. The angel tapped a long red fingernail against her full blood-red lips as her forest-green eyes studied Cyrus and me. She wore a black dress so tight it could've been a second skin, and her dark amber hair shone brightly. A glow similar to Rosemary's emanated from within her. It wasn't hard to figure out this was Rosemary's mother, Yelahiah.

"It's about time you arrived." A dark angel stood at the center of the table between Alex and another man I didn't know, towering over everyone. His wintery-gray eyes landed on me, and he glared. "I was wondering if they were actually going to show." His wings were midnight black, adding to his sneer. Even his spiked caramel hair and black suit heightened his intimidating presence, but a dark aura hovered around him. Not quite evil, but nowhere close to benevolent.

I take it that's the douchebag, Azbogah, I linked to Sterlyn and Cyrus.

Sterlyn's silver radiance overshone the purple in her irises. *Yep. And Ezra, the other wolf shifter representative, is next to him.*

It was good to put a name to the face. My attention flicked to the handsome wolf shifter. His sea-green eyes contrasted with his olive skin. He fidgeted and ran his fingers through the sable-brown hair that fell naturally around his face. He felt neither evil nor good—he was just there—but his demeanor screamed *guilty.*

"My pack was just attacked, so forgive us for not getting here as quickly as you'd like," Cyrus said without too much of an attitude. *I hate him more than I thought possible.*

A laugh bubbled in the back of my throat, but I swallowed it down. The timing wasn't ideal.

"I still can't believe that there are that many more silver wolves." A shorter woman sitting beside Sterlyn smirked and leaned forward, her black- and scarlet-streaked hair falling over her shoulders. Even from here, I could smell her herbal scent, telling me she was a witch as well as a member of the coven that were Eliza's enemies and the reason she didn't feel safe staying close by. "How many did you say you saw, Ingram?" Her thick black eyeliner made her misty gray eyes appear white. Something troublesome radiated from within her, and I understood why Eliza wanted to keep her distance and not let the witch connect Ronnie to her as her foster daughter.

"You could ask Sterlyn or Cyrus, Erin," Griffin said, making his way to the right side of the table. He took the seat at the very end. "She's their alpha, and Cyrus is her beta."

"Like we can trust Sterlyn," a woman with long burgundy hair spat from the seat closest to us on the left. Her rosemary scent assaulted my nose. "We had no clue there were more silver wolves."

So that was the other witch. Her inner light mirrored Erin's. I remembered Ronnie telling me that one of the three witches seemed genuine but in a difficult spot, but judging by this girl's attitude, she wasn't the one.

Cyrus ground his teeth.

Take a deep breath, I encouraged him. *Remember what your sister said.*

Following my advice, he inhaled deeply. *You're right. I can't let my anger get the best of me.*

"No one ever asked, Diana." A thin man leaned forward to look at her. She'd been positioned beside Gwen, Alex's sister, who sat between him and the witch. The man fluffed his white wings, which sprouted from his even whiter suit. He was paler than anyone I'd ever seen. The only colors on him were his butterscotch-blond hair and his piercing sky-blue eyes. "And why should it matter? It wasn't as if you would have advocated for them to rejoin our society inside these walls."

He must be Pahaliah, but he looked nothing like Rosemary. It was almost shocking. She must have gotten all the genes from her mother's side.

"Let's not forget we were told Annie was human." Ezra chuckled, and his eyes flicked up to me. "Now she's some sort of *demon* wolf that none of us have ever heard of. Much has been kept from us."

Ronnie sat upright next to Pahaliah and squared her shoulders. "When I mentioned her coming to Shadow Ridge a few weeks ago, I didn't know she was super-natural."

"When I was around her at Ronnie's wedding, I didn't have a clue, either," Gwen interjected, twirling a piece of her tousled white-blonde hair around a finger tipped with a long crimson nail. Her cranberry lips parted, revealing white teeth. Her chestnut eyes surveyed me. "But it's obvious now. She smells of musky, sweet lilacs."

"If they didn't know, how could they tell us?" a young

woman with waist-length dark brown hair said from her seat next to Ezra and perpendicular to Ronnie. The young woman leaned away from him toward Ronnie as her coffee-colored eyes met mine. She chewed on her black-stained bottom lip.

Erin laughed and stabbed her finger at the young girl. "Breena, remember whose side you're on. Of course Gwen is siding with her queen and sister-in-law. They're family."

"Yes, Priestess." Breena grimaced and stared at her hands.

"I take offense to that," Alex said, glancing at the priestess beside him. "Ronnie and I respect and value Gwen's opinion, even when it differs from ours. She doesn't get punished for telling the truth, unlike when Matthew reigned."

"And if you choose to remember, I spoke out against Matthew several times, especially at the end." Gwen arched her brow. "I'm insulted that you'd think I'm so easily manipulated."

"This is irrelevant." Azbogah banged his hand on the table. "The reason we're here is that Sterlyn, Ronnie, Alex, Griffin, and the silver wolves attacked an angel."

"You've got to be joking," Cyrus spat. "That angel," he said, addressing the council while gesturing at Ingram, "was working with the bear shifters that attacked our home and tried to kidnap her to take her gods-know-where."

"It wasn't only bear shifters." Sterlyn glanced at each councilmember. "There were wolves there, too, who aren't part of the Shadow Ridge or Shadow City packs."

Really? Confusion from Cyrus floated through the link. *Normally, there's a mix of supernaturals that work together. Only bear shifters attacked our house.*

Sterlyn tapped her finger on the table. *The men who stayed by the Suburbans were wolves. They didn't attack any other houses. They just kept anyone from helping you.*

Cyrus frowned. *That's disturbing.*

Trying to keep up with the two conversations was intense. I was afraid I'd say something out loud I'd meant for the pack link. But I had to ask, *Why?*

Because that falls in line with how Dick ran things, he answered. *It also confirms these were men I grew up with and trained.*

Dick was the man who'd kidnapped Cyrus, forced him to train the enemy that slaughtered his parents and the silver wolf pack, and tried to capture Sterlyn and hand her off to an alpha to breed an army of silver wolves. His mate, Saga, had also killed Griffin's father in the hope that Dick would become the alpha of Shadow City. Everything kept coming back to him, and I hated how it caused Cyrus to relive the past.

How is that possible? If Dick and his wife were dead, why were these fighters coming after us?

Because someone on this council is behind it. Sterlyn's irises glowed, and her chest heaved. *We must determine who.*

The implication of her words impacted me, and I hadn't been involved in any of that hell. *I guess we better watch everyone for clues.* I focused back on the external conversation, determined to help solve the mystery.

"Ingram, what do you have to say for yourself?" Azbogah stared the asshole angel down.

"I was flying over a neighborhood I'd never seen before when several SUVs drove inside and began firing at the houses." Ingram placed a hand on his chest and shuddered. "I've never seen anything like it, but as Sterlyn pointed out, they were shifters, so that's probably why it was so violent."

"Because angels aren't?" Griffin laughed and rubbed his nose. "You know none of us picture you all naked and playing harps, right?"

"I don't appreciate that visual," Alex grumbled, glaring at his friend. "I've always valued my imagination, but not anymore."

Ingram's shoulders tensed, proving he didn't like being made fun of. "What I *mean* is that angels would never attack in such a cowardly way. That's how barbarians like shifters and vampires fight."

But not witches. Odd.

Not only that, but Sterlyn had been right. He thrived off our anger, and us making fun of him in front of the council was turning the tables. Ingram was getting furious.

"If memory serves me right, at one time, you admired firearms." Rosemary stepped up beside me. "You even snuck into the guards' arms-training room and shot some pistols to see how it felt."

Yelahiah shifted in her seat and narrowed her eyes at Ingram. "Is that so?"

"That was years ago." Ingram cleared his throat. "And yes, I was curious. Not that I ever planned on using one."

Azbogah glared at Rosemary and said, "You aren't part of this council and weren't invited to discuss this matter. You're speaking out of turn."

"That's funny." Rosemary placed a hand on her hip and lifted her chin. "Because I was there, and as the only other angel at the scene, I'd think you'd want my account on the matter as well."

"You're biased," Azbogah retorted, his face turning pink. "Your friendship with the wolves and vampires hasn't gone unnoticed."

"Nor have you made it secret how *you* feel about them," Rosemary replied sweetly. "That's even more of a reason we should be part of this conversation—to balance each other out."

If I'd thought the dark angel had been angry before, I'd been so wrong. His face turned the color of a tomato, and I had a feeling things were about to explode.

CHAPTER SIX

"YOU DARE COME into a council meeting and lecture *me?*" Azbogah said through clenched teeth. "Yelahiah, you'd best keep *your* daughter in line."

The slight inflection intrigued me. Perhaps it was bitterness since he and Yelahiah had been together in the past. When you lived for millennia, watching an old lover find a partner and bear a child might be difficult to handle.

Could that be why he was so angry and bitter?

Angels reproduced only every century or so, and even then, it was a struggle. Their chaotic past—which included Azbogah orchestrating the death of Ophaniel, the angel creator of the silver wolves and Yelahiah's brother—had ruined their relationship. But maybe he still had feelings for her.

A thin line existed between love and hate. Could he be skirting that line and choosing to relinquish control to anger, similar to how Mila was handling her mate's death? Spewing everything negative into the world, not wanting to deal with the underlying issues—the loss they couldn't accept?

Or maybe I was looking for reasons to justify why people were assholes, and he didn't have any, other than enjoying the power it gave him.

"Is she wrong, Azbogah?" Yelahiah placed her hands on the table. "It always seems like you do everything possible to work against anyone you don't consider an ally here."

"Don't worry, love," he replied, and exhaled noisily. "You do plenty to undercut me all on your own."

Whoa. The supernatural world was more dramatic than the world I'd known working at the group home. This was next-level. If Sierra had been here, she'd be soaking up every minute. No wonder the others didn't enjoy the melodramatic movies and shows Sierra always favored—they lived it. It was probably like reliving their entire day over and over again. *Are council meetings always like this?*

Oh, yes. Sterlyn's stoic face gave nothing away, despite the frustration wafting through our bond. *Every damn time something happens.*

Somebody needs to put that dickwad in his place. Cyrus quivered with anger. *I don't understand how he's allowed on the council.*

He's been on it since it formed, along with Yelahiah and Pahaliah. Many of the angels follow him, and we have to be careful how we handle him, or we could start a civil war. Sterlyn rubbed her hands together. "We're digressing."

"I agree." Alex nodded, backing his friend. "If the angels want to discuss their personal differences, it shouldn't be done on council time."

Ezra steepled his fingers. "Please, Ingram, continue before Rosemary so rudely interrupts again."

"Yes, let's just ignore the fact that the angel testifying broke into the guards' training area to fire weapons without approval," Yelahiah murmured, but everyone had heard her clearly.

Nostrils flaring, Azbogah sucked in a breath. I expected him to say something to counter that, but he remained silent and gestured for Ingram to speak.

Fluffing his feathers, Ingram stepped forward so that his back was to us. The action reminded me of a toddler acting out in the only way he knew how. He must not fear an attack in the council room, but Cyrus was barely holding it together. Sharing the same room with the man who'd tried to kidnap me and not being able to kick the guy's ass was driving his wolf insane.

I squeezed his hand. I wished I could do more to comfort him, but anything else would look inappropriate and drive home Azbogah's point about our lack of maturity.

"Like I was saying, I was flying over the neighborhood and saw the shifters firing on the houses. They were focused mainly on the house that she and he"—he pointed his thumb over his shoulder at Cyrus and me —"were in. Naturally, I was inquisitive." He turned to the side and huffed on his fingernails, then rubbed them on his blood-crusted shirt. "That is a sign of high intelligence."

I could no longer hold in my laughter. My body shook as tears sprouted in my eyes. "Is that..." I paused to catch my breath. "*What* is it a sign of?"

Ronnie snorted and slapped her hands over her mouth as her eyes widened. But the corners of her eyes wrinkled, revealing she was still smiling.

"Is this funny to you?" Erin scoffed, and leaned forward. Her breasts bulged against the deep cut of her silky V-neck black top.

Cyrus stepped forward, instinctively attempting to block me from the witch's view.

Nope. Not happening. Eliza and Ronnie had treated me like a child for most of my life, and I was done with it. He knew better. I might be his mate, but I had to stand up for myself; otherwise, no one else would respect me.

Pivoting around him, I wiped away a tear trailing down my cheek. "Yes, it is funny, for so many reasons."

"Oh, do tell," Diana said, and tapped her fingernails against the table as if she thought the action and noise would throw me.

I lifted a finger. "For one, when the bear shifters were dragging me through the kitchen to the back door where Ingram was waiting, he said it was about damn time." Raising a second finger, I continued, "And the bear shifters willingly handed me over to him. There was no fight or scuffle. They expected him to be there."

Ingram scoffed. "They didn't say that."

"She never said they did." Griffin raised his brow. "She only described their actions."

He needs to defend himself but knows he must be careful about what he says so he's not caught in a lie. Cyrus's eyes glowed as his wolf tried to surge forward.

If he didn't calm himself, our situation would worsen. *Babe, remember what Sterlyn said. They're doing this on purpose. I know your wolf wants out to protect me. Believe me, I understand. I was the same way at the demon pack settlement, but I'm here next to you and safe. No one is threatening to take me away.*

Some tension released, and his body relaxed marginally, enough that his irises returned to their normal silver shade.

"If you can't be quiet, you'll need to be removed," Azbogah rasped, and glared at me. "Let Ingram speak. This disrespect won't be tolerated any longer."

Now that had my wolf surging forward. "I was *asked* to come here. Don't pretend it was the other way around." I struggled with authority figures. I'd seen firsthand what people in power could do to innocent children. I couldn't *stand* assholes with power, and that was exactly what this twatwaffle in front of me was.

"That was definitely not my decision." Azbogah pinched the bridge of his nose. "I was fine with the people we had here, and I'm not thrilled that outsiders have been allowed within these city walls."

"In order for us to truly understand what happened, the most impacted individuals involved must be here."

Yelahiah straightened her shoulders. "Otherwise, we won't get an accurate account."

"And here I thought we were opening the gates," Breena mumbled.

Erin leaned forward and glared down the table at her. The priestess's expression was clear, no pack link required. She wanted the young woman to shut up.

"I'm interested to hear what happened after Ingram took her." Gwen rubbed her chin. "Isn't that as important as what led up to it?"

"Maybe if I stop being so rudely interrupted, I could get to that part," Ingram said as he turned to me. "She acted like I was a monster, but I told her to hold on tight, that it would be a bumpy ride."

I bit the inside of my cheek, desperate not to laugh again. Sterlyn had been right, and Azbogah was going out of his way to prove we weren't reliable, but damn it, the way Ingram was skewing the story was comical. He was trying very hard to sound like a hero, and he was arrogant enough to think these people would believe him.

He did have a strong ally in Azbogah, so maybe some of that belief wasn't unfounded. However, we had allies of our own on the council. Shouldn't that worry him a little?

"Is that true?" Erin grinned at the idiot and looked at me. "Did he warn you it would be bumpy?"

"Yup, he did, right before he took off with me." There was no point in lying, and I didn't need to manipulate anything for my truth to stand true. "But Rosemary reached us before he could take me too far."

"And did you even question his intentions?" Azbogah crossed his arms, focused on Rosemary.

Apparently, my angel friend had permission to speak now. How kind of him.

I don't know how you put up with this, Sterlyn. Cyrus clenched his free hand into a fist. *This guy is full of himself and a complete menace.*

Most of the council agrees with you, but we must be careful. Sterlyn focused on Rosemary, though she was speaking to us. Her face remained a mask of indifference; we couldn't see any of the emotions we felt through the bond. *But more and more people are seeing it, and just like with the silver wolves reintegrating into society, our handling of him must be slow and methodical, or more chaos will erupt.*

"No, I didn't ask if he was attempting to kidnap Annie." Rosemary shook her head. "I told him to put her down, and he ignored me."

"We were in the air. She would've fallen." Ingram shrugged and placed his hands in his jeans pockets.

"You *did* let me go, asshole," I gritted out. The guy had some nerve.

He scratched the back of his neck. "When Rosemary said it a second time, I was just trying to oblige."

"Maybe I—" Cyrus took a menacing step toward Ingram.

I tugged him back, cutting him off. "I guess you aren't that inquisitive or smart after all."

Rosemary chuckled, and Ronnie's shoulders shook with silent laughter.

"Watch it, mutt," Ingram spat.

"Let's say you were trying to listen to Rosemary and help out." Sterlyn pursed her lips. "Then why were you fighting us instead of explaining why you were there?"

"And," Ronnie interjected, her head tilted, "why did you tell Rosemary she had no clue who she was up against?"

"Because I'm me." Ingram patted his chest. "And I was only fighting back to protect myself. Any sane person would do that."

"Not when they're up against a future councilmember," Alex said, gesturing to Rosemary, "and four active councilmembers. That's not very smart and *definitely* not inquisitive."

The angel would never live down that description of himself.

Ingram's chest deflated like a balloon.

"At the end of the day, there is one question I'd *love* to know the answer to." Sterlyn paused, building up the moment. Tension swelled in my chest. Right when I thought I might explode, she asked, "Why were you flying over the neighborhood to begin with?"

Uh...what? That was totally anticlimactic. I'd expected an earth-shattering or jaw-dropping question, but that was like, why'd you go for a run? At least to someone other than me. I didn't like running unless I was in wolf form.

"Good question." Pahaliah fidgeted. "The angels allowed outside of Shadow City aren't to go any farther than Shadow Ridge and Shadow Terrace, yet you were flying over an unknown neighborhood. That shouldn't be possible unless you were breaking a rule."

Oh, damn! I was impressed again. Sterlyn's question had merit that I hadn't understood.

"The same could be said about Rosemary," Azbogah growled. "She was in the same neighborhood."

My stomach dropped. The last thing I wanted was for Rosemary to get into trouble for helping me. Sterlyn, however, wasn't surprised or upset by the accusation.

"I was there because my friends needed me." Rosemary crossed her arms, scowling. "Sterlyn called me, telling me they were under attack and someone was using guns against them. They needed my help."

"*She* was asked to be there by a councilmember seeking additional help." Yelahiah's mouth pressed into a line. "Ingram, were you asked by a councilmember to go to that neighborhood?"

Ingram froze, and his gaze went to Ezra.

Son of a bitch. Cyrus's body shook, and his eyes glowed.

I should have calmed him down, but my heart was hammering. Ezra was the one who'd directed Ingram there? Did that mean he was behind the attack on our pack? But he didn't even know me. Why the hell would he be working with an angel to capture me?

My arms tingled, which happened right before my fur sprouted.

Hold it together, Sterlyn commanded, her eyes glowing as she stared at Cyrus and me. *We can't react. I know it's hard, but we have to be strategic and not let our animals control us.*

My wolf growled, but she backed down, listening to her alpha.

How do you expect me to do that? Cyrus's breathing turned rapid, and a faint spattering of silver fur appeared on his arm and face. *That asshole had that angel attempt to take Annie.*

Breathe deeply, Sterlyn replied. *Control yourself. Otherwise, they won't pay, and it'll be harder for us to get the councilmembers who are on our side to listen. You might as well hand Annie over to them now.*

This council dynamic was full of corrupt people willing to do whatever was necessary to further their own agenda.

"How do you know he didn't hear something or that he wasn't trying to save her?" Azbogah gestured to Ingram. "Maybe he shouldn't have been out that way, but something brought him there."

Yeah, like a councilmember. I swallowed down the words, but they sat heavy in my stomach.

"I flew there by myself—no one was with me," Ingram said cryptically, addressing Yelahiah's question, despite not actually answering it. "I was trying to remove Annie from the situation, and if my actions seemed less than heroic, I apologize."

Maybe he was smarter than I'd given him credit for. That irritated me more than I liked to admit.

"None of this will happen again." Sterlyn placed her hands in her lap. "There are homes available for the silver wolves to move into in the Shadow Ridge alpha's neighborhood. I'm sure no one would be brave or stupid enough to attack them there."

"Are you sure that's wise?" Breena asked.

Sterlyn pointed at herself, then at Cyrus. "We were created to protect Shadow City, and there is no reason we shouldn't follow through on that duty now, especially since Killian welcomed us to live among them and protect them."

"Then I see no reason to continue this conversation." Azbogah swirled a hand in front of him. "Ingram, you're not to leave the designated areas again, and the same applies to every angel here, regardless of another councilmember's request. Is that clear?"

"What about the attack on Sterlyn's pack?" Ronnie scoffed. "The angel's involvement isn't the only problem."

"Young *queen*," Erin said condescendingly, "that is a shifter problem, not a council-wide issue like an angel being accused of the attempted kidnapping of a shifter. That's something for Sterlyn, Griffin, and Ezra to resolve...if they can."

"They still haven't resolved the shifter attack at the capitol building when Matthew and I were assaulted." Azbogah exhaled and rolled his eyes. "Besides, her pack has been *relocated* to our safe town, so all is well." Sarcasm laced the last sentence.

Griffin glowered. "I was there during the attack, too, in case you forgot."

"I have a feeling whoever was responsible for the

capitol attack—which, you'll recall, resulted in my wife being taken from me—is also behind the attack on the silver wolves tonight." Alex lifted a brow and leisurely addressed everyone. "And when I find and prove who did it, I'll tear them apart, limb by limb."

I shivered. Alex had appeared truly vampiric to me. Even when he was vamped out and fighting, he didn't scare me, but the person in front of me was a mate desperate to protect the love of his life. Whoever was responsible for these attacks had better fear him, Griffin, and Cyrus, because this person had put all three of their fated mates at risk, and they'd make sure it never happened again.

"As long as it's a vampire." Erin laughed a little too loudly. "Because—"

"This meeting is adjourned." Azbogah banged a gavel on the table. "Get these two out of Shadow City. Now."

Yeah, he didn't even need to say that. Every cell in my body urged me out the door.

One second, Sterlyn linked. *We need to talk to Ezra.*

My blood ran cold. I'd thought we were going to leave, but apparently, the confrontation was happening now.

CHAPTER SEVEN

ROSEMARY GLOWERED AND CALLED, "INGRAM!"

He flinched but didn't slow down, and the door slammed behind him. He'd wanted to get the hell out of there and not answer any more questions. How suspicious of him.

"Rosemary, leave Ingram alone," Yelahiah whispered, heading toward the three of us. She clucked her tongue, which somehow sounded alluring.

I bet Rosemary's mother could dress as a pig and still look sexy. She radiated confidence.

Rosemary sighed. "Mother...he was dissembling the entire time and tried to make me look unreasonable. What did you expect me to do?"

"Rise above it and not fall for his tricks." Yelahiah pressed her lips together. "You know how the men are around here. They think women are stupid and irrational. Do not bend to fit that picture like I did for a very long time. I don't want you to have the same regrets."

All the other councilmembers except for Sterlyn rose from their seats.

"Yeah, too late for that." Rosemary huffed, her irises darkening in disappointment.

Her mother patted her arm. "You have not. You woke up quickly without making horrible decisions." Pain lined Yelahiah's face before her attention switched to me.

Sterlyn lifted a hand. "Wait. We still have to talk with Ezra and the council. We need another moment."

A frown crossed the wolf councilmember's face before he could smooth his expression into a mask of indifference. "Shouldn't they be escorted out, then?" He nodded at Cyrus and me.

That momentary look told me plenty. He was uncomfortable, which was both a good and bad thing. Bad because he'd be careful not to make a mistake but good because he was hiding *something*. We just had to determine what.

"It's regarding the attack tonight, but it isn't about Ingram." She smiled, not budging.

Pahaliah leaned over and said something in Griffin's ear. It was low enough that if I hadn't been watching everyone's body language, I might have missed it. I linked to Cyrus, *Did you pick up on what Rosemary's dad said to Griffin?* With the moon getting full, his hearing would be better than almost anyone else's in here, apart from Sterlyn's.

What are you talking about? Cyrus asked, glaring at Ezra.

Well, that explained it. Cyrus was focused on the third wolf councilmember and nothing else. I rolled my eyes, but I couldn't say much of anything. If I'd thought he'd orchestrated Cyrus's kidnapping, I'd be doing more than just glaring, proving Cyrus had more self-control than people gave him credit for, especially since I could feel his turmoil. His rage was intense, making it difficult for me to breathe.

I took a step closer to him, hoping that would ease some of his anger. When my lungs drew in a fuller breath, I almost smiled. My touch did affect him, even if he didn't realize it.

"I guess we can resume if Azbogah is okay with it." Erin turned toward the dark angel and leaned over so he had a full view of her cleavage.

Ronnie hissed, her emerald eyes turning a faint shade of crimson.

The witch was also giving Alex a view.

Poor Alex closed his eyes to avoid glimpsing more of her breasts than he already had.

"Back off my husband, or I will kick your ass," Ronnie warned.

I held back my laugh. For all of Erin's attempts to appear strong and secure, she was falling over herself to get the angel to notice her.

Surprisingly, the priestess was smart enough to listen to my sister, and she straightened, her neck turning red.

Yelahiah cleared her throat and retook her seat

between Sterlyn and Ronnie. Her attention remained on me. "This involves the silver wolf pack and the demon wolf I've heard so much about."

My hand tightened on Cyrus's arm. I wasn't sure if it was because that gorgeous woman's attention was on me or that she was discussing my heritage. Either way, my stomach fluttered.

Cyrus growled faintly. "She's *my* Annie. Don't call her a demon wolf."

He'd never called me his Annie before, but I *loved* the way it sounded.

"I didn't mean any insult, though I can see how my words could be misconstrued." Yelahiah touched her chest. "I'm sorry."

There was nothing patronizing in her tone, and she leaned forward, staring at me like she could see my soul. *Could* she see my soul? Angels and demons could see someone's essence...

"It's fine." I blew out a breath, trying to steel my nerves. "It's just that when I stayed with the pack I was born to, I realized they're egocentric and sexist, similar to —" I cut myself off, not wanting to say his name, but my gaze darted to Azbogah, my message clear.

The arrogant man furrowed his brows, looking confused about what I was getting at.

Yelahiah laughed, and the sound reminded me of my high school bell ensemble—light, tinkling, and mesmerizing. I'd thought about joining them my junior year, but I'd needed to spend my time focusing on school and saving for my future. But maybe there was more to it than that, like my demon side equating it to angel laughter, and Lord knew we couldn't have that.

"What the hell is going on here?" Azbogah barked, his dark gaze on me. He sneered. "It doesn't matter. I agree with Ezra—they need to go."

Griffin lowered his head and scowled. "First off, you don't get to make all the decisions. You were the only one on the council who demanded that they leave. And second, they'll leave with us when the meeting is officially over."

"I *know* how the council works," Azbogah rasped. "But since they don't live in the city, I figured you'd want to get them back outside the gates sooner rather than later."

"The gates are open now, remember?" Ronnie batted her eyes. "So we've got to start letting people other than Sterlyn and me in and out, right?"

"It's bad enough that there are so many people leaving to go to that damn school or work outside these gates." Diana scoffed and leaned back in her chair. "I don't know why anyone would want to leave this city."

"It's helpful to see how the world operates outside these walls." Gwen yawned and winked at me. "Besides, Annie and Cyrus are the family of councilmembers. I don't see a problem with them staying, much like Rosemary."

"Are we ever going to get to the point? I'd like to go home." Ezra had dark circles under his eyes. Was he tired due to the late-night meeting...or was he too stressed to sleep well?

Maybe I could make him squirm. "Are you okay?"

"Why wouldn't I be?" He chuckled, but no humor reflected on his face, as if he were trying to sound light-hearted but couldn't pull the act off.

"You do look pretty rough," Rosemary said with her usual bluntness.

He cleared his throat and averted his gaze.

Interesting. That body language indicated he was hiding something. Was it that he'd coordinated the attack on the silver wolves or something else?

"It's been a rough few weeks with the tensions between the shifter races." Ezra straightened his shoulders, his attention on me. "You may not all know what's been happening, seeing as your focus has been on things outside of our community."

"We're aware," Cyrus muttered. "We just had a group of shifters attack our neighborhood under somebody's orders."

The council members truly lived in a bubble. I bet if a war started outside these walls, they wouldn't care as long as they weren't impacted.

"Maybe so, but I don't see how this is worth the council's time unless Griffin recognized the shifters and couldn't get them to listen to him," Ezra said.

Griffin smirked and rubbed the back of his neck. "They weren't Shadow City wolves, and Killian didn't recognize them from Shadow Ridge."

"Which means it's not a Shadow City or Shadow Ridge problem, so again, your focus is diverted." Ezra shrugged and placed his hands behind his head. Sweat stains under his arms had turned his pale green shirt several shades darker, and my nose picked up sour body odor.

Sterlyn tapped a finger against her bottom lip. "I don't understand why you think the problem is irrelevant. If they're attacking shifters this close by, how do we know they won't attack the city as well?"

"Babe," Griffin chastised lovingly. "That would require him to be able to see the bigger picture."

Ezra bared his teeth. "I can see the bigger picture, but it's clear you've all forgotten that no one can reach us in here."

"What about all the shifters and vampires who live outside these walls?" Ronnie shook a finger at him. "You know, the ones who protect you while you stay safe in here? Are their lives not important to you?"

"The shifters who attacked tonight were from the same group Dick and Saga sent to slaughter my pack, and they attacked us in the woods that border Griffin and Killian's pack neighborhood." Sterlyn's voice had hardened.

Ezra's mouth dropped. "How do you know that?"

"Because I trained them before I was found. I recognized every attacker," Cyrus sneered, his body tensing even more.

Yelahiah touched her throat as she inhaled. "Oh, dear. That *is* problematic. Maybe we should—"

"No." Azbogah crossed his arms. "Unless they attack the city, we won't get involved. If we start inserting ourselves into every fight outside these walls, chaos will ensue. We need to settle things here first, which Sterlyn and Griffin aren't doing very well. Besides, you know we can't have angels leave these borders. Rosemary and Ingram have done enough damage."

His adamancy that angels couldn't leave had to be due to whatever agreement the angels had struck with the demons. Rosemary had mentioned that when the Shadow City gates closed about one thousand years ago, the demons had agreed to leave the angels and Shadow City alone if certain parameters were set. We just weren't sure what those parameters were.

"It's late, and we're all tired." Pahaliah raised his arms. "We can do nothing tonight, and we're just going to argue without coming to an agreement. The best thing we can do is head home and get some rest. We're all on edge, especially those who endured an assault tonight. If we feel the need to discuss this further, or if there is another attack, we can continue at our next meeting."

Sterlyn. Cyrus's displeasure coursed through the bond. *We can't just leave without answers.*

Pahaliah's right. We can't hound Ezra too hard, or he'll be more cautious. We need to watch him and see who's really behind everything. Sterlyn nodded. "I'm good with tabling the discussion, but I think his potential involvement should be addressed before another attack happens. The next attack could very well be on Shadow Ridge soil."

"And that would be your fault." Erin flipped her hair over her shoulder. "You decided to move them there."

"We all decided," Ronnie interjected. "And if they

aren't allowed in Shadow Ridge, we'll move them to Shadow Terrace."

"Surely Alex wouldn't approve of that." Azbogah laughed loudly, but when he glanced at the vampire king, he sobered.

Alex arched a brow and regarded the dark angel coldly. "She is my wife and queen, so my approval isn't needed. Annie is family, and Cyrus is her mate. Of course they and their pack are welcome in Shadow Terrace whenever they want."

"Unlike Matthew, Alex not only values his wife, but my voice as well." Gwen beamed at her brother.

Matthew, the former vampire king, had tried to force my sister to turn into a vampire, then tried to have her killed because she was Alex's soulmate. He'd gone so far as to find Ronnie's demon father to kill Ronnie when he and Azbogah couldn't.

"If we're all in agreement with my mate, I think we should head out." Yelahiah stood as she scanned every council member. "We can reconvene in three days and continue this discussion at our regularly scheduled meeting."

Murmurs of agreement echoed through the room, and everyone stood and made their way toward the door.

Ronnie, Sterlyn, and Griffin hurried toward us.

Let's get out of here, Sterlyn linked. When she reached us, she turned to Rosemary. "Are you coming back with us?"

"I'd better stay put," Rosemary said sadly. "But I'll come by in the morning."

I hated that we might have gotten our friend into trouble. I didn't want to cause problems with her and the angels. She deserved so much better than that. I wrapped my arms around her, my chest aching. "I'm sorry if this makes things hard on you, but thank you so much for saving me."

Rosemary's eyes widened for a second. Then she awkwardly wrapped an arm around me and patted my shoulder. "I will always protect this group. You're family in every way that counts."

Her kind words warmed my heart. She wasn't emotional and rarely showed affection, so her attempt to hug me back said wonders. "I feel the same about you."

She smiled and stepped away from me. "I know."

"Let's go." Ronnie looped her arm through mine and dragged Cyrus and me out the door.

In the expansive entry hall, I surveyed our group, counting Sterlyn, Ronnie, Griffin, Cyrus, and me. "Where's Alex?"

"He's talking to Gwen." Ronnie frowned and gestured at the doorway. "We're spending the night here to help organize things so we don't throw a ton of crap on Gwen, but we'll want to stay in the spare bedroom at your place tomorrow."

"Consider yourselves welcome." Sterlyn hugged her and headed for the door. "We'll see you tomorrow."

"Annie, if something happens or you need anything —" Ronnie started.

I kissed her cheek and promised, "I'll call you."

Her body sagged. "Good. Now, go get some rest."

I squeezed her arm and followed Sterlyn out of the capitol. I was ready for bed.

THE JOURNEY back to Shadow Ridge was made in silence. Cyrus and I checked in with Darrell, and the silver wolf pack had settled in fine. Luckily, Killian's neighborhood's houses were furnished.

I was learning that the pack took care of their own, and the homes we were occupying had been built for future generations. There was still land available to build more houses.

We pulled into the neighborhood full of Craftsman-style homes in varying shades of white, blue, green, and yellow, and my yawn broke through despite my best efforts.

We reached Griffin and Sterlyn's white, one-story house with its gorgeous wraparound porch. They pulled into the garage while Cyrus parked in the driveway, then got out of the car and snatched our black bags from the trunk.

I climbed out of the vehicle slowly and headed to the front door.

Sterlyn opened it as soon as I reached it. "Let's get you all settled," she said as Cyrus stepped in behind me. She led us through the small hallway and into her cozy living room. Even with the lights off, I could see the blue-gray walls and the pearl-gray couch that sat against the room's longest wall in front of a flat-screen television.

The matching loveseat sat perpendicular to the couch and across from the windows. The only illumination in the room came from the moonlight shining through the blinds. To the right of the windows was a doorway that led to their backyard.

The blinds were open, so I could see their backyard and the woods that abutted it. Killian lived next door, and even though it was early September, the moonlight glimmered off the still-open pool at his house.

We walked past the kitchen and down another short hallway to a door on the right. I'd stayed in the room before, so the familiar walls, a shade darker than the living room, felt like home. A queen-sized bed covered with white sheets and a charcoal comforter was centered against one wall, and a dresser with a television mounted above it sat against the opposite wall. The walk-in closet to the right was plenty big for both Cyrus and me.

"There are towels in the bathroom closet, as you know, with soaps, shampoos, and conditioners." Sterlyn stayed close to the door. "Let me know if you two need anything else."

Cyrus laid our bags on the shaggy brown carpet and leaned against the wall. "Thank you for letting us stay. If we—"

"This is your home." Sterlyn squeezed his arm. "Both of yours." Her eyes glowed faintly as she took me in.

My tongue thickened with emotion, and I couldn't speak.

"I'm going to bed. I'm exhausted." Sterlyn walked into the hallway and grinned. "Good night."

"Good night," I finally murmured.

When she shut the door, I crumpled onto the bed. Within seconds, Cyrus had scooted next to me and pulled me into his arms.

My head fit perfectly against his chest, and I listened to his steady heartbeat.

"I thought I was going to lose you tonight," he whispered, and his arms tightened around me. "I—I almost lost it." His turmoil rolled into me, mixed with his love for me.

"Hey." I pulled away slightly and stared at his handsome face. His cheeks were strong, and his lashes were full. He could easily be a model, though I'd have to kill any woman who looked at him. "I'm right here."

His silver eyes lightened, turning the color reserved only for me. "And you better always stay that way." His lips crashed onto mine, and he kissed me with so much passion.

All my fatigue faded as my body warmed. I opened my mouth, letting him slip his tongue inside. His cinnamon taste warmed me as his lips devoured me. Moments like this were perfect.

My hand slipped between us, feeling his hardness.

He groaned and pulled away. "Not tonight. You're tired. You need your rest."

"After." Not wanting to hear *no* again, I scooted back and removed my shirt.

His lips parted as his hands clenched. "Annie," he groaned, fueling my need further. "I'm *really* trying to take care of you."

I unclasped my bra and removed it.

He licked his lips as I shimmied out of my shorts and panties, completely naked for him.

"Baby," he whispered as I straddled him.

"You said you wanted to take care of me," I teased, but it was enough to crumble his resolve.

He placed his hand behind my neck and pulled me down to him. I kissed him as I rocked against him, and he rubbed me through his jeans.

He flipped me onto my back, and his hands slid between my legs. *You are a fucking goddess.* His lips captured one nipple, and he flicked his tongue as his fingers circled my tender area.

I unfastened his jeans, then slipped my hand inside his boxers. As he touched me, I stroked him. Our bodies were sweaty from pleasure.

The friction grew, and I yanked his hand away. "I need more." My wolf howled in my head, demanding it.

"Okay," he growled, eyes glowing. He stood and grabbed my waist, yanking me toward the end of the bed.

He kicked off his jeans and boxers while he removed his shirt. My eyes took in his rock-hard abs and lickable body. He was gorgeous, handsome, and all mine.

I spread my legs and arched against him, eager for him to fill me. I wasn't above begging.

When he finally entered me, I moaned, and the connection between us intensified. Every part of us collided. My heart grew in size as his feelings slammed into me. We completed each other, and we'd do anything to keep the other safe. This was the kind of love that most only dreamed of finding, and I was so damn lucky he was mine.

He hovered over me, watching me as we moved together. *I kinda love you so damn much, Annie.* He paused, cupping my cheek as he stared at me with adoration.

I kinda really love you, too. Those words didn't convey enough. This man owned me, heart, body, and soul.

He moved his hand between my legs, adding pressure as he slid in and out of me.

Needing an anchor, I grabbed the comforter and moved in sync with him.

When the friction built between us, he quickened the pace of his thrusting and his fingers. My head grew dizzy from the high, and I closed my eyes, concentrating on everything he made me feel. Sensations built, stronger and stronger, as our emotions crashed together and pleasure surged until orgasms ripped through us.

Cyrus slowly moved to lie on the bed next to me, his body coated with sweat. He pulled me to his chest, and I breathed in his scent as I fell fast asleep.

I NEED YOUR HELP, Darrell linked, waking Cyrus and me from sleep.

I opened my eyes, trying to remember where we were and what day it was. The urge to close them again overtook me when I found myself safe in Cyrus's arms.

Cyrus groaned, not happy about being disturbed. *What is it?*

Mila, Darrell answered simply.

That was equivalent to having a caffeine IV drip. Cyrus and I jumped to our feet.

What the hell was the woman up to now?

CHAPTER EIGHT

I RUSHED to my duffel bag and pulled out some clothes. I'd hoped to take a shower this morning, but that wasn't happening. I could only hope and pray the extra layer of deodorant I put on covered me for the rest of the day.

After slipping on my clothes, I enjoyed watching Cyrus put on his light gray cotton shirt. His abs contracted as he pulled it over his head, and my body warmed again. Last night hadn't been enough, but we had things to address.

Like Mila.

When would her shit ever end? I'd tried to connect with her. I thought I'd gotten through to her when she'd found Cyrus and me in a compromising position before we realized that we were mates. Everyone had thought I was human, and Cyrus and I had thought I was a demon, not a wolf, so he'd been fighting our connection. She'd promised not to tell anyone about us for a few days, but she'd thrown me under the bus at the first opportunity to gain leverage over Cyrus, setting off a spiral of attacks that had ended with her, Theo, Rudie, Chad, and Cyrus being taken by the demon wolves.

Despite Theo, Rudie, and Chad rejoining the pack, Mila was holding out, clinging to her anger over losing her fated mate, Bart, who was Cyrus and Sterlyn's uncle, instead of grieving and trying to move on.

Sterlyn, Mila is causing problems, Cyrus linked with us.

My mouth almost dropped, but I kept it closed. I couldn't believe what I'd heard. Had he actually informed his sister about a problem?

What? His eyes lightened to the color of his shirt. *Why are you looking at me like that?*

My chest expanded as my heart warmed. *I'm proud of you.* In moments like this, I could see we were both healing. Before, he would've marched out there and tried to hide the turmoil from his sister, wanting to prove himself to her. Whether he realized it or not, he was growing. He was relying on Sterlyn and me to figure out how to handle this.

I guess since I didn't handle Mila very well before, I should listen to my mate and my sister about letting them have my back. He bit his bottom lip and glanced at the floor.

Ugh, I'd made him feel awkward, and that was not what I'd been aiming for. I walked across the room and placed a finger under his chin, tilting his head up so he looked me in the eye. *I know, and I find it very sexy.*

He smirked, pulling me against his body. He kissed me and linked, *Maybe I could start doing things like that more often.* He pulled back, the corners of his eyes wrinkling. *Oh, babe. I can't reach my feet. Can you put my socks on?*

I laughed, enjoying this brief moment of happiness before we marched out there to handle the woman who would ruin my good mood. *Uh...good luck with that. I guess you'll be dealing with cold little piggies.*

Piggies? His brows furrowed. *You mean toes?*

Yes, like this little piggy went to the market? Eliza had told me the little nursery rhyme over and over as a little girl, making me squeal in delight as she tickled the bottom of my feet.

I have no clue what you're talking about. Cyrus ran his fingers through my hair as he examined my face. *Why would your toes be called piggies and go to any market?*

My heart constricted, and I tried to hide my hurt. He'd grown up with no one to teach him nursery rhymes, with no one to tell him they loved him, with no one to kiss his booboos and tell him that everything would be okay. I hated that his childhood had been stolen from him, but there wasn't a damn thing I could do about it. *It's nothing.*

He squinted at me just as someone knocked on our bedroom door.

Whew. Saved by the bell.

I didn't want him to think I felt sorry for him—I didn't—but my heart ached for him.

The signature freesia smell wafted under the crack, alerting us it was Sterlyn standing outside our door. She linked, *Hey, sorry. Killian was talking to Griffin and me. We need to go to the training area.*

Training area? I hadn't noticed anything like that nearby, but I hadn't been looking for it.

Cyrus opened the door. Sterlyn stood there in her usual jeans and black shirt. She wore dressy things on occasion, but her choices were similar to Ronnie's and mine, leaning toward more comfortable clothing.

"All of you ready?" Griffin asked, his voice gruff.

I glanced down the hallway to find him standing at the front door. His arms were crossed, and he was tapping his foot. He wore jeans, not his usual khakis, and a T-shirt. His muscles bulged, almost as big as Cyrus's, but no one could hold a candle to my mate. *What's wrong with him?* I asked Sterlyn as I hurried toward the Shadow City alpha.

Whenever someone gives me a hard time, he gets upset, and not being able to link with you irritates him, too. Sterlyn brushed past me and took her mate's hand. *This whole split-pack thing is getting harder to navigate, but it's too early to combine the packs. We need to get the silver wolves more settled and things straightened out in Shadow City.*

She was right. The silver wolves had been through enough turmoil, moving around as they had in the past year, then coming out of hiding and being forced to assimilate into a society they weren't comfortable with.

Things had to calm down before we made any other drastic changes. I also wondered what that would mean for Cyrus and me in the pack dynamics. Cyrus was acting alpha, but when the packs merged, how would that change things?

Something else to address later.

Cyrus held my hand as we followed Sterlyn and Griffin outside. We turned right, heading toward the entrance to the neighborhood.

We picked up our pace and rushed to join the others. When we reached the woods near the entrance, Griffin turned into the tree line between two redbuds and jogged straight ahead.

The sun was rising, and the heat warmed my back. The scents of magnolia and iris hung around us, further evidence that it was early September and autumn was approaching.

If the packs merge, what would that mean, exactly? I linked with Cyrus. My wolf surged through me, enjoying being in the woods and part of nature.

Cyrus ran a few steps behind me, keeping close. I could feel his heat, but it could've just been our mate link working. I could always feel him, especially when he was near me.

It won't change much. The Shadow City wolves will, for the most part, remain in the city until things become more resolved there. Cyrus's breathing was even, as if he wasn't exerting himself. *And the silver wolves will want someone sympathetic to lead. Even if I'm not acting alpha,*

I'll be beta and helping with the packs, especially when Sterlyn's preoccupied. I doubt the packs will officially merge, but we'll see. A lot depends on how we integrate into Shadow Ridge, too.

He was right—even with Cyrus as acting alpha, Darrell handled a lot of pack politics. He was still viewed as a leader. And Griffin and Sterlyn were amazing leaders, so whatever they figured out, I trusted it would be the best for everyone involved.

Mila's voice assaulted my ears. "I'm just saying maybe you should all reconsider who you ally with. The silver wolves are a good group, don't get me wrong. My fated mate was their alpha and an amazing leader. He died because of his nephew, who is now leading the pack. He trained—"

"That's enough," Killian growled. "Did you forget you're the reason three others defected from the silver wolf pack and were captured? Yet, after everything, Cyrus and the others came to save you. We exposed Annie to that pack, and Cyrus was captured because of everything *you* did."

The four of us broke through the last of the trees, and a huge clearing came into view. The Tennessee River bordered the opposite side. The open space was easily one hundred yards wide, and thick green grass covered the ground. The red roofs of Shadow Terrace were visible through the cypresses, oaks, and redbuds that densely covered the other side of the river as well. Unless someone was in the trees or on a roof on the vampire side, or a boat came by, the training grounds were hidden from view.

Mila stood between Killian and Darrell in front of twenty of Killian's shifters and twenty-three silver wolves. Her cognac eyes were wild as she pulled her cinnamon brown hair away from her face. The sun enhanced her dark olive complexion, but her eyes looked sunken, as if she were sickly.

"You have to stop," Darrell commanded and glanced over his shoulder at us. "This has gone on long enough."

"Bart would be—" Mila started, but Sterlyn didn't give her a chance.

She marched over to her aunt and frowned. "After everything that happened, we allowed you to remain with us without rejoining the pack. Look at you—you're falling apart, and being a rogue isn't helping."

"How could I rejoin?" Mila laughed harshly. "You two took everything away from me! Even my own daughter can't stand to be around me."

My limit for bullshit had been reached. "If you don't like it, leave." My time at the group home had taught me that sometimes tough love was the only way to break through to someone. It was hard, and Lord knew I didn't want Mila to leave because she was one of the few family members Cyrus and Sterlyn had left, but letting her continue to hang around us, spilling her hate, only made things worse. I'd hoped she'd wake up on her own, but it wasn't happening.

"Excuse me?" Mila's jaw dropped, her attention on

me. "You're the newest member of the pack, and you think you can talk to me that way? You might be Cyrus's mate, but I was Bart's, and I have more influence over these people, especially the women, than you do."

"No, you don't." Martha stepped forward, breaking away from the group. "Sterlyn and Annie are the women we follow. Not you, especially not anymore."

"Martha." Mila placed a hand on her chest. "After all we've been through, this is how you repay me?"

"Stop making this about you." Martha jabbed a finger at Mila. "You're angry and unbearable to be around. You attacked those dark wolves, starting the fight and putting people I love in danger. I agree with Annie. If you can't get your shit together, you need to leave."

"Is this how you all feel?" Mila's voice cracked, and she glanced at Chad, Theo, and Rudie, the three she was closest to. I only hoped they would remain loyal and not defect again. They'd become great allies after we'd saved them from the demon pack.

Rudie stepped beside Martha. Her irises turned navy as she gazed at me. "Mila, I love you and respect you so much. You know that, but you've changed. You blame Cyrus for Bart's death, but your recklessness led to my mate's capture because we followed you blindly. I can't keep doing that."

"And we'd all have died if Annie hadn't shown up to meet with that alpha," Theo agreed, and stood next to his mate. "How is what you did any different from what you're accusing Cyrus of doing?"

She sucked in a breath, and her face scrunched.

"You know you're like a mother to me, but things have to change." Chad placed his hands in his jeans pockets. "I'm sorry, but this is my pack and where I'm supposed to be. Where *we're* supposed to be." He gestured to him and her. "I miss him, too."

I scanned the rest of the pack. Most of the silver wolves had their eyes cast downward, uncomfortable with the scene. Killian's pack was a mixed bag, with Sierra standing in the front with her arms crossed. I was surprised she hadn't said anything, but with the glare she was directing at Killian, I suspected why.

"Mila, I agree with Annie." Cyrus took a slow step toward the woman, not wanting to intimidate her. "It would be best if you left to figure out what you want to do. You will always have a place in this pack if you want it. If not, I'm sure your father would be overjoyed to have you join his pack again."

She stumbled back a few steps, moving away from the shifters in front of her and the four of us. Her bottom lip trembled, and her eyes turned glassy.

Something hard settled in my stomach. I hated that she was about to break down, but sometimes hitting rock bottom was the only way for someone to pull themselves together.

"But...I can't go back to my dad's pack permanently. Jewel needs to be with this pack since she's silver, and I don't want to split off from her." She ran her fingers through her limp, greasy hair and tugged. "I...I need to stay here."

"You can't unless you accept Cyrus and me as your

leaders." Sterlyn moved beside me so she and Cyrus flanked me. The three of us stood tall together against the poor, broken woman.

I wasn't sure how she would respond. A desperate, fearful woman could do bad things—worse than what she'd already accomplished.

She frantically searched each face for something, and her jaw twitched. "Fine. I don't need you, anyway." She turned on her heel and took off, racing past us toward the houses.

I wanted to run after her, but that would negate everything we'd done. We had to stand firm—any sign of weakness, and she would continue to wreak havoc. Worse, she wouldn't take anything we said seriously again.

"Okay, does anyone else have a problem?" Killian scanned his pack and the silver wolves. "I want it to be clear that moving forward, our packs will be living and working closely together. We will have each other's backs in everything from this point on."

Sterlyn nodded and stepped up beside Killian. She lifted her head as she addressed both of the packs next. "The silver wolves were meant to protect Shadow City, and due to unfortunate circumstances, we failed to deliver on that purpose. Your pack," she said, addressing Killian's section, "took over that role with more dignity and grace than anyone could have hoped, and my pack will forever be grateful to you. Since we failed you and the residents who live here, we're honored that you're allowing us to assist you with what is now your rightful duty. We aren't and would never try to replace or diminish anything you've accomplished. We're humbled that your alpha and pack have gracefully opened your home and made room for us."

Her words were so simple and perfect. She'd addressed an issue I hadn't considered Killian's pack could be upset about—the one where we'd come to replace them and take over the purpose their pack had had for centuries.

A man in his mid-twenties nodded, his long pecan hair falling into his face. He scratched his chocolate-copper scruff as he straightened his shoulders. "I suppose we can get behind that."

The older man next to him smiled, and the action made sunlight reflect off his bald head. He was close to the same build and height as Killian. He chuckled. "I stand with my alpha. He's a true leader doing the best for everyone, just like his father."

Who is that? I asked. The older man held a proud look as he stared at the boy beside him and Killian.

Sterlyn moved to stand beside us again, now that the threat of an argument was gone. She linked, *That's Billy, Killian's beta. He was Killian's father's beta and helped handle the pack while Killian mourned his family. That's his son, Lowe, beside him.*

Having the acting betas on board with this plan alle-viated the knot in my chest.

"I guess it's time to start training." Killian clapped his hands. "This group will go with us to the demon pack, so we need to train with the silver wolves. Everyone, pair up with someone from a different pack."

"I'll take the girl," Lowe said, pointing at me.

Cyrus growled low in his chest, and his hands shook beside him.

Great, this was already starting out well.

CHAPTER NINE

I PLACED a hand on Cyrus's chest to calm his wolf. Despite wolves not liking the other gender touching their mate, there was more going on than that. Everywhere we turned, we were in danger, making his protective instinct that much stronger.

"You can train with *me*," Cyrus rasped, his silver eyes glowing. "Not my *mate*."

"Whoa." Lowe raised his arms in surrender. "I didn't mean to threaten you. I—"

Oh, dear God. This was getting worse.

"*I* don't feel *threatened*," Cyrus bellowed, patches of fur sprouting on his arms.

"Dude, I didn't mean it like that." Lowe flicked his gaze at Killian.

Killian smirked and rocked back on his feet. The message was clear—Lowe could handle it himself.

I appreciated the sentiment since the two packs had to learn how to communicate with each other. Killian and

Sterlyn couldn't get involved with every disagreement. They didn't do that within the packs, and they sure as hell couldn't handle doing it for two separate packs, especially when Sterlyn's attention was split between here and Shadow City.

Body quivering, Cyrus laughed. "It doesn't matter. If you come near her, I'll hurt you."

Hey, I don't think he meant anything by it. The last thing we needed was for a fight to break out between the two groups after we'd all agreed to work together.

Lowe huffed. "She just smells different, that's all." He tapped his nose as if that clarified what he was alluding to. "Her scent is like a combination of vampire, angel, and wolf with a musky, overly sweet flower. I'm not interested in her, just curious what she's capable of."

"Don't worry, babe." Sierra winked at me and sashayed over. "*I* think you're hot."

"I didn't mean she's not hot," Lowe said, and rubbed a hand down his face.

Another low growl rattled in Cyrus's chest.

The poor guy couldn't catch a break. If this had been happening to anyone else, I'd have found it funny, but I was most definitely not amused.

"You have a knack for adding tension and drama to any situation." Griffin nodded at Sierra and chuckled as he came to stand beside Sterlyn. The gold flecks in his hazel eyes were bright with mirth. "I've never seen anyone with half as much of your talent."

"I don't know." Sterlyn leaned against him. "Azbogah has his own natural flair."

"True, but his intent is malicious, while Sierra's is more..." He looked toward the cloudless blue sky. "*Playful* isn't the right word for it."

"Snarky," Killian offered. "Because it's not malicious, but it's not always from a place of kindness either like right now."

"I'm kind!" Sierra's jaw dropped, feigning shock. "He said she was ugly, and I was telling her she wasn't."

Lowe glared at her. "She's not ugly, but she's clearly taken. I'm not into someone else's fated mate. All I wanted to do was spar with her to see what she's got." He threw his hands over his head. "That's it. There's nothing more to it."

Cyrus's anger ebbed. He pulled me to his side.

I'll have to train with them. I looked up into his eyes. *I need to work with different people to practice different fighting styles. You can't act like this the entire time.*

His eyes narrowed. *Like hell I can't. Do you know what it's been like—*

Yes, I know what it's been like. I hated to argue with him, but we had to be smart and not let our emotions and bond override logic. *I watched them drive away with you in the back of a van, and I couldn't even communicate with you. Don't act like I haven't been through my own trauma when it comes to you.*

He exhaled, his body relaxing. *You're right. I just feel as if there's a target on your back all the damn time.* He placed his chin on my forehead, and guilt mixed in with his anger.

Him and me both. *Living in fear puts Tate in control.*

Besides, you're the only man for me. Surely you know that.
I wrapped my arms around his waist, needing to reassure him both physically and mentally.

The last bit of hesitation crumbled away, and the tension in my chest receded. He replied, *I know that. I'm being a jackass.*

Since I didn't have anything nice to say, I opted for the best alternative. *I still kinda love you.*

Cyrus kissed the top of my head, his chest shaking with laughter, and said to Lowe, "Sorry, man. Someone tried to kidnap her last night, and it has me on edge. If you—"

"Nope, I'm good." Lowe waved his hands. "I don't—"

"It's sweet that you two think you can make decisions for me." I got that they were macho males, but I had my own mind. "But I'm capable of making those on my own, and I would like to kick your ass—er—I mean, spar with you."

Lowe's eyes twinkled, and a smirk crossed his face. "Are you really going to talk shit?"

Cyrus grunted, not happy with the conversation, but he wisely said, "We're wasting time. Let's get moving."

"Get your partner, and let's start off in human form to get acclimated." Sterlyn clapped her hands and glanced at everyone. "We need to rotate and get comfortable with each other." She linked with the silver wolf pack, *In wolf form, we're stronger, so it's best if we start out this way so they can get a sense of how we move in human form before we take them on in animal.*

The angel descendants in wolf form would be even stronger, so it was best to stay in human form.

"Come on, Cyrus," Griffin patted his shoulder. "We've never fought each other before."

Everyone split up. Darrell and Killian teamed up, and Sterlyn walked over to Billy. It wasn't hard for me to notice that each alpha was sparring with a beta from another pack, including Griffin and Cyrus.

I headed to an area close to the water. The rushing sound of the river soothed me, and I rolled my shoulders to loosen up. I was weakening as the moon was waxing. Since it wasn't a full moon, or what the silver wolves called a Silver Moon, I was still stronger than a normal wolf shifter, but my magic was weakening, while the silver wolves' magic was gaining strength.

"Are you sure this is okay?" Lowe tugged at his ear. He was attractive, and I wondered why Sierra wasn't into him.

She'd never talked about anyone here, so I was pretty sure she wasn't romantically involved with any of them. With her love of romantic comedies, she was probably waiting for Prince Charming to sweep her off her feet.

Swallowing a chuckle, I pulled my hair into a pony-tail. The confrontation with Mila had fatigued me, but I was determined not to let it affect my training. "It's fine. Like he said, things have been tense lately, and we're newly mated, so our wolves are struggling to acclimate."

At least he had the decency to feel nervous and not downplay or disregard the way Cyrus had reacted. After the council meeting, with members purposely trying to upset each other, it was refreshing. Though I figured Killian wouldn't put up with that in his pack, seeing it for myself was encouraging.

Actions spoke louder than words.

That was the saying Eliza had beaten into me as a child.

"Even more reason this might not be a good idea." Lowe kicked at the ground. "I'm not trying to cause problems."

Maybe this was why Sierra wasn't into him. He looked strong and burly, but it seemed like he was one of those sensitive souls.

Whatever. I wasn't in the mood to chat about my feelings for Cyrus or vice versa. I didn't even know the guy. I balled my hands and held them in front of my chest. "If you don't spar with me, we're going to have problems." I set my feet shoulder-width apart and scowled. Smiling didn't seem like the right thing to do.

He blew a raspberry and cracked his neck. "All right. Let's do this." He didn't move urgently, as if he didn't consider me a real threat.

What an asshat. I had to prove him wrong.

My wolf brushed against my mind, and I threw a punch. As expected, Lowe blocked it, so I kicked him in the stomach.

His eyes bulged as he stumbled back a few steps and tripped. At the last second, he almost stayed on his feet, but he fell onto his ass.

Martha bumped her shoulder into mine, and I realized she and Sierra had moved to spar next to us. The older woman beamed. "That's what they get for thinking we'll hold back."

Though she wasn't a silver wolf, she was mated to one and had been part of the pack for who knew how long. Their daughter was around my age, so she and Darrell must have found each other shortly after Bart and the others had split from the pack for safety. Though she was technically weaker than the silver wolves, she was a strong wolf who I'd bet could challenge any alpha if she so desired.

"We're doing this?" Lowe asked as he climbed to his feet and stretched. He tried to come off as cool, but the corners of his mouth dipped downward. "I realize you're part of the silver wolf pack, but I thought it was because you were *his* mate."

That was true. "You assumed correctly." I smiled.

"That's what I thought. I didn't expect you to be so strong." He tilted his head, taking me in again. "You're the one those wolves are after."

I wasn't sure what Killian had told them, but he'd informed them of more than I'd thought he would. The color of my fur was bound to come out eventually, and it was probably smart that he inform them. That way, no one would be upset about secrets.

Lord knew we'd kept enough for eternity in the name of protection.

Cyrus moved toward me, obviously not liking where the conversation was heading, but I had to go with my gut. I'd seen how lies affected the kids in the group home —they made them not trust anyone. After being on the receiving end of half-truths and misrepresentations, I understood exactly how those kids felt.

Besides, if I lied, they'd all know. "Yes, I'm the biological daughter of the alpha."

Annie, we don't know if we can trust them yet, Cyrus linked, and his musky hydrangea scent filled my nose. When he stepped in front of me, I wasn't surprised. He wanted to protect me.

A few wolves near us watched curiously.

"I told you about her," Killian said leisurely as he walked over. "I told you that the demon wolves had attacked one of my family members and that they'd stolen women from other packs, forcing them into mate bonds. The people in charge of that pack have no morals, and there's nothing preventing them from attacking us if the mood strikes them. You are the group that volunteered to fight alongside us."

"Oh, I know. That's one reason I wanted to train with her." Lowe shrugged and grimaced. "I know you called them demon wolves, but I didn't expect her to be strong like the silver wolves. Now it makes sense, especially with the vampire smell mixed in with the floral and musk."

Two forms blurred toward us, and soon, Ronnie and Alex materialized. Alex's hair was a little messy, and he wore jeans and a hunter-green cotton shirt, which looked odd on him. He usually dressed more formally, likely because he was three hundred years old and had been raised as a royal.

My sister's emerald eyes sparkled, and she wore her

usual jeans and a pale pink shirt. Her copper hair was pulled into a ponytail, ready for training.

Alex nodded at the pack, and the middle-aged wolf closest to him took a jerky step back. It was clear that despite Killian and our group being acclimated to vampires, not everyone in his pack was.

Alex nodded at Lowe, then arched one perfectly sculpted eyebrow. "Demons turned a human into a vampire. They infused the human with some of their magic, and all magic comes with a cost that usually involves blood, which is why vampires crave it. We have a strong, sweet scent to hide the sulfur that pure demons have, a characteristic that helps to distance ourselves from them."

Another intriguing thing to know.

Not noticing the uneasy looks thrown her way, Ronnie ran over and hugged me. She pulled back and sighed. "I'm so glad you look normal! I was worried about you last night."

I returned her embrace. "I'm fine." And that was the truth. Surrounded by almost everyone I loved, I was the happiest I'd been in a while. We weren't currently under a threat, and we were working together to fix a long-term problem. My wolf was happy to be outside, and other than not being in animal form, I felt content.

"So...if they truly are demon descendants, that means they're stronger, too." Billy rocked on his heels.

Griffin waved a hand. "Yes and no. They're at peak strength during a new moon."

"Which is when we plan *not* to attack," Sterlyn said,

and slowly turned to glance at each wolf. "We'll attack on a full moon so the silver wolves will be at their strongest and the demon wolves at their weakest."

"Training with the silver wolves will make us better fighters and minimize the loss of life on our end," Killian said. "Eventually, once we get comfortable, we're hoping to train with Ronnie in her demon form so we can figure out how the non-silver wolves can fight a demon if it comes to that."

In other words, we were doing everything possible to prepare.

"Let's do this." Lowe smirked and rubbed his hands together. "We don't have time to waste."

THE NEXT FEW days went by without incident. The training was going well, and we'd progressed to sparring in animal form. Even though each silver wolf could kick their sparring partner's ass if they wanted to since the moon was nearing full, they were holding back enough so they wouldn't hurt the regular wolves too much. In exchange, Killian's wolves were growing stronger and acclimating to how silver wolves could channel their magic.

There was only one huge problem we couldn't figure out: fighting Ronnie in our wolf form.

It wasn't a problem for the silver wolves or me, but Alex and the regular wolves—including the female mates in the silver wolf pack—couldn't see her, and nothing in the air suggested she was there. The only thing they noticed was her scent, but since she was already in the area before she shadowed, they didn't realize she was attacking until she was already on them.

In human form, we had better luck because we could communicate with Killian and the others to tell them when she was near.

The sun was setting, and the day had been productive. Alex, Cyrus, Ronnie, Griffin, Sterlyn, Sierra, Killian, and I had hung back to discuss ideas about how to fix that problem when a branch snapped in the woods.

We tensed, and I sniffed the air for any hint of who it could be.

When I searched the woods, cognac eyes stared back at me. My chest tightened with fear or hope. *It's Mila.*

I know, Cyrus clenched his hands.

Sterlyn lifted her head. "Mila, what do you want?"

"I...I came here to alert you about something." She stepped from between an oak and a cypress into the clearing. "Something I think you might be interested in."

"And what's that?" Griffin asked, his brows furrowed.

She took one more hesitant step toward us and bounced on her feet. "I was running in the woods at the edge of Shadow Ridge when I saw a black Suburban park on a hidden section of road. I got close enough to hear two men discussing an attack that's happening tonight."

CHAPTER TEN

MY PULSE POUNDED against my skin. I must have misunderstood her. There was no way Mila would be coming here to be helpful.

"Why are you telling us this?" Cyrus asked, brows furrowing. "Is this a trick?"

She wrapped her arms around herself and averted her gaze. "I deserve that, but no, it's not a trick."

I sniffed, expecting to smell the stench of rotten eggs. The air remained clear, and her heartbeat stayed steady. She wasn't lying.

"And you came to us?" Sterlyn studied her body language. *She isn't lying.*

Cyrus replied, *Maybe she's spelled.*

Tensing, I inhaled sharply. *Are there witches around here?*

A few attend the university, but they wouldn't be able to hide her body language. Sterlyn stepped toward Mila. *There are no indications that she's lying.*

I had to agree. Also, the anger that usually flowed off her was missing. With her body language and the way she was withdrawing into herself, it seemed like she was ashamed.

She exhaled and rubbed her arms. "I could've gone to Darrell. I wanted to."

"Wow." Sierra placed her hands on her hips. "That's where you go?"

I agreed. If Mila was attempting to win any favors, that wasn't the way to go about it.

"What she means is, why didn't you?" Griffin asked, stepping next to his mate.

Mila grimaced. "Well..."

Ronnie laughed humorlessly and sneered at the shifter. "I'm going to need a hell of a lot more than that since you got my sister's mate kidnapped and made her hand herself over to the enemy to save your asses. *Well* doesn't cut it."

"My wife is right." Alex straightened, looking regal. "Why shouldn't we run you off?"

"While I was gone, I figured out something." Mila lifted her head, revealing pink cheeks. "I can't go back to my dad's pack without risking Jewel, and I can't remain alone."

I wasn't sure if she was angry or embarrassed, but we couldn't backtrack after everything she'd done.

She dropped her arms and puffed out her chest. "You're the people everyone looks up to, and when I heard their plans, I had to save my loved ones."

Killian ran a hand over his stubble. "You mean Sterlyn and Cyrus?"

Mila waved her hand at us. "I mean this group. All of you and your angel friend."

Out of everything I'd expected her to say, that hadn't been on my list. "Rosemary?"

"Yes, her." Mila nodded, looking relieved I'd supplied Rosemary's name. "Technically, Sterlyn is in charge, with Cyrus as standing alpha and Darrell as beta. But everyone looks at your group as a whole because you're family and you've created a pack beyond wolves."

Family.

Pack.

We were closer than family and stronger than blood, despite Cyrus and Sterlyn being the only true relatives.

"I came here to apologize to all of you, but especially to Cyrus and Annie." Mila focused on us, chewing her bottom lip. "I'm sorry. You were right." Her eyes glistened with unshed tears. "I was so damn angry, and I embraced it because I didn't want to fall apart. The crappier the stuff I did, the angrier I became, and the cycle spiraled until I didn't recognize myself anymore." A tear trickled down her cheek.

"You lost your fated mate." I had to say something. When hurt people finally reached out, they feared they wouldn't be accepted. The last thing I wanted was for Mila to feel like she wasn't worthy of love, because I understood that sentiment all too well.

Her eyes widened as I closed the distance between us and hugged her. "And of course, the people closest to

Bart and you would take the fall. Not that it makes it okay, but you didn't do anything that someone else hasn't done before."

A silent sob wracked her body, and my throat dried. I swallowed, attempting to keep my tears at bay. I didn't want to add more emotion to the moment. Mila was a strong wolf, and her coming here and admitting she was wrong was hard enough.

"But..." Her voice cracked. "I did so many horrible things."

"We all have." Cyrus made his way to us and placed a hand on my shoulder. "You weren't completely wrong. I did train the enemy, which is a mistake I'll live with for the rest of my life. I understand why it would be hard to trust me."

"And like Annie pointed out, you were a little boy and didn't know any better." Mila pulled away, snot dripping from her nose. "You have nothing to feel guilty about. You did what you had to do to survive."

"We all did," Sterlyn said kindly from beside me. "The important thing is that you're here now."

Mila sniffled as she pulled away and used the back of her hand to wipe her nose. "I...I'd really love to rejoin the pack. I belong here, even if I haven't acted like it."

If she'd been lying or trying to manipulate us, we would've picked up on it. Adding in that she wanted to rejoin the pack eliminated any reservations we had. Her rejoining would allow us to feel her, so if anything sketchy was going on, we'd know.

"You're always welcome here," Sterlyn assured her.

Mila smiled as she stared Sterlyn in the eyes, then averted her gaze to the ground. The cold pack link that had belonged to her sprang back to life, warm in my chest. Her presence there again was *right*.

The members of the pack murmured, and when Mila's eyes glowed faintly from the pack members linking to her, my chest lightened in a way it hadn't for a while.

Everyone was glad she'd come home.

"And you two"—Mila cleared her throat, glancing at Cyrus and me—"I won't cause any more problems."

I couldn't help teasing her. "Are you sure?"

"Fine, I'll speak my mind, but I won't cause turmoil in the pack anymore." She laughed, the warmth of her connection growing stronger inside me.

"I hate to interrupt this tender moment," Killian murmured like he truly meant it, "but we have the pressing matter of the impending attack to address."

He was right. We needed to focus.

"Are you sure you overheard correctly?" Alex asked Mila. "They could've been talking about anyone."

Mila rubbed her hands together. "They said Sterlyn's name and mentioned needing to capture Annie."

"Of course they did," Cyrus groaned. "The two most important women in my life are always targets."

"Uh..." Sierra gasped. "*Excuse* you."

Ronnie rubbed her temples. "That's his twin and his mate. What do you expect?"

"Don't even engage with crazy. That will only take us off topic," Griffin murmured.

Sterlyn must have been thinking the same thing,

because she said loudly, "Where exactly did you see them, and when?"

"About thirty minutes ago. I was running southeast in the woods and overheard part of the conversation. I didn't get closer because I didn't want to alert them to my presence." Between rejoining the pack and talking about the threat, Mila's washed-out complexion was already improving, regaining its healthy, dark olive glow. "I was half a mile away and upwind, so they didn't smell me."

That was a blessing. Maybe fate was tipping the scales in our favor. Though we were keeping watch in case of an attack, we'd also been training the strongest members hard, and actually *knowing* an attack was going to happen was beneficial. "Do you think they're still there?" I asked.

"There's only one way to know for sure." Ronnie faded out of view. "I'll go look."

"Wait. What if they can see you?" I didn't want her to go alone in case something happened. Losing her would be second only to losing Cyrus.

Ronnie's figure turned into shadow. "I'll keep to the treetops, but I'll need Mila to show me the way."

Alex shook his head. "You aren't going alone. If they're still there, maybe we can see who's involved and hear the rest of the plans."

"Fine, but we can't attack them. It might alert whoever they're working with if they don't make it back." Sterlyn glanced at the setting sun. "They'll probably attack at night to hide, but for them to time it when the moon's over three-quarters full tells me they're desperate."

"We don't need everyone to go if we're doing recon." Cyrus intertwined his fingers with mine. "They could be gone by now, or more could have joined them. Either way, only a handful of us need to go. The more people come, the likelier they'll smell us, and we need people here in case there *is* an attack."

That was true. We needed to stay undetected.

"If Ronnie is doing her shadow thing, I'm sure as hell going." Alex puffed out his chest, making it clear it was the only option.

Cyrus touched his chest. "I'm going, too. I trained the people who attacked us back at the old pack neighborhood. If it's the same group, I might pick up parts of the conversation that could elude someone else. Annie can stay—"

"Uh, no." If he was going, my ass would be right beside him the entire time. We'd been glued at the hip, and if he thought that was changing now, well...

"Look, we don't have time to debate this." Sterlyn moved her hand in a karate chop. "Griffin, Annie, Cyrus, and I will follow Mila."

Cyrus growled, but Sterlyn glared at him, her purple-silver eyes glowing. *They're talking about Annie. She deserves to be part of this, too.*

She was right. I'd told them everything I could remember about my time there, but I was sure I'd missed something that could pop up.

Besides, I wasn't asking for your permission to go. I

arched a brow at him, needing him to realize he was pushing a line. *You're my mate, not my father.*

"I'm going—" Alex started.

Sterlyn lifted a finger and interjected, "I know. I was talking about the wolf side. Killian and Sierra, go make a plan with the wolves while we're gone. Assume they'll strike around midnight when most of us would be asleep. I'll link with Darrell and give him a heads-up."

Killian exhaled loudly but nodded. "I hate not going with you, but this plan makes sense. Let us know if something happens and you need us."

Now that our plan was in place, my wolf surged forward, knowing the next thing Sterlyn was going to say.

"Let's shift." Sterlyn raced toward the woods.

Griffin ran behind his mate as Cyrus and I ran into another section where we wouldn't see them. My wolf rose within as I removed my clothes. My skin tingled, and fur sprouted across my body. Within seconds, Cyrus and I were on all fours.

We trotted back out to the others to find Sterlyn and Griffin already there. Killian and Sierra had left, and I could see Ronnie hovering in her shadow form next to Alex.

When Mila emerged, she stopped in her tracks to take Cyrus in. She linked, *How'd you shift so quickly?*

Ever since Annie and I mated, I've gotten more in sync with my wolf, Cyrus replied.

My chest swelled. His struggle to shift had made him feel unworthy. He'd come so far, and I was so damn proud that I'd been there to watch him grow.

Let's go. Sterlyn pawed at the ground. Her movements held an edge that let on to how worried she was.
*We need to determine who's involved and make it back to
get into position.*

Mila took off, and even though she ran slower than
Cyrus, Sterlyn, and me, she pushed herself harder.

We ran through the trees, listening as squirrels and
rabbits made their way to their homes, preparing for
twilight. My wolf enjoyed running, but the threat eliminated the playful mood. We were on a mission, and we
didn't have time to fool around.

I controlled my breathing, running behind Sterlyn
and Griffin. Alex was grumbling behind us since he
couldn't utilize his much faster vampire speed.

We had to follow Mila.

As we ran through the woods that abutted downtown
Shadow Ridge, I linked to Sterlyn and Cyrus, *Why do
you think Ingram tried to capture me and these men were
talking about me?*

Cyrus growled. *Doesn't matter. I'm going to kill
them all.*

That's not very helpful. I laughed, though it sounded
more like I was choking in animal form.

Sterlyn linked, *This happened after we alerted the
council that you were a demon wolf. I'm thinking someone
has hired these shifters to get you before the next half-
moon. They don't want to chance the demon wolves
attacking when they're stronger, and this is the weakest the
silver wolves will be before it gets too close to the next half-
moon. They have to act now.*

But how do these shifters know where we are?

If these shifters know about the demon wolves, then they're the ones who attacked my family pack, and they'll know to look for the location where I was raised. My gut thinks that someone from Shadow City contacted these enemy shifters to kidnap you and hand you back to the demon wolves, most likely before the demon wolves come here to get you. Sterlyn's large head glanced back at me.

My chest tightened. I hadn't considered that the demon wolves might figure out where we were. Of course, if they knew about Shadow City, they'd come to see if we were here, especially since the silver wolves' pack home had been close by.

Damn it. They won't stop, Cyrus snarled.

No, they wouldn't. *Not until Tate and his followers are dead.* The thought sat heavily on my shoulders, weighing me down.

We're getting close, Mila linked as we ran beside a huge wrought-iron fence.

Horrid memories of Eilam surfaced as I scanned the towering brick buildings of Shadow Ridge University. The campus was gorgeous, with views of the river and woods. Only six short months ago, I'd been so desperate to attend that I'd run away from my home with Eliza and Ronnie in Lexington to visit. That was when I'd met Eilam, and my entire future had changed.

Despite being used as the late vampire's personal blood bag, I couldn't regret the path that had gotten me here. Though it hadn't been pleasant, it had led me to Cyrus, and he was likely why I'd been drawn down here in the first place. If I hadn't made the decision to tour Shadow Ridge University, Ronnie and I might never have found our true homes and our fated mates.

We continued at a slower, steady pace as fatigue impacted Mila, but she continued to push onward.

About a mile past the university, the trees thickened.

I was here when I heard them, Mila linked. Disappointment wafted through the connection. *But I think they're gone.*

Let's be careful and head that way, Cyrus replied. *We can see if their scents are familiar.*

If they thought this place was a secret location, they wouldn't be worried about hiding their smell. *Good idea,* I interjected.

Sterlyn and Cyrus ran to the spot where the car had been parked. There were fresh tire marks in the grass, and the scent of musk lingered in the air.

One was a bear shifter, Cyrus linked as he lowered his nose to the dirt.

"Holy shit," Alex growled. "That wolf shifter scent is Ezra's."

Councilmember Ezra? I asked, already knowing the answer as I reached Cyrus and Sterlyn.

She nodded, and a deep snarl emanated from her. *The very one.*

I thought he never left Shadow City. Cyrus's brows furrowed, which would've been comical in wolf form if the situation hadn't been so serious.

The wind shifted, rustling the leaves, and something white caught my eye. My stomach sank.

CHAPTER ELEVEN

I BLINKED, hoping I was seeing things. But every time I opened my eyes again, ivory bones appeared about fifty feet away underneath some brush. It was hard to tell from here, but they didn't seem to have any skin left on them.

Someone is here? Cyrus tensed, surveying the area for the risk he assumed I'd seen.

I trotted over to the brush and used my head to move it out of the way. I winced, preparing for the horrible stench. *Something is.* I couldn't tell if the remains were animal or human. And hell, even if they were animal, would we be able to tell if it was a shifter or regular animal? Things I still didn't know.

The scent of herbs filled my nose, and I almost choked. I'd been expecting a horrible stench, not something pleasant, but I much preferred that one. *Do you smell witches?*

Sterlyn appeared beside me, and she whimpered. *Yes, I smell it. It's covering the bones.*

Which are human, Cyrus linked as he appeared on my other side. *Why are there human bones out here?*

Now that we were closer, I saw that the bones had been arranged in a pentagram-like shape. There was no telling how long they'd been out there. *Are they shifter?* I asked.

No. Sterlyn growled faintly. *If they were shifter, they'd have markings similar to animal bones, too. Shifter bones look both human and animal. These are all human, suggesting either a visitor or a witch.*

Whoa, I hadn't thought about how shifting back and forth between animal and human forms would affect our anatomy. *Why not angel or vampire?* Both had the same form as a human.

The spine, Cyrus answered and nodded toward the long, spiral-like structure. *If it was an angel, there would be an extra connection point for the wings. And if it were a vampire, their teeth would be longer and sharper.*

Ronnie's shadowlike figure lowered to the ground. "Of course there are bones near where the two assholes met."

Griffin started and huffed.

He and Alex were the only two who couldn't see her in this form since they weren't of angel descent. Alex, however, could link with her and sense her presence. Griffin had no clue she was near until she was close enough to smell.

Trying not to overthink it, I sniffed the bones. They didn't have a smell.

"Are these arranged like the bones you saw on

Thirsty's roof?" Alex asked, talking out loud for our benefit.

Thirsty's? The bar in Shadow Terrace? I asked Sterlyn and Cyrus. I hated that we couldn't all talk, but even if Griffin and Sterlyn merged our packs, that wouldn't solve the issue with Alex and Ronnie. They weren't wolves, so we'd always struggle with communication, especially when in wolf form.

The first time Ronnie shadowed, Sterlyn answered, *she floated above the bar and saw bones on the roof.*

I wasn't surprised that Sterlyn knew this. She was instrumental to the group and had been involved in all the happenings since before Ronnie had come to town. I'd been so jealous of Ronnie's connection with this group, feeling excluded, but now I understood why. Being with them, my life was in constant danger, and they'd been trying to protect me. Not that it made it right, but it didn't matter. Cyrus was my mate, and I was meant to be part of this world.

Ronnie exhaled loudly. "I didn't get a good look that day, and I haven't thought about it since. I remember it looked like the skin was flaking off, but there was no smell."

"We need to get out of here in case they're nearby." Alex's jaw tensed, and he turned around. "Something isn't right here, and I don't think we understand what we're up against."

Yeah, the herbal scent didn't fit. Why would that smell be here? *Could a witch from Shadow City have been with them?*

No guards have ever seen the witches leave the gates.
Sterlyn lifted her head and glanced at the treetops. *Either
it's a witch who's attending Shadow Ridge University, or
Ezra and his friends brought in witches to attack us.*

If witches join the attack... I trailed off, not wanting to
think about the implications. I remembered seeing the
damage Aurora and Lux had done to the demon wolves
when Cyrus, Mila, Theo, Rudie, Chad, and I had
escaped. Despite being two of the youngest witches in
their coven, the women had made a huge impact. We'd
only gotten away because of their help.

Years ago, Saga, former council member Dick Hard-
ing's mate, had kidnapped Eliza's granddaughter, Aurora.
Saga had proposed a trade to Eliza—baby Cyrus for
Aurora. Eliza was the only one who could make that
trade because her coven lived close by, and she'd assisted
the alpha silver wolf in delivering their children. She'd
spelled Cyrus at his and Sterlyn's births to make it seem
as though his heart had stopped. Their parents had
grieved his death, and then Eliza had sneaked him away.

That same spell had been cast on me two years later
when my mother, Midnight, had stumbled onto that
same coven and asked for their help. By then, ashamed
of her actions, Eliza had banished herself and was living
on her own in Lexington. The coven had told my mother
they wouldn't help, but they had spelled me the same
way. That night, my parents had thought I'd died, and
when Midnight had left to dig my grave, the witch
who'd been tracking me took me. Midnight hadn't
known I was alive until a few weeks ago. The witches

had brought me to Eliza to raise, and the rest was history.

Cyrus's life and mine had started out eerily alike. Our parents had thought we were dead, and surrogates had raised us. The only difference was that Eliza loved me as if I were one of her own, whereas Cyrus had been forced to train and become a fighter.

Despite Eliza's love, I'd always felt unworthy, believing my parents hadn't wanted me. Cyrus had been told that his parents had rejected him and only wanted Sterlyn.

No wonder we were perfect for each other.

Mila walked over to Cyrus, looking at the bones, and linked, *If a witch is involved, they could be watching us now.*

A shiver ran down my spine. *Let's head back. If they think we're on to them...* We didn't need our pack to be attacked while we were gone.

Cyrus and I headed back the way we'd come, Griffin and Sterlyn right behind us. I wondered how we were going to tell Alex, but he figured it out just fine. He and Mila took the rear as we took off in a quick jog.

Something heavy settled in my stomach. We still didn't know so much, and every time we turned around, we were missing yet another piece of the puzzle.

Hey, it's going to be okay. Cyrus moved closer to me. His silver irises darkened to granite as he glanced at me. *I promise I won't let anything happen to you.*

My heart increased its pace. *I'm not worried about myself. I'm upset that I don't understand how we can fight an enemy we know nothing about. When the demon pack attacked, we were clueless, and people got captured. Now we have a council member who's never left Shadow City before sneaking out to meet with people you likely trained, and witchy magic is floating around human bones.*

It's not comforting, but you're right. We don't know what Ezra is up to, but we know more than we did four months ago. He faced forward, his body rigid despite our speed.

What do you think Ezra wants? I linked Sterlyn in since she'd been around the wolf shifter a lot.

Sterlyn growled faintly behind us as she answered, *I know one thing he's after, and that's making Griffin and me look bad. He coordinated that shifter attack on Matthew, Azbogah, and Griffin so that Griffin would appear like he didn't have control. I think that's what he's trying to do, and he's teamed up with Azbogah.*

He wanted to replace Griffin. Standard alpha wolf move, which was one reason I was so surprised our group of friends worked. Griffin didn't hate that Sterlyn was stronger than him, and Killian didn't bother to prove he was just as strong as Griffin. Cyrus wanted to support his sister, and I didn't doubt that those four were the strongest wolves I had been around—except maybe Tate, unfortunately.

You think that's what this is about? Making the shifters attack so it looks like we can't protect Shadow Ridge and someone else needs to take over? Some people might call that driven, but I called it narcissistic twatwaffling. *How does that involve me?*

I don't know. Sterlyn's unease filtered through the link. *I'm worried that might have something to do with Azbogah, since the angel tried to take you the same night he found out about you. I just don't see how they could've coordinated that so quickly. Ezra would've had to figure out how to contact Saga and Dick's old network, now that the two of them are dead.*

What about their daughter? Cyrus asked. *Isn't she in prison? Maybe he got the information from her.*

They had a daughter? I couldn't believe what I was hearing. From what I knew, Dick and Saga were *not* great people.

Sterlyn huffed. *Yeah, they do, but after the night everything went down, I have a hard time believing they involved her. Her mom talked down to her and constantly insulted her. Saga didn't think Luna was smart or could accomplish anything.*

My heart grew heavy. That was how the demon wolf males treated their women—emotional abuse that could easily become physical. I hated that people got off on making others feel powerless. Usually, abusive people were insecure and needed something—anything—to prove they were powerful. Little did they know that revealed just how damn weak they were.

Maybe, I replied. *But she could have overheard something useful. They'd have disregarded her because they thought she was useless.*

That was why I had to save all those women from the demon wolf pack. They didn't deserve to be beaten and made to feel worthless.

No one did.

They were worth so much more than they realized, and they were never far from my mind.

We reached the university as the sun descended behind the murky Tennessee River, the sky swirling with pinks, purples, and oranges. If I'd been a child, I would've thought the sun had touched the water, considering the way the colors reflected off the currents.

Even in my current frame of mind, I appreciated the sight. The world had a way of reminding us that no matter the bad things going on, beauty could be found in any given moment.

That damn balance. I hated that every good action was offset by a bad one. I understood that we had to experience pain to appreciate happiness, but did the world need to include horror and terror, too? Couldn't a stubbed toe be the worst thing that could happen to someone?

I hadn't thought of that. Sterlyn continued the conversation, pulling me back into the moment. *But you're right. She might have overheard something. I'll see if Kira will talk to her. She's in charge of the cops now, and she's pretty good at getting information.*

Kira? That name sounded familiar, though I couldn't place it.

She was with Darrell and me while we were tracking you and Eliza when Matthew and the demon were after you, Cyrus answered. *The fox shifter with the bright red hair.*

A snarl left me before I could hold it back. I didn't

like thinking of a girl I didn't know hanging around my mate. Yes, it was irrational since we hadn't been together, but damn it, my wolf had a mind of her own.

Uh...I was only around her that one time, and you have nothing to worry about. Cyrus's eyes lightened nearly to the gray color I loved.

I know. I'm sorry. It was so damn ridiculous, and if what Ronnie had said was true, she was the reason Cyrus had been following Matthew. Otherwise, the vampire king and Ronnie's demon father could've attacked Eliza and me before we'd had a chance to get away.

Kira talking to Luna made sense. *Since she's with the cops, she can go to the prison, right? It won't come off as strange.*

She could easily come up with an excuse, Sterlyn agreed. *And it would be better than Griffin or me strolling in there and talking to her. Less of a red flag. I'll call her when we shift back to two legs.*

At least we had a plan, though I wasn't sure what we would do with it once we got some answers.

The rest of our return to the pack neighborhood was done in silence. People walked downtown, chatting, and engines rumbled by. We stayed in the woods in animal form so we wouldn't alarm any visiting humans.

Soon, we rounded the bend to the pack neighborhood, and the tension in my chest loosened. There was still a little daylight, and the neighborhood hadn't been attacked.

We reached the places where we'd left our clothes,

and within minutes, the five of us were back in human form and dressed.

Alex stood at the edge of the clearing near the river, talking on his phone.

"Everything okay?" I hoped it was. I wasn't sure we could take on anything else at this juncture.

"He's getting vampire guards to help in case we're attacked tonight." Ronnie removed her own phone from her back pocket. "I'll call Eliza to see if she knows anything about the bones."

Mila frowned as Sterlyn and Griffin glanced at each other.

"Yeah, that's our best bet," Cyrus agreed.

If it was witch-related, she could give us some insight.

The phone rang, and Eliza picked up within seconds. "Hello?" Her strong voice warmed my heart.

"Hey. Are you busy?" Ronnie paced in a small circle in front of me.

"Never for you and Annie." Eliza's voice deepened. "Is Annie okay?"

Of course she'd think I was in trouble. Despite my best efforts to show my maturity, Eliza still viewed me as the baby she'd saved.

"She's fine and standing right beside me." Ronnie turned on the speaker and held her phone out.

I didn't say anything until Ronnie waved her hand, telling me to speak.

"Hey," I said awkwardly.

"What's going on?" Eliza sighed. "I haven't heard from you in days."

"We were giving you time with your coven and family," Ronnie said with sincerity.

"I did, but you two are my kids, too. I don't have to choose between you." Eliza *tsk*ed. "But I spent some time with them, and I'm heading back to Lexington. We have a home there, and I can't just leave everything behind."

"You're going back permanently?" I'd hoped she would stay with the coven and not be alone anymore.

"Not sure. I have some research to do first, but I won't stay away like I've been doing." Eliza's car engine purred in the background.

"I hate to change the subject, but we need to ask you something." Ronnie glanced at me. "We're about to be attacked, and when we scouted the place our enemies met to make plans, we found human bones with a faint herbal smell of witch. Do you have any suggestions—"

"Dear goddess!" Eliza gasped. "*No.*"

CHAPTER TWELVE

MY STOMACH SANK. Whatever was going on was worse than we'd contemplated. I couldn't control my tone as I snapped, "What does it mean?"

She didn't scold me. Instead, she answered, "Nothing good. That's black magic."

Because having a normal witch after us would have been just that—normal. We had to get an expert in the black arts.

"Do you know who it could be?" Cyrus asked, his body vibrating.

I touched him, needing the connection more for me than for him, the calming effect benefiting us both.

"No." Her breathing turned ragged; it was like listening to the wind blow. "I'd need to tap into their magical essence."

"Magical essence?" That was insane. "Tell us how to do it, and we can go back and give you the information you need."

Sterlyn frowned. "It's not that simple."

"It never is." Griffin's face was lined with worry.

"How is it not?" Mila asked.

"The descendants of angels can feel people's essence," Eliza said matter-of-factly. "And witches can feel the essence of someone's magic, which is similar but not the same."

"I'm not following." I stepped closer to Cyrus, needing to feel more of him. "You can tell what a person is by being around them?"

"More like when they exert their magic, so when a shifter transforms or when a witch uses their magic." A ticking noise sounded over the phone. "Anyway, I'm on my way there now." I realized we were hearing Eliza's turn signal.

Ronnie bit her bottom lip. "You don't have to come here. I know it makes you—"

"I need to get a read on the magic before it dissipates." Eliza was back to her curt ways. "I was heading toward Nashville already, so I'll be there in two hours. Should I come to Shadow Terrace?"

"No, we're in Shadow Ridge at Sterlyn and Griffin's." I hated that she was coming here when she'd always done her best to stay away. Whatever had happened between the Shadow City coven and Eliza's all those years ago had left quite an impression on her. Their grudge had stood the test of time on Eliza's end.

Alex strolled over. "It's a good thing she's coming here if witches are involved in the attack tonight."

"Why do you think they might be?" Eliza's voice

grew rough. "More importantly, tell me about this coming attack."

Ronnie filled her in on what Mila had overheard.

"We aren't sure that witches are involved," Sterlyn interjected as she looked out across the lake. "But the bones were located close to where the two men met, so we're concerned."

"Were the bones easy to see?" Eliza asked.

That was a trick question. "Not really," I replied. "They were hidden under some brush, but my eyes were drawn to them."

"And they were definitely not shifter, angel, or animal," Sterlyn added. "They were human."

"With the smell of the magic, I would bet they were witch bones." Eliza clucked her tongue. "And my gut reaction says they weren't meant to be found. If a witch or coven is helping your enemies, they want to remain hidden. It could be a coincidence, but I'd need to see the setup myself."

I sighed and placed my head on Cyrus's shoulder. "Eliza, you don't need to risk—"

"I'm coming, and that's the end of the discussion. You and Ronnie are my family. You're my girls, just like Circe and Aurora are, and I am *done* being afraid," she said sharply.

My heart doubled in size.

Ronnie snorted and shook her head. "I guess we know that arguing with you is futile."

That was damn sure. Eliza was strong. Once she made a decision, it took the goddess herself to get the older woman to see reason. Hell, she'd cut herself off from her entire coven because she couldn't forgive herself for helping kidnap Cyrus to save her own granddaughter. Though it hadn't been a good decision, a situation like that didn't have a right or wrong solution. Unfortunately, what she'd thought best at the time had resulted in Cyrus growing up the way he had.

Despite the odds, he'd become an amazing person. Yes, he still struggled with feeling unworthy, needing to prove himself, and understanding that love should be given and never taken away. He was doing a damn good job of working through those issues, and he was realizing our friends would always have his back.

No matter what.

"What is it you girls say?" Eliza chuckled. "'I'm old enough to make my own decisions.' Well, so am I, and you should respect your elders."

"Then I guess we need Alex to tell you to go home and stay safe," Ronnie teased, turning to her husband. "He has, what, two hundred and forty years on you?"

Alex's irises darkened to cobalt as he glared at her. "Sierra pokes fun at my age enough. I don't need you encouraging her."

Smirking, Griffin added, "She's not around."

"Okay, I'm on my way. It's approaching seven-thirty, so I should roll in around nine-thirty." Her tone turned disapproving. "It might behoove you to talk battle strategy instead of poking fun at each other." And she hung up.

Mila's jaw dropped. "Uh...is she mad? We need her help."

I patted the woman's shoulder. "Eliza never says goodbye, and she's almost always serious."

"Very true." Ronnie put her phone back into her pocket. "This is her normal. She's an amazing person, just a little rough around the edges."

"Aren't we all?" Cyrus exhaled.

No truer words had ever been spoken, at least not in the past few minutes.

"She's right, though. We need to get back to the house." Alex nodded toward the trees. "Twenty vampire guards and Joshua are heading here to help patrol tonight."

"Are you sure you want to bring vampire guards here? The council will give you hell since it's a *shifter* problem, and what if they attack your side of the river, too?" Sterlyn asked with a deep frown.

That was yet another way she was so different. Her friend was bringing people over to help fight, and instead of just taking the extra help, she remained concerned about the vampires' safety. Again, her compassion extended to everyone, not just her own group.

Mila inhaled sharply, and her bottom lip quivered. "You sound just like Bart. It's uncanny. He was always worried about everyone, even outsiders. It used to upset me because, to my father, his pack was the most important one."

"Of course I'm concerned about the pack." Sterlyn closed her eyes for a moment. "Though we may be three separate groups, we're all the same at heart. But we can't have everyone else risk their safety for us. If we do, we're no better than the enemies we fight."

Her words struck something deep within me and pulled at my soul. She was right. The demon wolves would do whatever it took to win. We couldn't stoop to that level, and I firmly believed by not doing so, we could beat them.

"And that is why Ronnie and I don't hesitate to help." Alex took his wife's hand. "Sterlyn has our best interests at heart, and we know she would return the favor without hesitation."

"Besides, my sister is a demon wolf and mated to a silver." Ronnie winked at me. "Even if we wanted to distance ourselves, we couldn't. We're all family."

Griffin cleared his throat. "We do need to head back. I'm reaching out to a few Shadow City wolf guards to see if they can do some digging on their end without alerting anyone."

Something clicked in my head. "Are any of the wolf guards coming to help?" We had Killian's pack, the silver wolves, and some vampires, but Griffin wasn't bringing anyone over from his side.

Sterlyn headed toward the trees and waved for us to follow. I obliged as Griffin sighed loudly.

"That was something Sterlyn, Killian, and I were discussing on the way back." Griffin's face turned serious, and the brown in his eyes stood out more than the gold. "I could have some of the Shadow City guards come here to help, but since we're sure Ezra is involved, he'd be alerted, too. If not through the pack links, then from people talking to one another. Plus, people would talk about a large portion of the guards leaving the city."

If Ezra guessed we knew about the impending attack, they'd strike harder, or worse, withdraw and plan to attack another time, and we wouldn't know when. We needed to lie low.

"What about Rosemary?" Cyrus asked as he took my hand.

We stepped into the trees. The area was quiet with the daytime creatures settled in for the night and the nocturnal creatures having yet to rise. Dusk and dawn were the silent moments of nature. The time when a person could see the true balance that Earth had to obey. When the world was neither light nor dark and there was just...gray.

The balance was both comforting and infuriating, which had been the constant state of our life here lately.

"I texted her, and I'm about to call Kira," Sterlyn answered. "Rosemary will be here in twenty."

"Won't that alarm someone?" Mila asked as she followed behind the group. "If we're trying to keep Ezra in the dark, anyone leaving Shadow City will raise suspicion."

"She hangs out with us regularly." Griffin glanced over his shoulder. "Her not coming to visit would seem odd."

I'm glad she's coming. If Rosemary hadn't been there when Ingram kidnapped me, I had no clue where I'd be that second. He'd glanced at Ezra while the council had been questioning him, but that only confused things further. I had no idea why Ezra would want to capture me.

Cyrus squeezed my hand lovingly. *Me, too. We're lucky to have her on our side.*

When we reached the neighborhood, Chad, Theo, and Rudie were waiting outside. They rushed over to Mila, and Rudie hugged her tightly. Mila's cheeks turned pink, and a huge smile spread across her face.

Everyone was happy she was finally home.

Giving them some time alone, our group continued toward Sterlyn and Griffin's. When their house came into view, Killian and Darrell were waiting in the front yard.

Sterlyn stopped two houses down and said, "I'll call Kira and be right there. Go ahead and fill them in on everything."

I'd never met the fox shifter, but they seemed to trust her. I just hoped nothing had changed and that contacting her wouldn't backfire on us. Our luck tended to do that.

Griffin nodded to the two men as we walked up to them. He filled them in on everything that had transpired since we'd left.

"I'm just glad Mila came back and alerted us. I was beginning to worry she wouldn't come around." Darrell's shoulders sagged, but his face remained tense.

Though we'd all like to celebrate Mila rejoining the pack, that wasn't happening tonight.

"Did you come up with a plan?" Alex asked as he walked beside Ronnie.

She stopped next to me and tapped her fingers on her thigh.

That was one of her nervous tics. Even though she hadn't said anything, she hated me being in danger. All her life, she'd protected me and taken care of me. I hadn't noticed how much she'd done for me until she'd stayed in Shadow Ridge and I'd returned to Lexington without her. She'd prepared my food, handled my dishes, and done so many other things I'd taken for granted. She was fiercely loyal and protective of the ones she loved, and having her beside me was almost as comforting as having Cyrus.

Killian crossed his arms. "Yeah, we'll have the normal number of guards, but we'll have four or five silver wolves included in the mix. They'll stay a little more hidden since they can hear and see better than we can."

"Chad and I will keep an eye out in the woods behind the house where the shifters attacked from last time via boats." Darrell rubbed his hands together. "That way, they can't surprise us. If we hear or see any boats heading this way, I'll link with you and the other wolf pack, and we can go from there."

Ronnie glanced at the sky. "Shouldn't we have more people on guard?"

Twilight had descended. The moon was rising, its beauty breathtaking. If a threat hadn't been looming, I'd have loved to stare at the moon and stars. The moon outshone every star, making it almost magical.

Sterlyn marched over to us, her olive skin glowing in the moonlight. "No, having a group of vampires join us will appear odd enough."

"Don't worry about that. I told them to take three of our large SUVs to minimize the number of people heading over. They're leaving at staggered times to stay under the radar." Alex looked at his watch. "The first one should be here in ten minutes."

"Can you call the first car and tell them to pull into my garage?" Killian surveyed the area as if he thought a threat might pop out at any second.

The back of my neck tingled. I glanced over my shoulder but didn't see a damn thing. His paranoia was rubbing off on me.

"Yeah, I can call them now." Alex took out his phone and punched in numbers.

Ronnie exhaled loudly. "Just text them." She took the phone from him and typed out a message. "Not every-thing has to be a phone call."

Alex tugged at his ear. "That just doesn't seem right. With a call, I can hear their voice, which is strange in itself. Sending letters on a phone is damn weird."

"Letters?" I was missing something. "You mean texts."

"This is why you need to start attending your classes at Shadow Ridge University again." Griffin chuckled and shook his head. "You need to adapt to technology already."

Given how young Alex looked, I often forget he was three hundred years old until someone or something reminded me. He had a slight accent that wasn't quite British and was old-fashioned in some ways, but he was relatable for the most part. I had a feeling that was mainly due to Ronnie.

Ronnie closed her eyes. "We need to arrange the vampire classes after this threat is over."

If it was ever over. Surely, at some point, it would be.

"Until Eliza gets here, we need to rest up," Sterlyn pinched the bridge of her nose. "The more rested we are with the few lookouts on duty, the stronger we'll be when they get here."

"If these are the same shifters, we'll also need guns and ammo." Cyrus smoothed his strained expression. "Since they're a mix of shifters, they'll stay in human form so they can communicate more easily."

He hated guns, but this was how he and the enemy were trained. If we wanted to be on equal footing, we needed to be prepared.

"They'll also have a tranquilizer gun for anyone they were instructed to take but not injure," Cyrus spat. "Sterlyn and Annie could be targeted."

Griffin nodded. "They've tried to use one on Sterlyn several times."

"I'll have the next group of vampires bring weapons so Killian's pack won't have to raid their supplies in case we're being monitored." Alex reached for his phone.

"I can send a letter," Ronnie teased.

He pulled her against him and growled, but it wasn't in anger. "I only like to be teased in bed. You know that." He snatched his phone away.

"Okay, if they're watching us, it'll be soon." Griffin gestured to the house. "We need to act as normal as possible."

"The next SUV of vampires can park at the house where we're staying," Darrell offered.

I was thankful for that. Few shifters were comfortable with vampires, so his offer not only made things easier but also showed the rest of the silver wolves that he was embracing their help, which would hopefully encourage others to follow in his footsteps. Either way, fighting alongside the vampires would bond us all.

"And the next ones can go to Sierra's," Killian groaned. "She's with her family and demanding to help in some way."

That worked, too. Sierra got along with everyone, even if she drove them crazy.

"Now that we have everything decided for the moment, I need to talk to Annie," Cyrus rasped and tugged me toward the door. A strange emotion wafted off him, and my chest tightened.

Something was wrong.

CHAPTER THIRTEEN

MY HEART POUNDED hard as Cyrus's emotions crashed into me. I didn't know what was going on, but the impending battle had him on edge.

And he wasn't the only one affected by it. All of us were.

Sterlyn gave me a tight smile as we passed everyone and entered the house. I didn't speak out loud or through our mate link as we walked through the living room toward our bedroom. He wanted to talk, so it made sense for him to begin the conversation.

I tried taking deep breaths, but his caginess added to my anxiety. The temptation to bite my nails took hold, but that would only make me bleed.

He opened the door to our room and waved me inside. I stepped in, not bothering to turn on the lights. I could see just as well at night as I could during the day, the handy little trick of the wolf inside. Most of the time, we used the lights out of habit, but I wanted to feel partially hidden by the darkness. Even if it was an illusion, it was one I'd cling to for the moment.

When he shut the door, it reminded me of the gavel hitting the council desk. I didn't know why my palms grew so sweaty—it was just Cyrus—but I couldn't get over the odd sensation surging through us.

I turned to him, his silver hair bright in the darkness, and wiped my palms on my jean shorts.

He rubbed his fingers along his lips and exhaled. *There's no chance I could talk you into going to Shadow Terrace or away from here tonight, is there?*

What? I shook my head, thinking there had to be cobwebs or wax clogging my ears.

His jaw twitched. *You heard me, but I'll say it again if I need to. I want you to go somewhere safe tonight.*

Loud laughter escaped me. He couldn't be serious. *That's funny.*

Annie, I'm not joking. A vein bulged between his eyebrows as he swallowed hard. *They can't get you. Not again.*

Correct me if I'm wrong, Cyrus. Ugh, I'd wanted to convey my displeasure by using his name, but it fell flat. Sometimes, sarcasm worked better out loud, but I didn't want the others to overhear our argument. *But you were the first one taken.*

He sucked in a breath, completely taken aback, but damn it, he didn't get to treat me like that.

Refusing to feel remorse, though I knew it would come, I continued, *Tate took you, and if I hadn't come, I don't think you would've gotten out.*

I'd never seen his face turn red; he was usually good at appearing even-keeled when it came to his anger, but not this time. His nostrils flared, and he marched toward me.

My wolf surged forward, both angry and upset. Upset that we were fighting with our mate, but furious that he was treating us like we were weak.

Like we were human.

Like we were incapable.

You think I don't know that? he snarled, his breathing turning frantic. *But if they have witches or an angel involved, I'm afraid I won't be able to protect you.*

I don't need you to protect me. I was done with being treated like I was fragile and too inept to handle my battles. I'd promised myself I would never be treated like that again. Now my mate was attempting to treat me that way. He should've known better. *I'm a wolf shifter and can fight, too. Don't make me feel like I'm a liability. I've been training out there every day with everyone.*

His expression fell, and he hung his head. *That's not what I'm getting at.*

Oh, really? He didn't get to say all that and then pull at my heartstrings. The most annoying part was that my heart thawed and tugged me toward him. *Then what are you getting at? Please, tell me.*

I had to stay strong.

I had to stay upset.

If my resolve crumbled, he'd continue to treat me this way, and that was unacceptable.

I know you're capable. You're so damn capable, but

you shouldn't have to be. His eyes softened as he stepped toward me and cupped my face. *Seeing that angel fly off with you while I couldn't do a damn thing to stop him has haunted me every minute of every day.*

He was scared.

The anger was knocked out of me, but it was important for me to remain firm. He had to understand that he needed to come to grips with this, just like I had to. *I felt the same that night Tate took you. The thought of you fighting again makes me sick to my stomach, and all I want is for you to run away so nothing like that will ever happen again.*

But...that's different. His nose wrinkled. *You can't compare the two.*

The knot in my chest reformed, and my temperature rose. I stepped out of his reach and placed a hand on my hip. *How so?*

He dropped his hand and frowned. *Because your point doesn't work in my favor.*

So? They aren't any different. Why are you acting like they are? I hadn't wanted to smack and kiss him at the same time in quite a while. Those conflicting emotions were back, and they were more extreme than when we'd been fighting the mate bond without realizing it.

His body sagged, all the fight leaving him. *Because I'd take your fury as long as you were safe.*

My heart warmed. Damn traitorous heart once again. *As long as Tate is out there, I'll never be safe. If I left, who's to say they wouldn't be watching and attack when I was alone?* A chill ran through me. I hadn't considered that. If they suspected we were here, they could be staying back and watching for evidence to prove it. They wouldn't be dumb enough to come into town until they were ready to attack.

I know. I didn't really mean what I said. If you left, I'd be worried sick because you wouldn't be by my side. He ran his fingers through his hair and pulled. *Ever since I saw you, my emotions have been split when it comes to you and danger. I just love you, and I wish I could take you away from all this.*

But you can't.

Look, I know you can fight. You're more capable than half the silver wolves, and that's with the moon magic on their side. He took my hands and squeezed. *It's just that I wish you didn't have to be so strong.*

Butterflies took flight in my belly, and though I still wanted to be mad, I couldn't. I understood what he meant. In a perfect world, none of us would be under constant threat, but this was not a perfect world. *You can't ask me to do something like that again. Do you understand?*

His plump bottom lip stuck out, and he batted his thick lashes. *Fine. I was an ass. I'm sorry.*

Not able to resist, I sucked his bottom lip into my mouth and bit a little hard. *Good. That's your punishment.*

Punishment? He chuckled and pulled me against his body. *If you don't want me to do that again, this is definitely not the way to punish me.*

My body warmed, and all my frustration turned into

sexual energy. *I'll have to think of something more rigorous.*

I'm all about that. He pulled far enough away so that my teeth lost traction on his lips. Then he kissed me.

As his tongue slid into my mouth, his cinnamon taste became all-consuming. I didn't know what was wrong with me, but all I could think about was his body over mine. *I should be mad at you.* I groaned and sucked on his tongue.

It's our mate bond pulling us together since we sort of argued. Our souls need to reconnect. His hands slid under my shirt, his skin hot on mine.

I'd heard about makeup sex, but I'd never had it before. There was a first time for everything. *We'd better oblige.* I jumped on him, wrapping my legs around his waist.

His free hand cupped my ass as his other one slipped underneath my bra. He turned around and pressed my back against the wall. Kissing down my neck, he rolled his fingers over my nipples. My breathing turned ragged as I leaned my head back. His musky hydrangea scent surrounded me, thick with arousal. The combination was like a drug, and I grew lightheaded.

Gods, you taste good, he linked as his teeth raked my neck. I placed my feet on the ground and pushed him slightly off me. I took hold of the hem of his shirt and pulled it over his head, watching his abs flex as he helped me remove it from his body.

My hands ran down his perfectly sculpted chest, my fingertips tracing his muscles. His body quivered at my touch as he unfastened my bra. He tugged my shirt and bra from my body, and I begrudgingly pulled my hands away long enough to eliminate the last barrier between us.

You're so breathtaking, he linked as he perused my body. He captured one nipple with his lips and dragged my shorts and panties down.

Between his tongue and him placing his hands between my legs and circling, warmth crashed over my body. The pleasure was already building as he applied the right pressure and slipped a finger inside me.

I moaned, not able to hold it inside. If anyone was in the living room, they'd know what we were doing, but I couldn't bring myself to care.

All I needed was him.

Nothing else mattered.

I unfastened his jeans and pushed his pants and boxers to the floor. We removed our shoes and stumbled out of the clothes around our ankles.

Even through all that, he kept his pace and worked my body.

As I stroked him, he moved his hips faster. On a high, we opened ourselves to each other.

The friction built, and I couldn't take it any longer. I needed to connect with him in the way our bond demanded.

My fingers threaded through his hair, and I fisted it, making him groan. His hand gripped my waist, digging his fingers into my skin and turning me on even more.

Are you ready? he asked, but he knew the answer.

Wanting something different, I pushed him away and got onto the bed. Instead of the normal position, though, I grabbed a pillow and propped myself up on my stomach.

He climbed behind me and settled in between my legs. As he got into position, he wrapped an arm around me, rubbing the same sensitive spot. Still circling, he slipped inside me, hitting me deeper than ever before. *Is this okay?*

Yes, I replied, and pushed against him as he withdrew his hand and filled me completely. *It's perfect.*

We moved slowly at first, but soon, we quickened the pace.

I opened myself up to him through our link, letting him feel my emotions and sensations. When he responded, my chest expanded like it might explode. We loved each other so much, and in moments like this, it was hard to know where I ended and he began.

He thrust inside me as his fingers dug a little deeper, making me crash over the edge. An orgasm rocked my body, and then he released himself, adding to the pleasure.

Our bodies shook together as we rode the high.

When the moment was over, he quickly snatched our clothes off the floor and held mine out to me. *We should get dressed in case someone attacks earlier than anticipated.*

I flopped over and stuck out my tongue at him. *I kinda wanted to lie against your naked chest.*

And I want you to. His irises lightened to my favorite

color. *But unless you want to risk us running out there naked—*

No! I growled. The thought of another woman seeing him undressed made me irrational. I was the only one who got to look at him this way.

I agree. I don't want another man to see you like this, either. He held out my clothes again. *So let's get dressed and cuddle.*

That worked, though I wanted to pout. I quickly put on my clothes, and when he slid into bed beside me, my eyes grew heavy. Sterlyn would wake us when Eliza got here or the attack began. We couldn't do much else before then.

THE SOUND of the familiar Camry engine stirred me from my slumber. I woke up safe in Cyrus's arms, and though part of me didn't want to leave them, Eliza was here. Hopefully, that would get us closer to some answers.

I moved, and Cyrus groaned.

He pulled me against him and linked, *Shh. It's a figment of your imagination. Eliza isn't here.*

Even though I'm tempted to play along, you know we can't. If someone got hurt, we couldn't live with it.

He kissed my forehead and released me. He scrunched his face as he booped me on the nose. *I hate it when you talk reason.*

Same. I sighed and winked at him.

Keep looking at me like that, and we won't be leaving here anytime soon, even if there is an attack. He waggled his brows.

I laughed. It was rare for him to be in a playful mood like this, and I hated that we had to cut it short.

Hearing footsteps heading toward the front door was the equivalent of a cold shower. Dread pooled in my stomach, and I hurried out.

As I reached the living room, the front door opened, and Griffin and Sterlyn entered. I inhaled sharply as Eliza came into view, flanked by Ronnie and Alex.

Eliza's caramel hair was pulled into its usual haphazard bun, and her sea-green eyes were tense. The past month, she'd begun to look her age, which was close to sixty, with her wrinkles becoming more pronounced. Time and stress hadn't been good to her. She was the only person here shorter than me, but only by two inches.

"What did you all figure out?" Cyrus asked, cutting to the chase.

Eliza placed a hand on her chest and exhaled, and I wanted to hide. She knew Cyrus and I had been having sex. I wasn't ashamed of it, but I didn't want the woman who was essentially my mother to know what we'd done.

She rubbed her hands together and stepped into the house. Ronnie and Alex followed suit and shut the door behind them.

"I couldn't get a read on anything at the site," Eliza said sourly. "The magic was centered around the bones and not where the two shifters were speaking, so I doubt the coven that placed the bones there wanted them to be found, but magically, a coven was definitely involved."

"What are the bones for?" Sterlyn asked, gesturing for us to follow her into the living room. She and Griffin sat on the loveseat while Ronnie and Alex took the end and middle spots on the couch. I'd have sat down, but I was too nervous to stay still.

Eliza walked to the windows that overlooked the backyard. Her eyes went to the moon, which was still rising. It had to be close to ten, which meant the attack could begin soon.

She kept her attention skyward. "Those are witch bones. Someone from that person's coven placed them here so they could connect with the bones when they desired."

"How do you know that? And do they not bury their dead?" Griffin asked with disgust. "That's horrible."

"Most witches do, but their bones are still part of nature, and they also serve a purpose." She slowly turned around, her eyes darkening. "One that only a handful of witches know."

CHAPTER FOURTEEN

HER DEMEANOR HAD my throat closing and dread pooling in my stomach. She got like this when she had bad news, and the childish part of me wanted to plug my ears.

That wouldn't change the situation. If I wanted to be treated as an equal, I had to act like an equal. Maybe I did play a role in the way they'd treated me.

Self-awareness was part of the journey.

"Spit it out," Ronnie rasped. "Or I'll pull it out of you."

Eliza lifted a brow. "You may be a demonic vampire queen, but I can still whip your ass, little girl."

Ha. For once, Ronnie was getting on her bad side instead of me, which was a little crazy.

Alex growled low. "Do *not* threaten my wife."

Oh, dear God. We were spiraling. "Guys, can we focus, please?" I exhaled, trying to remain as calm as possible. "You know how Eliza is. All you're doing is dragging out her explanation."

Ronnie scoffed and snapped her head in my direction. "Who *are* you?"

Wrapping an arm around my waist, Cyrus kissed my forehead. "My smart mate."

"Eliza, what do they use the bones for?" Sterlyn asked to get us back on track. "Should we be worried about this?"

"Yes, we should all be." Eliza clutched the chest of her sky-blue dress. "You see, since they're the human remains of someone from their coven, the magic left in the bones is linked to the coven, plus there was an M— the rune of Ehwaz—etched into one of the bones. It was small and where most wouldn't notice, but the magic was strongest there."

Griffin scratched his head. "I'm not following."

"They mark the bones to connect a living witch to the dead one so they can access the location of the bones to see things easily without having to astral project. Even though astral projection is relatively harmless, it takes a lot of concentration to find the location you seek, and your body is paralyzed while your spirit is suspended." Eliza's face turned a shade paler. "By using the bones, they see around that area while staying safe and mobile in their present location. All they have to do is link to the magic in the bones, and it's as if they're looking into a mirror, but they see what's going on near the bones instead of seeing their reflection."

"Are you saying they can watch us anytime?" Sterlyn asked, on edge. "How far can they see?"

Cyrus's body tensed as his worry mixed with mine.

"With that kind of magic steadying them, they can see for several miles." Eliza paced in front of the window. "It could be more—it depends on the witch's remains. The stronger the witch, the farther they can watch."

"What about a former priestess?" Alex's voice grew terse.

Eliza paused, her face lining with more concern. "They could reach here. Why do you ask?"

"Just a guess, but there are also bones on top of Thirsty's Bar in Shadow Terrace." He grimaced. "That can't be a coincidence."

"Do you think Erin is involved?" Griffin leaned forward, placing his elbows on his knees.

My stomach soured, and I rested my hand on it. "Wait. From the way Diana spoke at the council meeting, it sounded as if none of the coven members had ever left the city."

Griffin nodded. "The guards on both sides keep a docket of everyone who has gone in and out of Shadow City. None of the coven members have left. Male or female."

That comment wasn't odd since males were members of covens. I'd met a handful of men in Eliza's coven while we'd stayed there to get Cyrus.

"I'm not saying it's the Nightshadow Sisters." Eliza lifted a hand. "Though that is the type of magic they'd use. That was one reason our covens didn't get along. Evil magic might be strong, but it's not as pure as magic performed with good intentions."

Good and evil.

Balance.

It always came back to this. Hell, even the demon wolves and silver wolves had been created at the same time for that very reason. If a wolf race was tied to the full moon, to have balance, a race had to be created for the new moon.

Couldn't there be a balance within each person instead of people taking it to extremes?

My mind raced with that feeling of walking into a room for a specific purpose and forgetting what I needed. I couldn't grasp hold of any coherent thought.

Cyrus was obviously not struggling with that problem because he asked the perfect question. "Can they leave Shadow City without anyone knowing?"

Eliza inhaled sharply. "Yes. I don't know why I didn't think of that. They could, and it would be hard to prove."

"I think it's safe to assume that Erin is in on whatever is going on." Sterlyn leaned back against the couch. "We can't accuse The Nightshadow Sisters or eliminate the possibility of someone else working against us, but we need to keep them in the equation."

Ronnie's emerald irises darkened. "Erin is desperate for Azbogah's attention, and the best way to get it is by helping him gain control over the coven. Maybe he strings her along behind closed doors to get her to do his bidding."

Alex sneered. "And we wouldn't consider that her

coven might be involved because they stay behind the gates, as far as we know."

Things still weren't adding up. "But they had to leave to get the bones out here, right? How could they do that without being seen?"

"A very powerful witch can do a cloaking spell." Eliza chewed on her bottom lip, looking toward the moon. "It's possible, but they'd have to pull a lot of magic from the coven and only use it in short bursts—long enough to get out and back in."

So not only could our enemies be working with an outside coven, but they could also be partners with the coven inside Shadow City, which we wouldn't have previously considered. Instead of our list of potential enemies narrowing, it was growing larger.

Hey, what's wrong? Cyrus linked, feeling my turmoil.

It's just aggravating. Every time I think we're finally getting somewhere, like realizing Ezra is involved, we add another enemy or complication to the equation. At some point, things have to start making sense.

Actually, I think this does. Cyrus stepped behind me and placed his hands on my shoulders. *The Nightshadow Sisters make perfect sense. They were close to Dick and Saga, who started most of the chaos. And if Eliza has held a grudge against them all these years, I'm sure Erin's coven feels the same way. That much hate is rarely one-sided.*

He was right. Maybe finding the bones was the missing element that pieced everything together. I hadn't been looking at it from the right angle. That had to be why Sterlyn had said to assume that the coven tied to the bones was them but not to eliminate anyone else yet.

"Do you think the witches will be involved tonight?" We would be attacked. If Azbogah, Ezra, and Erin were working together, part of their goal was for the silver wolves to leave and Griffin to step down as alpha.

Eliza shook her head. "No, they won't. These two shifters met at the edge of town and didn't expect to be overheard. The witches don't want to risk exposure until they have to."

Griffin sat upright, his shoulders straightening. "How do we know they didn't see us find the bones?"

Good question. If they'd been watching us, we might have spurred the witches into action.

"The magic had dissipated, meaning they weren't connected. When the coven connected to the bones to watch those two, the magic was strong enough that I could've picked up their essence and determine who it belongs to. In other words, I'd need to be around if they connected again, but then that would put me at risk of them seeing me." Eliza rubbed her arms. "The only good thing about not being able to read their signature is that it confirms we aren't currently being watched."

"We've found human remains here and in Shadow Terrace, too. There's no telling where else more bones might be." Ronnie clenched her hands. "But if it was coven and silver wolf targeted, why on top of Thirsty's?"

"I don't know, but they could've been placed there with Matthew's help," Alex growled, light red blending into his soft blue eyes. "Didn't you say there was skin flaking off? If that's the case, the death could have been more recent."

"The flaking could be due to herbs or just being on top of the roof." Eliza shrugged. "I'd have to see them, and it would be better during the day, since my eyes aren't as good as the rest of yours at night."

All of this was insane. My mind was still trying to catch up when I realized there was another piece missing. "Did you ever hear back from Kira?"

"Not yet." Sterlyn frowned. "Ezra showed up at the police department earlier, and she didn't want to leave while he was there. She'll have to go tomorrow to visit Luna. Going this late could raise questions."

Yet another occurrence preventing us from getting answers. "Do you think he did that on purpose?"

"I don't know." Griffin stood and tugged at his shirt. "He said he was stopping by to check on the status of the shifter attack investigation. That was the same shit Dick used to pull when he was being shady, but Ezra's position on the council makes those questions relevant. It's just so convenient. A shifter I trust who was guarding the gate today pretty much confirmed Ezra had left."

"Pretty much?" Cyrus's shoulders stiffened. "What the hell does that mean?"

"He didn't tell me outright that Ezra left, but he told me I could always verify the logs. He wants me to come to the gate so people can say they saw me," Griffin rasped, his voice dangerously low.

That didn't clarify anything. "Then how do you know?"

"It was his way of telling me Ezra had left without directly answering. Ezra must have threatened him." Griffin's jaw twitched. "I'll head over there tomorrow and look at the log so the guard doesn't look like he told me."

This was all too complicated. "Will that look suspicious?"

"No, because I'll do it." Alex flicked his wrist. "I regularly review the list of vampires who have requested to leave the city. It won't raise any red flags."

"Why are vampires requesting to leave Shadow City?" Eliza's nostrils flared. "They've never been around humans before."

Ronnie lifted a hand. "We know, but we're developing a class to help vampires learn how to control their bloodlust. We asked for anyone interested in attending the university to apply to leave. The council isn't happy, but we're hoping to move forward with this once we have the class up and running. Hopefully, in the next few months, we'll have a trial run."

"The supernaturals can't stay hidden in the city forever." Sterlyn leaned forward and placed a hand on her mate's arm.

Griffin was always serious, but he was tenser than usual. It couldn't be easy hearing that someone in your own race was working against you again, only to learn that the powerful coven within Shadow City might be working against you as well.

Wings flapped outside the back window, and I jerked my head around. If Ingram was here to grab me, at least we had Eliza to help fight.

When Rosemary landed, my lungs expanded again. I hadn't realized I'd frozen. Her eyes met mine, her face drawn.

Almost on cue, a howl filled the air.

Three boats are approaching, Quinn linked with the silver wolf pack. *They look like large jet boats with an enclosed cabin in the front and bench seats in the back.*

The hair at the nape of my neck lifted. The time had come.

Sterlyn jumped to her feet. "They're here."

"What?" Ronnie pulled out her phone and glanced at the time. "It's only eleven."

I couldn't believe we'd been talking for almost an hour.

"Go on out there and tell them they're early," Griffin groused, his face turning red.

Alex glared at the alpha wolf. "You don't have to be an ass."

"We're all a little tense, and they caught us off guard by attacking earlier than we suspected," Sterlyn said, her eyes glowing. "But fighting with each other is a waste of energy, and we need to direct our anger at the enemy, not each other."

She was right.

"Killian is alerting his pack. We need to get out there." Griffin headed to the back door. "We need to attack so we can get this over with."

"Wait!" Cyrus shouted. "If we attack while they're still on the boats, they'll fire from the water, and we won't be able to get near them. We should wait until they're coming through the woods."

That was a good plan: make them think they had the element of surprise until they were right on us or could smell us. No reason to rush out in animal form.

"Tell Killian to let the vampires know to meet behind Griffin and Sterlyn's house," Alex commanded. "That way, we can coordinate."

Griffin lifted a brow, but his eyes glowed. "Be glad we're about to go into battle, or I'd be pissed at you telling me what to do."

Our group headed toward the back door, Cyrus and me following Eliza.

"Are you up for this?" I couldn't hide the worry from my voice. Eliza looked worn out, and I didn't want to make things worse for her.

She *tsk*ed and pointed a finger at me. "I'm fine. Don't you treat me like I'm an old woman. I've still got a lot of juice left in me."

Cyrus chuckled, though tension rolled off him in waves, and I wasn't foolish enough to pretend not to know why. He said, "Can you stay close to Annie? If an angel tries to take her again, you and Rosemary are our best defense."

You've got to be kidding me. Heat flushed through my body. *Last time, I bit him and shot him. Don't act like I was useless.*

I didn't mean that. He grimaced as his guilt washed over me. *I meant in addition to you. He flew you high in the air before you could hurt him, and I don't need you falling to your death.*

That melted some of my tension away, and I moved my jaw to work out the discomfort. *Fine, but that's not what you said.*

I know. I'm sorry. He held the door open, waving Eliza and me through.

"I'll stay close to her." Eliza walked nearer to me as if that would make a difference.

"Four boats are approaching," Rosemary spoke low, but we could all hear her. "The one at the end looks different from the first three, and I'm assuming they're backup."

Blurry forms approached, and when they slowed, the vampires came into view. Each vampire had two guns around their waist. Several wolves were running our way, too, but our core group was in the center, talking as the others circled us.

"Wait, I thought it was only three boats," Cyrus said as he stood beside me.

Rosemary fluffed her dark wings. "One is trailing about a half mile behind."

"Wouldn't they assume you'd be watching for them?" a vampire with a medium-brown complexion asked as his mocha-brown eyes scanned the woods. The wind blew through his espresso hair, making it stick up in different directions.

"They wouldn't, Joshua." Alex answered.

Ah, this was the vampire who Ronnie and Alex trusted to run things in Shadow Terrace. He'd helped them shortly after Ronnie had turned and was the first one to witness her turning into her shadow form when a grenade had been thrown at Alex's SUV with her inside.

"We're going to shift and wait for them in the woods to get off the boat." Sterlyn slowly spun around, looking every person in the eye. "We stay upwind so they won't smell us until they're on foot and heading our way."

"What about the bloodsuckers?" Sierra asked, pushing through shifters already in animal form. "Are they going to get furry, too?"

Alex rolled his eyes. "Now's not the time."

"Our people need to get into a position where they can fire at the enemy. Our attackers are probably wearing armor. The wolves will need to break through the body armor enough so the guns can leave their mark," Ronnie interjected, stopping Alex and Sierra's bickering. "Hold off until the wolves let us know when it's time to move. Most importantly, make sure you don't hit the wolves. Try your best to only injure and incapacitate, not kill. We need a few people alive to question."

"But do everything you must to survive." Griffin lifted his chin. "Though we don't want to be like our enemy, we have to make sure our sympathy doesn't hurt us."

Killian bellowed as his wolf surged forward. "Is everyone clear?"

Murmurs of *yes* could be heard.

"I'll take to the air and make sure they don't have more boats coming behind the last one." Rosemary flapped her wings and took off. "And ensure there aren't any angels heading this way," she called back.

We needed to get going. To remain undetected, we needed to be in place before the boats reached land. My heart hammered as I took off toward the right side of the woods, away from the vampires and the wolves in animal form. I called over my shoulder to Eliza, "I'm going to shift."

Eliza hurried toward a redbud where everyone else had gone. "I'll stay right here and wait on you."

Like she'd promised Cyrus, she planned on staying by my side.

Cyrus ran beside me as my skin tingled and fur sprouted. When we got to a private area, I removed my clothes and my wolf surged forward. My bones broke, and within seconds, I was on four legs.

Stay close to me, too, Cyrus linked as he trotted over to me. *I don't want to lose you.*

That was fine with me. Every time we split up, something bad happened to one of us.

We ran back to Eliza just as Sterlyn and Griffin ran out from behind more redbud trees. The sound of engines grew louder.

Killian charged past Eliza, racing to catch up with the pack, while Sierra stood waiting by Eliza, pawing at the ground, ready to go.

Cyrus ran to my mother and bent down, lowering his almost horse-sized body for Eliza to climb on. She frowned for a second and crossed her arms. My heart sank. She was being stubborn.

I'll catch up with them, Sterlyn linked as she took off in a run, following Killian. *We need to make sure they all stay in line.*

Sierra huffed at Eliza, making it clear she wasn't happy, and ran after Sterlyn and Griffin. That was enough for Eliza to realize she didn't have a choice or she'd get left behind.

"Dear goddess," she grumbled, and climbed onto Cyrus's back. "You have a horrible sense of humor."

If the situation hadn't been so dire, I'd have been laughing, but not even a grin passed my wolfy mouth.

Cyrus glanced at me and linked, *Go in front. I'll need to run slower with her on my back. I don't want to toss her.*

That was his nice way of also guarding my back, but his logic made sense, so there was no reason to argue.

I took off, not bothering to run slowly. Cyrus was tied to the moon, which was over three-quarters full, so if I ran as fast as possible, he could keep up, even with Eliza on his back. Thankfully, we'd been running these woods enough that we knew the land, giving us an advantage over the attackers. Surprise was all they'd had on their side, and we'd taken that leverage away.

Eliza grunted every few steps, not impressed with riding a wolf.

The river came into view. Two boats were already pulling up to the shore. Cyrus and I ran to the right, between thick trees, and joined the silver wolves there. They made room for us as we all hunkered down, the tree branches hiding their silver fur from the moonlight.

With a deep sigh, Eliza climbed off Cyrus. He inched his way beside me so that I was between the two of them.

Everyone, stay calm, Sterlyn linked. *We'll let you know when it's time to go. The vampires will follow our lead.*

I surveyed our group and noticed that Theo, Quinn, and Darrell were right next to us. The wolves that had been on patrol were waiting for this very moment.

None of us said anything, everyone on edge, waiting to attack.

The three boats dropped anchor, and I watched as forty shifters slowly climbed off. They weren't in a hurry, and they had weapons strapped all around them. They were quiet, probably to ensure they didn't give us any warning.

The tallest and bulkiest guy walked to the front of the group and gestured in our direction. He was telling them to move.

This was it. There was no going back.

The forty men ran toward us. As they drew closer, I could hear every breath they took. They wore black face paint to blend in with the night and bulletproof vests and helmets, ready to defend against gunfire.

They were scanning the area when the guy in front stopped dead in his tracks. His eyes widened, and he turned his head as Sterlyn linked, *Attack.*

CHAPTER FIFTEEN

MY EARS POUNDED SO LOUDLY, it was a wonder I could hear the pack's snarls. The overwhelming noises made me a little lightheaded, but we didn't have time for weakness.

Sterlyn, in true leadership form, charged first, with Griffin and Killian only a moment behind her. She went straight for the bulkiest guy, wanting to take out the one in charge.

Eliminate the commander, and their group would fight chaotically.

The rest of the wolves sprang into action. I leaped to my feet and rushed forward. Out of the corner of my eye, I watched as the bulky guy raised his weapon and aimed right at Sterlyn's chest. Though she was fast, she was several feet away, and a bullet could travel faster than any supernatural.

No!

I pivoted, desperate to help Sterlyn. If something

happened to any of them, it would devastate the packs. Though Griffin and Killian had been friends before Sterlyn, she was the glue that had settled them down and helped them become the alphas they were always destined to become.

Cyrus's fear slammed into me as he rushed past me, pulling magic from the moon. His large tail swooshed in my face, and I wanted to tell him to stay back.

But how could I? I was doing the same thing. That would be super hypocritical, and Sterlyn was his twin, after all.

Gunshots rang in the air, and my stomach roiled. I waited for Sterlyn to fall to the ground, but the big burly guy dropped instead.

My head swung toward the vampires, and I caught Joshua pivoting the barrel of his gun away from the burly man to another person behind him.

The vampire had saved Sterlyn.

Thank God.

My lungs began working again, though each breath was painful, like a saw hacking away at the tissue. If I didn't get oxygen flowing, I might as well hand myself over to the enemy. I had to keep a level head.

Six silver wolves and four regular wolves were locked in battle with the men in front while the other twenty-nine reached for their guns.

Charge as many as you can before they can engage their weapons, Cyrus linked.

Sterlyn pounced on the man who'd been standing behind the burly one. He was raising a gun at Griffin, and

Sterlyn snarled and sank her teeth into his jugular. She yanked her head to the side, ripping his throat out.

Blood had already been spilled, and the battle had just begun. Our side might have been the first to draw it, but there was no way we were getting out of this unscathed.

Griffin jumped on the man who'd attempted to shoot Sterlyn and thrashed at his chest. The rage was clear on his face, even in animal form.

We all had a part to play, so I needed to focus on helping my friends and family instead of watching them. I locked eyes with an enemy near the shore who had reached the tree line. The guy was scanning the area for something. I wasn't sure what, but damn it, I'd make sure he didn't find it. I took off in that direction, ready to end his hunt before it began.

"Annie," Eliza murmured, but I could still hear her. "I'm supposed to stay close to you."

She'd promised Cyrus, but I hadn't. Besides, she could cast a spell from several feet away; she didn't need to be right up on me.

I couldn't communicate with her in this form, so I continued running. She was a smart woman; she'd figure out the message.

As I drew closer to the man, I realized he was bigger than I'd thought. When the scent of grass tickled my nose, his height made sense. Bear shifter. Blond hairs spilled out of his black helmet, and blondish chest hairs poked from the top of his black shirt. The strangest part was that he was clean-shaven, unlike most bear shifters, I guessed to keep the black paint on his face.

Musky scents hit my nose, telling me our enemies were a mixed group of bears and wolves. I wondered why there wasn't more variety, but maybe that was yet another piece of the puzzle.

He didn't reach for his gun. Instead, his copper eyes focused on me, and he raised a hand almost in surrender.

Yeah, I wasn't falling for it. Like Sterlyn had recommended, I wouldn't kill him...unless he made me. But I'd make sure I got his weapons.

I'd crouched low, readying to lunge, when footsteps rushed me. I jerked my head to my right as something slammed into my side. I stumbled and caught my balance. Then I spun around, baring my teeth.

A wolf shifter with platinum hair and a buzz cut smirked at me. He lifted his gun to my head, finger ready to pull the trigger, and snorted, "That was the last touch of a man you'll ever feel."

My breath caught. I was screwed unless Eliza helped me.

"Are you a fucking idiot?" the blond bear shifter scoffed and smacked the gun down right as Platinum fired.

The bullet hit the ground mere inches away from me. Dirt burst into the air, and my fur stood on end. My body twitched as I realized how close I'd come to dying.

"What the *hell*?" Platinum rasped and shoved Blondie Chest Hair away. "You had your chance to kill her."

"No, moron." Blondie Chest Hair smacked him in the back of the head. "That's one of the girls we're supposed to capture. If you kill her, there'll be hell to pay."

The corner of the wolf shifter's mouth tilted downward, and he lowered the gun. "How the hell do you know that?"

"They said the one wolf would be silver with lavender eyes and the other would have dark fur with a bluish tint," said the bear shifter. "If you'd listened, you'd know."

Why was he spelling it out for me? Was he trying to get me to think he was an ally? *They're looking for Sterlyn and me.* We'd already assumed that, but since he'd confirmed it, I wanted to inform everyone.

How do you know? Cyrus's displeasure wafted through the bond, then his displeasure turned into anger. *You're supposed to stay close to Eliza.*

I wouldn't humor him with a response. He was being an asshole, and I was part of this pack and his mate. I would have fought everyone the same way Sterlyn, Ronnie, Sierra, and all of our packs were.

"Wade!" Platinum yelled. "One of them is here."

Shit, Wade's here. Cyrus's anger surged into me as he linked with the entire silver wolf pack. *The one Joshua killed, who attacked Sterlyn, isn't actually the asshole in charge. Wade is.*

Then why was he leading the charge? Darrell asked.

Sterlyn's disgust churned my stomach. She replied, *I bet the jerk is still on one of the boats.*

He was a trainer like me, but he was the favorite. They let him direct things from wherever he wanted, and he always picked a safe place. Cyrus ran toward me as he continued, *He's got great aim, and he's smart. We can't underestimate him.*

Using Platinum's momentary distraction to my benefit, I stood on my back legs and sank my claws into his chest. My nails raked through his protective gear. They'd come here, knowing Cyrus was on our side, and taken precautions. He knew that we could use guns. They probably hadn't expected us to be in animal form with vampires as the shooters.

The more vests we could destroy, the easier it would be for the vampires to take them down. The vampires had bulletproof vests, too, but not us wolves. Maybe we should consider getting them designed for our wolf forms in the future if fights like these continued.

As my claws ripped his vest, Ronnie's shadowy form appeared beside me. Her emerald eyes locked on the asshole, and she swung her demon dagger into the twat-waffle's chest. His eyes bulged, and he stumbled back, glancing down. The dagger was also in its shadow form, so he couldn't see it. However, he could *feel* it.

Blood trickled from his mouth and down his chin as he glanced from me to Blondie Chest Hair. He asked, "How?" before his legs gave out and he fell.

My mate reached me, placing himself between the dying man and me. His attention flicked to the boats. *You need to get in the damn woods. If they tranq you, you won't be able to protect yourself, and one of us will have to watch over you the entire time.*

And we'd be down two fighters.

Ronnie leaned over the dying man and wrapped her hands around her dagger. She jerked upward, yanking the blade from his chest. My stomach revolted at the sickening suction noise, and Blondie Chest Hair backed away.

"Look, I don't want to hurt you or anyone," he whispered, his bottom lip quivering. "I don't know what you just did, but please, I'll tell you whatever you want to know."

The air didn't smell like rotten eggs. We needed answers, and maybe we'd found someone to give some. *What do we do?*

Dave's a good guy, Cyrus replied. *I believe him, but we keep an eye on him. One shady move, and I'll kill him with no hesitation.*

Dave, I guess, was a better name than Blondie Chest Hair, but only marginally. I kept forgetting that Cyrus knew many of these people. *He doesn't seem to recognize you.*

Because when I was with them, I couldn't shift. Cyrus growled at Dave, making his threat clear. *And remember, Dave thinks my name is Julius since that's what they called me when I was with them.*

A smaller man with a vest stepped from the covered cabin, tranq gun in hand. I could see the tranq's clear liquid as he loaded it. I assumed this was Wade. He was about Sierra's size, which surprised me, since he was in charge. Something besides brute strength must have elevated him to leadership status, and I didn't want to know what.

A vile and icky aura drifted to me, similar to what I'd felt from wolves in the demon pack. It had to be his essence.

Ronnie blurred as she flew to the man. No one on their side could see her, meaning none of them were angel descendants. At least we had that advantage on our side.

His soot-colored eyes focused on me as an evil grin filled his face. He raised the gun when sturdy footsteps sounded and Eliza's herbal scent filled my nose.

Before Ronnie could reach him, Eliza yelled "Flare!" and flicked her wrist.

The tranq gun flew out of Wade's hand and into the air.

"What? No!" he yelled and tried to catch it, but just when his hand was within inches, Ronnie's shadow form barreled into him.

He fell backward, eyes bulging in horror, and the gun fell past the boat and splashed into the water.

He landed on his back, and Ronnie raised her arms, ready to strike.

Wade growled, "You stupid bitch." He thrust out his arms.

Ronnie's shadowy form flew out of the boat, and she landed hard on the embankment. Wade stood and ran to the edge of the tree line, surveying the shore. "You think we don't know about you?"

He was insane.

Be careful. He doesn't scare, and he's ruthless. Cyrus ran toward my sister. *He'll do whatever it takes to wind up on top. He's killed kids, families, whatever it takes to break someone.*

Great, he was essentially a vampire who'd lost his humanity. *Don't get too close to Ronnie,* I told him. *He can't see her. Maybe move so he thinks she's somewhere she's not.*

Before Cyrus could get too close, Wade pulled out a regular gun. No one was near the embankment, and he fired at random, probably hoping to hit Ronnie.

To my horror, he wasn't far off. He fired shots within a few feet of her and kept moving in her direction.

"*Inherere!*" Eliza screamed, and pushed her hands out, palms facing Wade.

Wade's face scrunched, and his jaw clenched. He fired another shot, but then his hand shook. "Shit." He groaned and eventually dropped the gun. He blew on his hand as if it was hot.

The gun landed right in front of him and fired, and the bullet lodged in his vest. The asshole was saved.

We had to take this guy out, even if it was the last thing we ever did.

I ran toward the boat, flying past Cyrus.

Annie, what are you doing? he linked, his panic wafting through me.

There was only one way to answer that question. *We have to end this.*

Smartly! Just wait. Eliza is handling him, he linked,

his panic increasing and swirling between us. He then included the entire pack, saying, *Whoever can help, get to the boat. We're going to take away their means of escape.*

That was smart. They might stand down if they were trapped. I paused, waiting until we came through with a plan.

Ronnie was floating toward me, no longer dodging gunfire, so I took a moment to reevaluate. Two wolves were dead from Killian's pack, their bodies shot full of bullets, and five bodies on the enemy side were full of bullet holes, too. A lot of the enemies' vests had been shredded or weakened enough for a bullet to make an impact. Our numbers were more than quadruple theirs, so many wolves had teamed up on them.

We're all heading that way. I informed Killian and Griffin of the plan, Sterlyn replied. *That will force them to reconsider their entire strategy. The vampires can distract the shifters with gunfire as we run through. Killian just told Sierra to shift back to human and tell Alex the plan. Everyone, get out of the line of fire so the vampires can shoot without risking injuring one of us.*

Uh...Sierra would be naked. Finally, she'd have to stop teasing me about saving Alex while I'd been naked—I'd have my own ammunition.

The wolves retreated toward the tree line, and the enemy hesitated. Gunfire assaulted them.

As the wolves charged toward the boat, I checked on Eliza. Sweat covered her forehead, and she was still and focused, holding up her hands. I realized Wade and the men on the other two boats were frozen as if they couldn't move. She had to be holding them.

"Hurry and do whatever you're thinking," Eliza rasped. "I can't keep this up much longer."

That was all I needed. I let my wolf take control, and when Cyrus rushed past me, I was determined not to get left behind. The silver wolves took the lead, and the standard wolves ran diligently behind them.

Our pack split, with Sterlyn, Cyrus, Darrell, Theo, and Chad—five of the strongest—heading to one of the boats. I followed my mate, determined to stay with him. We were in this together, a team to the bitter end.

Quinn jumped on the boat, following Cyrus, with me on their heels. The boat was large, and the three of us easily fit on it, even with Wade lying on the ground in the doorway to the cabin.

Something tickled the back of my neck—something like dread.

Something was off.

Something wasn't right.

The crack of a bullet rushing toward us churned my stomach. I had no idea where it was coming from, but it wasn't from the boats.

Everyone, duck! I yelled.

My warning came seconds too late.

CHAPTER SIXTEEN

QUINN'S large silver wolf body slammed onto the deck's smooth floor. He whimpered as the stench of blood filled my nose. The pain that flowed from him into the pack bond was mind-numbing. I'd never experienced a connection like this before.

His whimpers pulled at me. He needed help, and damn it, someone had to do it. I'd started running toward him when another shot erupted.

No!

I had to protect him. He was part of my pack.

Annie, stop! Cyrus linked, his terror flowing into me. *They're shooting from the backup boat.*

Realization crashed over me. They were positioned where they could see us through the trees. I spun in the opposite direction and saw the boat floating a hundred and fifty yards away, around a tree-covered bend.

They were using hunting rifles.

We couldn't leave Quinn there to die.

Though I didn't know the young man well, my few interactions with him had been positive. He tended to fade into the background, but he was a rock Darrell could lean on.

From the ground only a few feet from us, Wade chuckled darkly. His soulless eyes danced with mirth, despite his paralyzation.

He was enjoying our pain.

"I can't hold them much longer!" Eliza yelled, her voice cracking.

Get down, Darrell linked urgently with our pack. *They're snipers.*

Something smashed me hard against the floor. The buzzing in our connection informed me it was Cyrus, and he pushed me toward the side of the boat for shelter.

The link with Quinn began to grow cold, and I tried to scramble to my feet to reach him.

We have to stay down. Cyrus nuzzled my neck to calm me. *If you run out there, you'll get hit.*

Wade is right there, too! The asshole's focus was locked on me, and I could swear the corner of his mouth had tipped upward. He was lying near the edge of the boat, but he didn't seem worried about being hit. Either he believed the others were aiming to kill, or he was fearless like Cyrus had described. I had a feeling it was a mixture of the two, but who the hell knew?

The gunfire between the vampires and the enemy raged on. This plan wasn't as good as we'd thought, but we'd had no way of knowing the outcome. We were just trying to eliminate their getaway boats before the backup got here.

None of us could have known their backup had never planned on arriving.

What do we do? Cyrus had trained with them. Surely he'd have an idea about how to get out of this situation and save Quinn before it was too late.

Cyrus tensed. *I...I don't know. They never had snipers, or I would've prepared us for them.*

Damn it. That meant someone had taken control after Dick's and Saga's deaths.

The sickening, salty taste that usually came before vomiting filled my mouth.

Blood from Quinn's wound trickled toward us. From his position, I thought the injury was somewhere in his chest. There was so much blood, and my own turned ice cold.

I'm going to climb off you, but I need you to keep your head on straight, Cyrus linked. *They think Quinn's dead. They won't hit him again unless you give them a reason to think he's still alive.*

His logic sank into my head. *Okay, I understand.*

He inched off me as a whining noise, like a bomb dropping, sounded from the sky. My heart lurched into my stomach, and I braced myself for impact.

This was it. We were all going to die, including the enemy, over whatever purpose they clung to so desperately. I wasn't sure if the blast would kill us or if we'd die from the aftermath. Whichever was less painful would be my choice.

Right when I expected the impact, the noise transformed into flapping wings.

It's Rosemary, Sterlyn linked with relief. *Hopefully, she can fight the snipers so we can finish what we started.*

This was insane. What kind of enemy were we up against?

Bullets filled the air from both sides, and Cyrus inched out from under the bench. Out of the corner of my eye, I noticed Wade's fingers twitch.

Eliza had said she was weakening. Things would only get worse from here.

What are you doing? I asked Cyrus. He'd just tackled me so that I would stay hidden, and now he was climbing out. *You told me to stay put, and Wade is beginning to move.*

Since there's one boat, that likely means at least two snipers are on it, judging by the timing of the shots. Each one will have someone helping them lock on targets. Cyrus ran toward Quinn. *They'll be focused on taking out Rosemary, since she's an angel. Stay put. I'll handle everything from here.* He reached the downed wolf, whose connection was lukewarm, indicating he hadn't passed away yet. The coolness was unnerving. The only comparison I had was when Cyrus had been kidnapped and taken out of our bond's range.

Since Cyrus would be focused on Quinn, I'd handle Wade and secure the boat.

Ronnie's shadow figure appeared beside me. "I'm going to help Rosemary. Holler if you need me."

Before I could respond, she flew toward the boat we

couldn't attack. I watched as Rosemary spun, fending off bullets as she made her way toward the snipers. They should've known that bullets were no match for an angel, but she'd been hanging out in Shadow City over some pressing angel issues. Maybe they hadn't expected her to be here.

Ronnie is helping Rosemary, I linked with the rest of the pack. *We need to focus on securing the boat.*

As if fate had bowed to the challenge, Eliza cried, "I can't hold them anymore!"

At shifter speed, Wade reached for the tranq gun.

Hell, no. Not today, twatwaffle.

I jumped toward him, trying not to overthink. Once again, I'd be forced to kill. There was no way this man would hand himself over willingly.

My teeth sank into his arm as he reached for the gun with his other hand. I shredded his skin, wanting him to feel pain.

The prick didn't even flinch.

Something was seriously wrong with him.

Rage swirled inside me as Cyrus realized what was going on. *Damn it,* he growled.

Wade swung the tranq gun at my face, and my body went numb as if my brain couldn't comprehend what was going to happen.

Refusing to give up, I released his arm and lunged for his neck. Maybe I could make him bleed a little bit and give Cyrus the advantage.

I watched as Wade moved his finger, and I braced for

impact. At the last second, Cyrus jumped in front of me, taking the dart instead.

"Fuck!" Wade screamed and rushed to stand.

Get... Cyrus thudded to the floor. *Him...* His eyes grew unfocused, and his head bobbled.

Wade glanced back into the cabin, his hands twitching. He stepped toward it, but he moved as if he were off balance.

Maybe the blood loss from his arm was getting to him.

My eyes followed where he looked, and I saw another tranquilizer dart sitting next to the steering wheel in a container.

He hadn't expected to miss or for someone else to take the blow.

Cyrus got hit with the tranquilizer, I informed the others. I still couldn't believe he'd done it, but I knew why he had. He didn't want me weakened in case something did happen. He needed me to be able to protect myself, which meant more than he'd ever know.

We've secured this boat, Sterlyn responded, though she didn't sound thrilled. *I'll head over to help you now.*

Normally, I'd have said I could handle it, but Cyrus and Quinn were down for the count, and this crazy-ass man knew no fear or pain. When Cyrus had said he was ruthless, I hadn't expected this. This was next-level insane shit.

Wade shuffled his feet, stumbling as the boat rocked from the current. The rocking wasn't anything major, but enough to tip us over if we weren't careful.

I steamrolled into him, smashing him into one side of the cabin doorway. He grunted, the first sign of discomfort, confirming he could feel some degree of pain. He moved his good hand, pulling at something in his waistband.

Using the distraction, I clawed into his vest. If we were going to kill these pricks, we had to expose their hearts, neck, and anything else that could help kill them quickly. We didn't have the luxury of letting them bleed out.

An evil chuckle left him as something sharp sliced into my side. I swallowed the howl of pain that wanted to escape, not wanting to give him any encouragement. If he knew he'd hurt me, that would only fuel him to keep attacking. If I acted unscathed like he had, hopefully that would frustrate him instead of making him more determined.

Agony burned through my side, and my vision spotted, but I controlled my breathing. He hadn't hit anything that would kill me, which he must have done on purpose. They wanted to capture Sterlyn and me alive.

Though that didn't mean unharmed.

My belly churned as nausea took hold. I tried to push through the discomfort, but if I couldn't, I'd puke on him as I had on Nyko when Tate had beaten me. It would be a win either way.

His face turned red as he attempted to pull the knife from my side, but I jerked away, keeping it lodged in. I didn't want him to remove it and stab me again, and only one of his arms was good, since I'd destroyed the other.

We were in some sort of dominance pissing match, reminding me of when Theo and Chad had challenged Cyrus for the position of alpha of the silver wolf pack. Mila had influenced them, making them think they were stronger than Cyrus and worthier to lead. Cyrus had put them both in their place.

Just like that, this was not a fight I could afford to lose. Not only did I need to keep my friends and family safe, but I also had the women from the demon pack to help as well. I couldn't do that from wherever the hell they wanted to take me.

Wade's nostrils flared as he fought, and my link to Quinn continued to fade. I wasn't sure how much longer it would feel lukewarm. My chest tightened, and my throat closed, reminding me of the day I lost my childhood best friend, Suzy.

He moved for the knife again, and I bit down on his forearm. Blood coated my mouth, mixing with the salty taste. I dry-heaved but held on tight.

My wolf surged, taking more control, and I let her. Maybe with her in charge, my stomach would be less sensitive.

Using the arm I'd mauled earlier, he punched me in the snout. My jaw slackened, and my head snapped back. This must be what it felt like when a guy got kicked in the balls. The pain whited out my vision for a moment, and I pawed at my nose to lessen the agony.

He spun and headed toward the cabin again.

I shook my head, knowing I couldn't let him reach the tranqs, and rushed past him. I bumped into him, and he bounced off the doorframe, growling, "Stupid bitch. You have no idea who you're up against."

Wow. He wasn't even clever with his insults, and the thing was, our group was pretty damn sure we did. If Dave was as sincere as Cyrus expected and had just gotten stuck working for the wrong side, maybe we could convince him to come to our side and tell us everything he knew.

Wade hit the tranq gun as he fell to the deck, and he screamed, grabbing a handful of my fur with his bloody arm and hand. He yanked, pulling at the roots, and gritted his teeth.

I'd experienced worse pain—like from the knife still stuck in my side.

I kicked with my back legs, hitting him in the chest hard enough that he fell against the railing of the boat and tipped over into the water with a splash.

Well, okay, then. I hadn't expected that.

As of now, the boat was secured, and I had access to the tranqs I needed to destroy. I ran into the cabin, focusing on one thing at a time. With all the gunfire and commotion, the noises were overwhelming, but I could still hear Wade in the river. He'd be trying to get back on board, so I needed to move.

Paws hit the deck as Sterlyn linked, *Oh, dear God. I should've come with you.*

I didn't need to feel her horror on top of mine. This had been a horrible fight, and it wasn't over yet.

Clutching the black container with my teeth, I dropped the box, and the three tranqs inside hit the ground. I stomped on them, careful to hit only the container. The liquid spilled onto the floor.

There. If they wanted Sterlyn and me, they'd have to take us fighting or kill us. *I destroyed the tranqs.*

Good job. The other boats are secured, and it looks like this boat was the only one with tranqs. Sterlyn raced into the cabin. Her eyes widened as she took me in. *You have a knife stuck in you.*

Yeah, he stabbed me a few minutes ago. I didn't want to focus on it because doing so increased the pain.

Let me get it out. Sterlyn ran over and bit down on the handle. *On the count of three. One...*

I braced myself. When I expected her to say *two*, she yanked out the knife.

Pure agony surged through me, and I yelped. Tears flowed from my eyes, and my chest heaved. *You said you were counting to three!*

She opened our pack link so I could feel her regret. *I'm so sorry, but it would've been worse if I'd waited. You'll start healing now, so the pain should recede soon.*

Maybe I'd made it worse by staying with the silver wolves. Quinn's link was too cool, and Sterlyn rushed to him while I went to Cyrus. His eyes were closed, but I could feel consciousness returning.

I looked for Rosemary and Ronnie and noticed that neither one was in the air. *Are Ronnie and Rosemary okay?*

Yes. They took out the snipers. Sterlyn sighed. *Griffin informed me when I reached you. They've eliminated the threat. The shifters that are still standing are surrendering.*

Uh...what are we going to do with all the shifters? This was a nightmare.

My head turned at the sound of something climbing onto the boat. Wade stood there, water pouring off him. Teeth gritted, he lifted a gun, aiming right at my chest.

Gunfire erupted, and I closed my eyes, bracing for death.

CHAPTER SEVENTEEN

WHEN NO PAIN burst through me, I opened my eyes and saw Sterlyn charge at Wade. He dropped to his knees, and my attention homed in on the bullet hole in the center of his forehead. His body fell forward as the gun clattered to the floor.

His head landed near the back of Quinn's, and I could only think it was karma. Blood trickled from his wound, mixing with Quinn's.

My eyes flicked toward the embankment in time to see Dave lower his gun. The blond, hairy-chested bear shifter had saved me. Was he playing us? This could be a ruse so he could infiltrate us and take me to Ezra, or whoever was in charge, and solidify his role in whatever this organization was.

Whatever his motives, it was a victory, and we had enough drama to deal with before addressing anything else. The fight was over, but we had to be ready in case someone changed their mind again.

Rosemary flew toward us.

Sterlyn howled slightly to get her attention. The silver wolf hurried over to Quinn and whimpered, placing her snout on the wolf.

Black wings grew larger as Rosemary headed to the boat, and her rose scent hit me as she touched down.

Had I not seen her with my own eyes, I wouldn't have known she'd landed. The boat didn't budge under her weight.

As she kneeled beside Quinn, the pack link went cold. A sharp, piercing pain ripped through my chest, and I threw my head back and howled. Other pack members followed suit, their pain mixing with mine, the emotions like the current surging toward a dam.

Howls from both packs mourning their losses made a sob wrack my chest.

Rosemary's mouth mashed into a line as her hands glowed, and she reached for Quinn. The light was so bright I almost had to close my eyes, but when she touched Quinn, the brightness redirected inside him, making it bearable.

Knowing that Rosemary was Quinn's best chance to live, I rushed to Cyrus. His eyes fluttered open as he regained consciousness. I nuzzled him, trying to ignore the piercing pain in my side. The last thing he needed was to worry about my injury, especially with the drugs raging through him.

Sterlyn, where's Wade? Cyrus linked, his mind working slowly. He was groggy, and his eyes kept closing, no matter how many times he opened them. *You have to get out of here.*

He's dead. I licked his face to help him become aware, and I wanted to taste him, too. I'd come too close to dying. *Dave shot him when he was—* I stopped. Nothing good would come from telling him I could've died while he'd been knocked out.

Tension stormed through him, spilling into me. His eyes popped open, adrenaline burning off the rest of the drug. *When he was what?*

Rosemary's low groan interrupted us. I turned my head as her eyes tensed, and she clenched her teeth. Her skin glowed moonlight white as she channeled more of her magic into Quinn.

I wasn't sure what to do. *She's struggling to save Quinn.* I jumped to my feet and winced as I tried to reach him.

Cyrus slowly climbed to his feet, his attention diverted for now. I knew he'd eventually find out what happened, and though he couldn't do a damn thing about it, he'd blame himself.

Is everyone other than Quinn okay? Cyrus linked as he stepped toward the fallen wolf. His legs quivered, still affected by the medicine, but his breathing and heartbeat had returned to normal.

There are a few minor injuries, but we're okay, Darrell replied. *Rosemary and Ronnie sank the sniper boat.*

I glanced toward it and saw only the roof and front of the boat sticking out of the water. The back end sunk first. The snipers must have died, too. The people on that boat had seemed to be the most skilled, probably in case we managed to escape the group here on land.

They'd truly thought we'd be taken by surprise and hadn't expected us to fight back so effectively.

A shadowy form drifted toward us. Though Ronnie could fly like Rosemary, they moved differently. Ronnie traveled fast in shadow form, but it was more jerky than fluid. That could be because she was still learning her powers. She'd come a long way in a short time.

She landed beside me, her shadowy form solidifying until her full body appeared. Her copper hair was blowing away from her face in the slight breeze. "What can I do?"

"Nothing," Rosemary gritted. "I...I can't bring him back. I didn't get here in time."

My heart broke, even though I already felt the loss of his connection. My throat constricted, and my eyes burned. When Mila had left the pack, there'd been a coldness where her link had been, but it didn't compare to this. This was icy, as if the link was freezing over to sever it permanently.

As if the loss was irreversible.

Death.

This was the first pack death I'd mourned, and the pain suffocated me.

No wonder Mila was so bitter.

Maybe I'd judged her too quickly.

If losing Quinn hurt like this, I couldn't imagine the pain of losing her mate.

God, I hoped I never had to experience it.

Sterlyn lowered her head and brushed her side along Rosemary to let the angel know she'd done everything she could.

Though we mourn the loss of Quinn, we have an enemy we must stand up to, Sterlyn linked, her heartbreak coursing through the connection. *We can't let his sacrifice be in vain and lose the fight he gave his life for.*

Her words caused something within me to change fundamentally. The frigidness of the dying link remained, but my mind cleared as her words connected with my wolf. My wolf rallied, her determination mixing with mine.

We wouldn't let our packmate down.

We'd honor his sacrifice.

And when it was time, we'd honor his life and wish him well in the afterlife.

"Guys, the vampires want to know what to do with the shifters who surrendered." Ronnie cleared her throat, and her gaze locked on me. When she tensed, I grimaced.

I knew what was coming next.

"Oh, my God." She blurred the short distance to me and examined my side. "You're hurt."

What? Cyrus jerked his attention to me and moved to see my injury. Their attention on the knife wound made the pain slam back into me.

I almost stumbled from the burning sting, but that sensation had to be more psychosomatic because I was paying attention to the wound.

"What happened?" Ronnie asked.

That's an excellent question, Cyrus growled.

I blew out a breath. It wasn't like I could actually tell Ronnie in animal form, and I hated that she'd alerted Cyrus to it. We had enough going on without the extra attention. *It was Wade, but it's fine. He's dead, and I'll heal. He made sure the wound wasn't fatal.*

"Rosemary, do you have enough strength to heal her?" Ronnie asked, and raised her wrist to her mouth. "Or should I use my blood?"

The nausea that had receded came back. I'd drunk Ronnie's blood before, and it tasted good, but I couldn't get past the fact it was *blood*, even if it tasted like sweets.

"Let me." Rosemary closed her eyes as she hovered over Quinn's body. She whispered, "I'm so sorry I couldn't help you. I didn't realize there were snipers on the backup boat until it was too late. I hope your soul finds peace."

No one should feel responsible for Quinn's death. There'd been so much going on, and it had been hard enough for me to keep track of those fighting around me, let alone those in other areas. I wished I could convey those thoughts to her.

Sterlyn walked to the edge of the boat. *I'll head to the embankment and shift back to human form so I can talk with Alex and the enemy shifters. We need to determine our next steps. Unless you two need me here?*

No, we'll be right behind you, Cyrus replied, guilt swirling between us. *Once Rosemary heals Annie, we'll be on our way. I want to talk to Dave. I need to hear why he saved her.*

Do you know him? Sterlyn's purple-silver eyes glowed.

Cyrus nodded, coming off human with the gesture. *We grew up together and became close a few years ago while I trained him.* Sadness filled his expression.

Then yeah, you'll be good at reading him. Sterlyn jumped off the boat and headed toward the woods. *I'll bring your clothes back with me.*

"It might take longer than normal to heal you," Rosemary rasped. There were faint circles under her eyes, which weren't her norm.

I'd seen her look this rough only one other time—when we'd escaped the demon wolf pack. Lux, one of our witch allies, had spelled the demon wolves to fall asleep so we could get away. The magic had taken its toll, so Rosemary had channeled her healing magic into Lux, reenergizing the witch's magic to keep it flowing. The two of them working together was the only reason we'd escaped without losing Alex. He'd been injured trying to help Ronnie, and if we hadn't made it to safety in time to get him blood, he would've died.

Rosemary sighed. "I channeled a lot of magic into Quinn, so I'm depleted, but I have enough left."

My heart twisted, knowing she felt obligated to explain.

"Take a second to recharge." Ronnie rubbed her hands together. "I don't want to leave her like this. I can wait a few more minutes before getting back to Alex."

Warmth flooded me at my sister's words. Even though her soul wanted to be next to Alex, she didn't want to leave me injured. Ronnie loved with her whole heart, and she'd always put me first to a fault. But maybe fate had done that on purpose because she'd followed me here and found her soulmate.

Or maybe I was romanticizing the situation, but this was the happiest I'd ever seen her, even though we were under constant threat.

"I can do it." Rosemary's hands glowed once more, and when she touched my fur and pressed her hand against the wound, warmth spread through me.

The pressure was uncomfortable at first, but after a few seconds, the discomfort eased. My wolf welcomed the angel magic, and despite my magic feeling cold against hers, something felt familiar. After all, demons had been angels before they gave up their humanity. That had to be the reason.

The white light filled me and concentrated on the injured area. My skin tingled like when I sprouted fur.

Are you okay? Cyrus asked, his eyes locked on Rosemary's hand. *Do I need to make her stop?*

No. My eyes closed as peace surged through me. *Why?*

You feel funny. Cyrus nudged his head into my neck. *I don't understand what it is.*

It feels...nice. I wasn't sure what other word could describe it. *Her magic is warm, and it collides with the coolness of mine, but then they merge. Like, the two temperatures conflict, but then they work together. It's strange, but it doesn't hurt. I can feel myself mending. I* probably sounded insane, but I wasn't sure how to describe the sensation.

The magic inside receded, and Rosemary said, "You can go. It's healed now."

When I looked into Rosemary's face, I found that she'd paled like she had on the night of our demon pack escape. She'd flown back, carrying one of the witches, and crash-landed into the ground, barely making it to the coven. After some sleep, she'd gotten back to normal.

I stood up. Cyrus and Ronnie needed to stop worrying, and I wanted to talk to Dave and see what we could figure out. *Let's go so we can question the corrupt shifters.*

"I'm glad you're okay." Ronnie ran a hand through my fur, then blurred, disappearing from my side.

Yeah, she wanted to get to her soulmate.

Rosemary stepped over the dead bodies at the edge of the boat. Her hair hung in her face, and her shoulders sagged. She wasn't the strong Rosemary I knew.

Sensing me watching her, she raised her head and smiled. "I'm fine. Go talk to them. I'll get Quinn off the boat. I just need a minute to rest." When I still hesitated, she waved me on. "I promise, I'm fine. I'll be back to somewhat normal in a few minutes. It didn't take as much out of me as the night I fell from the sky."

She's not lying, Cyrus reassured me as he trotted to the edge of the boat. *We really need to get over there.*

Since the air was free of the signature smell of a lie, I turned and hurried after Cyrus.

We jumped off the boat, and our paws hit the shallow

water. Being able to move without pain was freeing, but I wished none of this would've happened.

The enemy shifters were contained in a circle with the vampires and our wolves surrounding them. Killian stood next to Alex and Ronnie, who were in front of Dave. The bear shifter glanced at me, concern etched across his forehead. When our gazes met, some of the tension smoothed from his face.

Odd.

Your clothes are here, Sterlyn linked to Cyrus and me.

Cyrus trotted toward a copse of redbuds, and I tore my focus away from Dave to follow him. Sterlyn and Griffin stepped from between the trees and pointed deeper into the woods.

I didn't need any further encouragement. I was eager to get back into human form so we could get some answers.

Our clothes lay on a large branch at shoulder height. Within seconds, Cyrus and I had shifted back into human form and dressed.

"Hey," Cyrus said, and took my hand, pulling me to him. I blinked, staring into his granite-colored eyes—the shade that revealed he was stressed or worried. *I'm sorry I wasn't there to protect you from Wade.*

Annoyance flared through me, and my pulse pounded. I had to remember how I felt when I was in his position and unable to help him. *There is nothing to apologize for. He wanted to use the tranquilizer on me, and by blocking him, I was able to destroy the rest of the tranq darts.*

And get knifed. He wrapped his arms around my waist, pulling me against him. *I almost wish you hadn't killed him so I could.*

Dave killed him, not me. I'd only mangled his arm and hand, and that hadn't prevented him from trying to tranq me.

My body melted into Cyrus's. I wrapped my arms around his neck and laid my head on his chest. He had a foot in height on me, which I loved. My head nestled against his chest perfectly, and he placed his chin on top of my head.

I felt safe in his arms, and I hadn't realized how desperate I'd been to have this moment with him. I'd truly thought I would die and likely would have if Dave hadn't saved me.

At the thought, my body broke into a slight sweat. I hugged Cyrus tighter and breathed in his musky hydrangea scent. *I kinda love you.*

His chest shook with silent laughter as he placed a finger under my chin and tipped my face upward. He winked. *I kinda love you, too. Just a little.*

He leaned down and kissed my lips briefly. We both knew we had to get back to the others.

Cyrus, Sterlyn linked. *We need you out here. Dave is refusing to talk to anyone but you. By the way, I told him you go by Cyrus now.*

Good. I never want to hear that other name again, he linked, and took my hand before we headed out to confront the enemy together.

When we stepped into the clearing in front of the river, most of the silver wolves were back on land.

My stomach dropped. *Who's protecting the boats?* I hated to think that someone might have sneaked away to alert Ezra that they'd been captured. We needed to keep him out of the know. *Are we sure none of these are Ezra's pack?* If any of them were, Ezra would already know, and more enemy backup could be on the way.

They aren't, Sterlyn assured me. *Griffin is the alpha of Ezra's pack. He'd know if any of these men were his pack, and if Ezra created his own pack, his pack link would feel removed because he'd have shifters accepting him as alpha.*

As long as we were sure, that was good enough for me.

"Man, I'm so sorry." Dave tugged at his shirt as he stared at Cyrus. "I had no clue that was you in wolf form. You smelled familiar, but I thought you couldn't shift."

"I couldn't shift until I found my pack and learned I'd been kidnapped at birth." Cyrus tugged me after him as we walked over to stand by Alex, Sterlyn, Griffin, Killian, and Ronnie. "Why did you help us?"

Eliza stood in the back, her face pale and her arms wrapped around her body. She looked so tired. Between using her magic and stress, she needed to take better care of herself.

"When I saw the silver wolves, it clicked that these could be your packmates, and...I remember you telling me you had a sister who was destined to be alpha, so they got rid of you." Dave gestured to Sterlyn. "I figured that was her, which surprised me, since you seemed to hate her. But clearly, they're your pack, so I saved the girl because I didn't want to do something you might not recover from. I couldn't do that to you."

Why would he care? Sterlyn asked, her eyes narrowed on the bear shifter.

The same people took him from his pack, too, but not because they wanted him to train others. Cyrus's face hardened as he stared the bear shifter down. *They took him because his father couldn't deliver the guns they'd demanded. It was an unreasonable, last-minute request, and his father had never worked with the pack before and had no clue what they would do. He had to give up his son because he couldn't follow through.*

And Dave stayed? As soon as I could, I would've gone back to my family.

They told him that if he left, they'd kill his family. Cyrus's eyes darkened to steel. *And they said that if his parents really loved him, they would've found a way to get all the guns they needed. That this was his family's way of getting rid of him.*

Emotional abuse. Sterlyn's eyes glowed. *Like they did to you.*

Exactly. That's why we bonded. We both felt like we weren't wanted. Cyrus's hand tightened on mine. *And that's why I'm inclined to trust him. But I'm not completely sold yet.*

"If you want my trust, you need to earn it." Cyrus lifted his chin and glared down his nose. "Why do the people you work for want my mate and my sister?"

"The demon wolf is your mate?" Dave's eyes widened. "I thought girlfriend, but your actual *mate*?" He sniffed the air, and his jaw dropped.

Wait. He knew about the demon wolves. That couldn't be a coincidence.

"Demon wolf?" Ronnie laughed without humor. "How do you know about them?"

"The people I'm *forced* to work for know a lot more than you realize. Like, the person who wants the silver wolf is the shifter she was supposed to mate with before she bonded with Griffin." Despite answering Ronnie, Dave kept his attention on Cyrus. "He has a plan to eliminate their mate bond, and they're desperate to do something with the demon wolf. I'll tell you everything, but it'll cost you."

"What the fuck, man?" The wolf shifter standing next to Dave shoved him in the arm. "What the hell are you doing?"

"Going after what I've wanted all along." Dave smirked, his irises darkening.

My heart sank. I worried whatever his price was, we might just have to pay it.

CHAPTER EIGHTEEN

SWEAT COVERED MY PALMS, and I wiped them on my jean shorts.

"What is that?" Sterlyn asked Dave, her head tilted. Instead of looking worried, she appeared curious.

"What we all have to deal with." Dave swirled his finger around, indicating the group. "I just want to go back home and for my family to remain safe."

"That'll never happen, idiot." The wolf shifter next to Dave ran his hands through his shaggy apricot-red hair, getting it out of his eyes. His rugged features made his scowl more menacing. "You're going to fuck us all over."

Cyrus tensed, his neck cording. "Yes, because the ones who trained you and forced you to serve them do *so much* for you. I can see how trying to break free from the terror would seem stupid, Richie."

The wolf shifter's crystal-sage eyes darkened to a gray. "You had to leave because you turned on the people who'd fought alongside you. They told us everything you did."

They viewed Cyrus as a traitor who'd attacked his own and left them behind.

"That's not fair." Cyrus released his hold on me and inched forward. "They were going to hurt my twin sister, and I couldn't let it happen. The others wouldn't back down. I didn't mean to kill them."

"We were the ones who did it," Griffin said, stepping next to Cyrus. "He didn't kill any of them, but he took a bullet for Sterlyn. If you're going to blame anyone, blame me. I went there to get my mate back, and I didn't care about the cost."

Killian nodded and patted Griffin on the back as he stood beside him. "Me, too. I helped fight them, but my sister was taken, and there was no other choice. Just like you attacked us today and we had to stand our ground."

Sterlyn arched her eyebrow. "Besides, you killed some of us tonight. How is that any different?"

The wolf shifter exhaled. "We didn't have a choice."

"Nor did we." I got that Cyrus wanted to keep me out of the spotlight, with them knowing I was a demon wolf and all, but I was part of this, too. I had something to say, and I could help. I'd learned how to reason with the kids in the group home, and I'd watched so many damn television law shows that the interrogation skills were ingrained in my brain. "Did you expect us to hand ourselves over without a fight? You're attacking for survival. Why would you think we wouldn't defend ourselves?"

"Uh..." Richie blinked, his mouth hanging open.

"Great reasoning." Sierra snorted. "Ronnie, you should take royal lessons from him so you can become more eloquent in the fine art of conversation."

"Dear gods," Alex groaned, and pinched the bridge of his nose.

Ronnie grinned. "I'll take your advice under consideration."

Sierra's eyes sparkled, and she pointed at my sister. "Oh, I see what you did there."

Eliza grunted and shook her head. "Even in a situation like this, you run that mouth of yours?"

"See, someone finally agrees with me." Alex gestured to his mother-in-law and sighed. "Thank you. Everyone else finds her charming, for some reason."

"Eliza's the only here who's even remotely close to your age." Sierra pursed her lips and shrugged.

She loved ragging on Alex and how old he was. His mannerisms often showed he was far older than us, but just looking at him, you could never tell. That was part of the allure of the vampire's immortality. He looked to be in his early twenties, and he fit in well, but occasionally, his old-fashioned ways sneaked through, or he'd speak more formally, reminding us he was three hundred years old.

Sterlyn cleared her throat, redirecting everyone's attention. She found Sierra humorous under most circumstances, but she also knew how to keep everyone on a serious path. "How about this?" She lifted her arms. "You tell us one important piece of information so we know you actually have some, and if we're intrigued, we can work out an agreement."

Do you think he has something? I linked to Sterlyn and Cyrus.

Cyrus nodded his head slightly. *He has a knack for getting along with others, and that's gotten him inside information before. He can handle his wolfsbane better than the rest of us, too, and get people's tongues to loosen. Also, when I left, they probably moved him up in rank so he'd have access to higher-level intel.*

The knot in my chest eased. Maybe Dave's demands would work in our favor.

"Fine," Dave rasped. His attention went to Cyrus. "I can tell you the name of the wolf who wants to mate with Sterlyn."

Griffin's irises glowed as his wolf surged forward, and he bellowed, "She's already mated and *mine*."

"Whoa." Dave lifted his hands as sweat beaded on his upper lip. "Everyone knows that, but this guy is determined."

"I have a fated mate. How would any sort of relationship with him be possible?" Sterlyn's nose wrinkled, and she gagged. "Unless he—"

"Yeah, he doesn't give a shit if you belong to him as long as you bear his children." Dave shivered, his eyes closed. "He's a sick fuck."

Rage wafted through my mate connection with Cyrus. He didn't want to process what that man wanted to do with Sterlyn because there was no way it would be pleasant or friendly. He growled, "Who is it?"

"I'll tell you, but you need to calm down." Dave lowered his hands and glanced at me.

The look was clear—he wanted me to calm my mate down, but I would never dream of doing that. I'd seen kids come through the system who'd had unforgivable things done to them, and that was something this alpha was considering doing to Sterlyn.

Everyone had a right to be enraged.

"Dumbass," Richie groaned. "What did you expect to happen? For everyone to be intrigued and nicely ask for you to tell them more? That's her fated mate, for God's sake."

He had a point. Maybe starting with their plan for me would've been safer.

My stomach roiled.

Dear God, was their plan for me worse than the plan for Sterlyn? Was it a way for the man to get back at Cyrus for deserting him? Still, they knew I was a demon wolf—were they planning the *same* thing for me? I almost wanted to ask, but if Cyrus hadn't thought of that, I didn't want to jump to that conclusion since I *could* be wrong. He was already having a hard time holding his wolf back over Sterlyn.

Cyrus bristled as fur sprouted along his arms. I had to get control of my emotions because I was egging on his transition.

"Who the hell is it?" Griffin marched over to Dave, getting into his face.

"Look—" Dave started, but Griffin punched him in the jaw.

Dave's head snapped back. I linked only with Sterlyn, *We need to get our men under control, or we won't get anything more out of these guys.*

She glanced at me. *You're right. I'll handle Griffin. You get Cyrus under control.*

Sterlyn slid between Griffin and Dave, facing her mate. She placed her hands on his chest, and her eyes glowed faintly. She was talking to him through their mate connection.

I turned to Cyrus. *Babe, we need to remain levelheaded.* I winced. That sounded critical, which was the opposite of what I was going for. You'd think after all my time working with highly emotional kids that I'd be better at this.

He laughed bitterly. *That's easy for you to say. The idea of what they're planning for the two of you—* He cringed like he hadn't meant to say that.

I realized he was having the same thoughts as me but was trying to keep me from worrying. *It would make sense if they wanted to breed with a silver wolf and a demon wolf, which is why we can't beat the shit out of Dave. We need him to talk before whoever's in charge realizes things haven't gone according to plan. You said you were friends—use that.*

I touched his shoulder. His body relaxed slightly, and some of his rage dissipated from the bond.

He inhaled deeply. The fur patches on his arms vanished as he rolled his neck. "Dave, man. Dragging this out is making things worse. Who is it? Just tell us what you know."

Blood trickled from Dave's nose as he pinched the bridge. "I'm trying to be helpful. I'll tell you everything if you promise to help keep my family safe."

"That's a no-brainer for us." Ronnie crossed her arms, staring at Dave. "Whoever is organizing the kidnapping of my sister and my best friend won't be in a position of power much longer. We *will* take them out, along with every one of their allies."

"And if you don't?" Dave chewed on his bottom lip.

Alex stepped forward, placing a hand on his heart. "Then I promise we will do whatever we can to ensure that no innocent person is harmed."

I noticed that he'd said *innocent*. Knowing Alex, it was a tactical decision, but Dave seemed relieved.

"Fine. The man who took over for Saga and Dick is named Ezra," Dave said hurriedly. "He's—"

A few men groaned, and one even muttered, "You just got my family *killed*."

"Wait." Griffin lifted a finger. "You're saying *Ezra* wants to *breed* with my *mate*?"

"Uh...do you know him?" Dave clenched his jaw.

Richie snarled, "Of course he does. He's the Shadow City alpha."

"Why do they want Annie?" Sterlyn remained calm and glanced at Dave. She didn't remove her hands from her mate, afraid of what would happen if she did.

The question had needed to be asked, but I wasn't sure I wanted to hear the answer. My stomach churned as Ezra's face popped into my mind. I remembered thinking he was handsome, but now I wondered how I could've thought that.

"Well—" Dave bounced on his feet.

"Why hold back now, nut sack?" Richie hissed. "You've already told them who's in charge."

Dave spun around and put his finger into Richie's chest. "Now listen here—"

"I'm not scared of you." Richie rolled his eyes and puffed out his chest.

Shaking his hands, Cyrus exhaled and said sincerely, "Dave, please. Tell me why they want my mate. We already promised to protect your family. You know we aren't lying. What more are you angling for?"

Dave's hesitation slipped away as he dropped his hand from Richie's chest. The bear shifter rubbed his hands together. "This is hard. For the past ten years, all I've done is please them to protect my family."

"I know." Cyrus stepped toward him. "I get it. Had I stayed, they would have killed me for failing to stop Sterlyn from leaving. Making that decision was difficult, which is crazy. I *do* understand what you're feeling. And I promise it'll get better. They messed with our minds to create a warped bond with them." He took a moment to glance at the other captive shifters. "That goes for all of you, if you choose to leave. We'll do everything in our power to take down Ezra and whoever else stands in our way."

His words made my heart grow, and I wasn't even one of the people he'd been talking to.

Dave's demeanor changed. He rubbed his fingers

together as he said, "He wants Annie so we can take her back to the demon pack."

My body stayed motionless. I was neither relieved nor more traumatized. It felt like the emotion remained steady because there wasn't a lesser evil. Either way, their plan was to push me onto another man—wolf shifter or demon. Hell, I wasn't sure Ezra wasn't a demon.

"How does he know the demon pack's location?" Eliza asked, her face lining with worry.

If they knew about the demon pack, they could know about her coven. I hadn't considered that.

"A demon told a vampire that Ezra is connected with." Dave scratched his head. "I don't know their names because we never saw or talked to them. I think they died."

Alex hissed as crimson bled into his irises.

Dave had to be talking about his brother and Ronnie's father. They'd told Ezra about the demon wolf pack. My heart stopped. What if demons were close by and the enemy was protecting them? The night we'd escaped the demon wolves, Tate had gone to meet with a demon, and that strange energy had filled the air. It had been stronger near the edge of the demon wolf neighborhood where I'd worked in the garden with Midnight and the other captive mates.

"I'm not sure if I should be relieved or more worried," Eliza murmured.

I felt the same way.

"Okay, so what was the plan?" Cyrus tapped his

fingers on his legs. "Where were you supposed to bring Annie and Sterlyn?"

I could feel his anxiety. He was ready for this situation to be over, and I was right there with him.

"Wade was supposed to take the boat to the edge of Shadow Ridge and hand them off there. The man's going to be there waiting with a van." Dave's body sagged as if he'd come to grips with his decision to switch sides.

Finally under control, Griffin asked, "How do you know this?"

"Wade told me in case something went wrong. I was his backup plan." Dave glanced at Cyrus. "Since he's no longer with us, I'm next in command."

That's what I thought. Cyrus took my hand and pulled me close to him. "How many guys were supposed to go with Wade?"

"Just him." Dave licked his lips. "We didn't want everyone knowing the plan, in case you tortured them into turning."

"Little did they know it would be you who betrayed them," an olive-skinned wolf shifter spat from the back.

Most of these men weren't thrilled that Dave had told us everything, but they couldn't do anything about it.

"We'll need to pretend to be unconscious," Sterlyn said, and pointed at me. "Dave will need to take us to the meeting place. We don't want to alert Ezra that anything is off until the last possible moment."

"There's no way in hell I'm not going with you." Cyrus shook his head. "I'll hide in the boat's cabin or something."

Griffin crossed his arms and looked into Sterlyn's eyes. "Me, too. You aren't going anywhere near that asshole, especially with his plans for you. I'll kill the jackass before his eyes can even focus on you."

I didn't like the idea of the guys putting themselves at risk, but I couldn't blame them. I'd be the same way in their shoes.

"We'll ask Rosemary to fly over and watch in case we need backup," Killian said. "And a second boat can follow and stay back. I'll be on it, and you can link with me if you need help."

"Uh...I'll be shadowing and going, too." Ronnie's jaw set as she stared Killian down. "Rosemary isn't the only one with flying powers."

We didn't have time to argue. Killian hadn't meant to hurt her feelings. "It'd be best if Eliza, Alex, Killian, and maybe one or two vampires you trust come in another boat with Rosemary and Ronnie in the air."

Sterlyn nodded. "Killian, do you have a place to hold the rest of these shifters while we're gone? We don't need one of them running off to contact Ezra."

"We can tie them up in the training area." Killian glanced behind him, and I wasn't surprised to see his beta, Billy, heading this way. "Billy will coordinate. I'm hoping Darrell and the rest of the silver wolves won't mind helping out..."

"That won't be a problem," Sterlyn said. "When we get back, we'll bury and honor Quinn."

Wings flapped as Rosemary flew in behind us. She looked better, but blood stained her silky white shirt. "I heard everything. I placed Quinn's body in the training area and threw Wade's in the river. I'm ready to go when you are."

We had a set plan. Now it was all about executing it.

Cyrus turned to Dave and asked, "Are you okay with this plan?"

"If it gets me away from this organization and allows me to have a normal life, I'm in." Dave's face was set in determination. "We need to go. Ezra will be waiting for us. He didn't expect it to take long."

That was the advantage we needed. Not only was Ezra narcissistic, but he was also arrogant, which fit his profile.

"Go ahead, but one wrong move, and I'll kill you with my bare hands," Griffin rasped, his hazel eyes glowing. "If this is a trap—"

"It's not. I swear," Dave vowed, and the air stayed stench free.

Cyrus linked with the silver wolves, informing them of the plan and what they needed to do as we headed to the boat.

Blood stained the boat's deck, but it didn't matter. Sterlyn and I would lie down and pretend to be unconscious as soon as we got close to the meeting place.

As promised, Rosemary and Ronnie took to the sky while Alex, Joshua, Eliza, Killian, and Sierra got on the second boat. We were out on the water within minutes, heading south of Shadow City.

Cyrus pulled me to his chest. *I swear I won't let anything happen to you.*

I was more worried about Ezra figuring this out and hurting him. I closed my eyes, enjoying the smell of my mate and the river, with the warmth of the night flowing over my skin. Fish jumped in the water, and I could hear raccoons and flying squirrels in the trees.

For a moment, things were peaceful, and I latched on to that. We didn't experience times like this very often.

Dave stuck his head out of the cabin. "You two need to hide, and Sterlyn and Annie need to pretend to be knocked out."

"I'll tell Killian to stop back there," Sterlyn said.

I opened my eyes to see the second boat one hundred yards behind us.

If you feel uncomfortable, tell me. Cyrus looked deep into my eyes and kissed me. *You need to trust your wolf.*

I promise. I kissed him back, licking my lips to taste his cinnamon flavor.

Come on, Sterlyn linked, and patted the space beside her. It was in the stern of the boat, as far away from the blood as we could get. *Close your eyes. We don't know if he'll have someone watching from afar to ensure nothing seems odd.*

Ugh, I hadn't even thought of that. Pushing away my fear, I lay on the deck next to her and breathed in her musky freesia scent. We rested side by side, our arms brushing, needing to feel each other. It took everything I had to close my eyes, my wolf not wanting to eliminate one of her senses.

After a few minutes, the boat slowed, and the sound of a car engine idling tickled my ears.

230 JEN L. GREY

The urge to open my eyes overwhelmed me.

Take deep breaths, Sterlyn linked, and intertwined our pinkies. *I'm right here, sister.*

Sister. My chest expanded. I hadn't considered that, but we were family now.

"Oh...I see you brought my surprises," Ezra cooed, and the warmth in my chest vanished.

I prayed the situation didn't go south.

CHAPTER NINETEEN

EZRA HAD CALLED us his surprises as if he hadn't expected us to be brought to him. I wanted to laugh, but any sudden moves might alert him that I was conscious. I tried swallowing around the lump in my throat.

Movement from the cabin told me Dave was stepping onto the back of the boat where we were. He cleared his throat. "This is where you said you wanted them." His voice sounded unsteady.

"Where's Wade?" Ezra's tone turned harder.

He didn't seem alarmed, which meant that though Cyrus and Griffin were squashed in there, they were hidden...for now.

My heartbeat picked up its pace, and Sterlyn squeezed my hand.

Try to stay calm, she linked. *If he senses anything abnormal, it could alert him that this is a trap. Take deep, calming breaths, and clear your mind.*

If only it were that easy.

Terror clawed into me, and my heart raced harder. There was only one way to get a calming presence. I linked with my mate, *Hey. Are you okay there?*

I'm fine. You don't need to worry about me. Are you okay? he asked with concern. *I can feel your panic.*

I was a jackass. I hadn't meant to worry him. *I'm scared, but I'll make it through it. I needed to connect with you to find some calm.*

I'm always here for you, Cyrus vowed. *And I'm only a few feet away.*

That wasn't close enough, but it was for our safety.

Sterlyn linked with Cyrus and me, *Killian says Rosemary and Ronnie rode with them part of the way. Rosemary healed Eliza enough that she isn't exhausted, so if we need extra backup, she can use her magic.*

That eased the knot in my chest a little. All my friends and loved ones were here, and I trusted them to keep us safe.

"Wade died," Dave muttered. "He got cocky and tried to take on the demon wolf and silver wolf on his own with no backup."

"I told him not to underestimate them." Ezra *tsk*ed. "They're more capable than most give them credit for, unfortunately. Not only that, but Sterlyn is the alpha of the silver wolves, and the demon wolf is the alpha heir of the demon pack. Of course they aren't weak, especially the silver wolves with the moon growing in their favor."

Something heavy settled into my core. I'd never considered that I was the alpha heir of the demon wolf pack. Even though I had the title and eventually would have the transfer of power, the men would refuse to follow me, but I didn't care. I'd never wanted that kind of responsibility, but I'd take it if it got the pack's women out of that situation.

"Wade was always reckless, and his desperate need to prove he was stronger than Julius made him worse." Dave shrugged. "That was what caused his death."

"It's a shame. He was reliable and good at ensuring tasks got done. I'm glad he shared the location with you, though, or I might not have been able to finish things on my end." Ezra exhaled. "Hand them off to me. Then make sure the other shifters head back to the house. I need everyone on standby for the next attack."

Dave's voice dropped low. "Next attack? You told us this was our final mission."

If he believed that, why did he agree to work with us? I wasn't following his logic, and I wasn't sure we'd been smart in trusting him.

Because he suspected it would change, Cyrus replied. *And we're friends. They've told us something like that several times, and it always wound up being a lie.*

Sterlyn's confusion wafted through the link. *But you could have smelled the lie.*

At the time, I think the person telling us that truly believed it. In my case, it was Dick, right before they sent the shifters to your—er—our pack neighborhood.

My skin chilled as the urge to comfort him washed over me. He didn't know whether to say *my pack* or not, and I understood the dilemma. He still felt like in the past, this hadn't been his pack, but in the present, it was. I wished I could comfort him, but I couldn't right now.

Anyway, after you escaped when the pack got slaughtered, things changed, Cyrus continued, bringing me back to the present. *So...obviously, Ezra has additional plans now.*

"I know what I said, but after I take the demon wolf back to her pack, we have to handle Griffin so Sterlyn can take her place at my side." Ezra almost sounded regretful.

"You want us to kill the Shadow City alpha?" Dave asked coldly.

"Though this situation isn't ideal, it's the only way to regain peace among the shifters. It's really for the best." Ezra scoffed, and I heard him move closer to the boat. "We've wasted enough time, and I don't have to explain myself to you. You know what will happen if you don't obey. Move so we can unload the girls before they wake up. I need to secure them in the van."

This was it. My breathing tried to pick up, but I forced myself to control it. I didn't know what would happen.

"Fine." Dave groaned and took a few steps toward Ezra. He stopped beside me. I could feel him hovering over me, and his scent grew stronger as he bent down.

Ezra growled, "Hand me the silver wolf first. Her tranq will wear off faster since the moon is strengthening her healing power."

Ah...so that's how Cyrus had woken so quickly after he'd been shot. Interesting. Sterlyn probably would've had enough time to wake even if they had captured us.

They must have had no clue how much to give us, especially with our magic being tied to the phases of the moon.

Another little bit of information that benefited us, and we needed to make sure neither Azbogah nor Ezra figured it out.

"Of course you'd want the one who's more difficult to reach first," Dave murmured loud enough that Ezra could hear.

Dave's grassy scent hit my nose as he slowly reached over me and picked up Sterlyn. Knowing I was blocked from view for a few seconds, I squinted and got a nice view of his blond chest hair sticking out of the top of his shirt.

Ew. I could've gone without a close-up, but I was curious about what was going on. Dave's face was still painted black despite all the sweat, which mildly impressed me. He cradled Sterlyn in his arms, and I swore I heard a faint growl from the cabin.

Ugh, Griffin needed to get it together.

I closed my eyes before I could get caught, and I heard Dave take slow, steady steps toward Ezra. "Here she is."

"Good. Give me a second to secure her, then I'll come back for—" His words cut off as I heard a loud smack.

"Sterlyn?" Ezra asked with surprise. "Look, I can explain. It's not what you think."

I sat upright as Griffin barreled out of the cabin. His hazel eyes glowed as he pivoted toward Ezra. Griffin snarled, "We know what's going on. No explanation needed."

My attention landed on Ezra. Sterlyn stood between him and the van.

Cyrus rushed to me, and Griffin ran past Dave and jumped off the boat. He punched Ezra in the face, snapping his head to the side.

My mate pivoted toward the embankment as Ezra stretched his jaw and said, "It's not what you think."

"Oh, it's exactly what we think," Sterlyn rasped. "You want to use me as *your* breeder. You were working with Dick and Saga the entire time."

"At first, I didn't even know it was *you* or that the silver wolf they were talking about was Griffin's *fated mate*." Ezra rubbed his jaw and winced. "All they asked was if I wanted a strong female mate to elevate my status in Shadow City and help do what was best for the shifter community since Griffin was too busy chasing—"

"You finish that statement, and I'll hurt you even more," Sterlyn snarled, her chest heaving.

Ezra was focused on the past, though, and not the present.

"That was your excuse then. What about now?" I held his gaze, a challenge in mine.

Ezra's irises darkened to emerald as he glared at me. "Every time you two add to your group, it's someone who causes more problems."

A dark laugh escaped Cyrus. "My mate doesn't cause trouble. That's what happens when people are power-hungry."

"She hasn't caused *trouble*?" Ezra lifted his chin and dropped his hand. "She's a demon wolf here in Shadow City. What else would that do?"

"I didn't know what I was at the time." That was true. We'd thought I was a plain old demon, but I had a feeling that detail would help his point, so I kept my lips sealed.

The corners of Cyrus's mouth tipped upward. *You sneaky girl.*

My body warmed at his approval, despite the horrible circumstances.

"I'm still waiting for the answer to Annie's question." Griffin's body shook with anger as his face turned tomato red.

"You've lost control of the shifters," Ezra sneered as he turned so he could see Sterlyn, Griffin, and the boat. "What did you expect?"

"Because you've been undermining us." Sterlyn crossed her arms and glared. "Don't think we aren't aware. You're the one behind the shifter attack on Matthew, Azbogah, and Griffin at the capitol building."

"*What?*" His voice rose. "You can't know that."

Yeah, if that wasn't a guilty response, I wasn't sure what was.

"We do. You aren't as careful as you think, talking in a shifter bar about your plan. The VIP section isn't soundproof." Griffin fisted his hands at his sides. "We were just waiting for the perfect opportunity to expose you. This seemed like the right time."

Ezra's attention landed on Dave as he threatened, "I hope your family's death is worth it."

Eyes wild, Dave tensed.

"That's it," Griffin bellowed with a half snarl and punched Ezra again.

The shifter's eyes widened before he crumpled onto his face.

"Do you think he meant it?" Dave's bottom lip trembled.

Sterlyn shook her head. "We have everyone in custody at the camp, right?"

Dave exhaled loudly. "Yeah, you do."

"Then Ezra hasn't had a chance to send word to hurt your family." Sterlyn glanced back at the van on the small dirt road that went through the woods.

Ezra had picked a remote location for the pickup, no doubt to stay off the grid. I wondered how the hell he even knew about this place.

"We need to keep him knocked out." Griffin hovered over Ezra, the vein in his neck bulging. "If he gets desperate, he might alert someone in Shadow City about what happened. I don't think he has yet, or he would've gloated about it. Azbogah would certainly use this to his advantage to discredit us."

"Very true. If they decided to have a trial, none of those shifters would talk because of the leverage Ezra and his allies have over them," Cyrus explained, pulling me to his side. "But our bigger issue is if they were going to take Annie to the demon pack, Tate could get antsy and attack us here when she doesn't show up, and they'll be ruthless."

We had to attack the demon pack before they came

here. My stomach soured. We'd been planning to attack, but I'd thought we'd have another week. This upped our timeline, but at least we'd fought alongside each other and the vampires fairly well tonight.

"Annie, Dave, and Cyrus, can you three get Ezra in the boat while Griffin and I pull the van deeper into the woods to hide it?" Sterlyn asked. "We'll be back in a second so we can rejoin the others. We need to get moving. The attack on the demon wolves needs to happen tomorrow night. Hopefully, they'll be worried when Ezra doesn't show up with Annie."

"What if we take the van? They're probably expecting it. We could pull in and catch some of them off guard," Dave said.

"We?" Cyrus's brows furrowed.

"I figured I could help." Dave tugged at the collar of his shirt.

That must be his nervous tic.

Any additional help would be good, and I doubted the demon pack would expect a bear shifter in our mix, but I didn't trust the guy.

"You're right." Sterlyn bit her lip. "Rosemary? Ronnie?"

I looked skyward in time to see a shadowy form descending and huge black wings heading toward us. Both Ronnie and Rosemary landed in front of Sterlyn a few seconds later.

Sterlyn glanced at the two women. "Can one or both of you drive the van close to the road and meet us back at the house?"

"Uh...there's only one person standing there," Dave whispered.

Like Griffin, he wasn't an angel descendant, so he couldn't see my sister. "Ronnie is in her demon form. You can't see her when she's like that."

"Oh. Is that how some of us were attacked and no one could see the attacker?" Dave froze, uncomfortable with that information.

"Yeah, man." Griffin rolled his eyes. "Welcome to the club. The silver wolves and demon wolves can see her, but we regular wolves can't. It's about having angel magic inside you."

"Sure, I can do that." Rosemary nodded. "I'll meet you back there in a second."

"I'll go with you in case something strange happens," Ronnie added. "I'd hate for you to get attacked and not be able to reach us. I can use my connection with Alex if needed."

That was true, and one of the handiest things about having a mate. Alex was the only one Ronnie could connect with like that, whereas we wolves could connect with our pack as well.

Griffin bent down and tossed Ezra over his shoulder. "Then let's move."

Rosemary ran to the driver's seat of the running van while the rest of us headed back to the boat, ready to get on the road.

Wɪᴛʜɪɴ ᴛᴡᴏ ʜᴏᴜʀs, our group was on the road. It was around one in the morning with the slightly over three-quarter moon high in the sky. We expected to arrive at Eliza's coven's cabins around three in the morning.

Eliza had spelled Ezra to keep him knocked out the entire time we were gone, and we had Killian's pack guarding him, although only a witch could wake him. As long as no one outside of Killian's pack stumbled upon the training location where we were keeping the shifters and Ezra restrained, we would be safe from Ezra getting in touch with someone.

Only twenty members of Killian's pack had left with us, leaving the majority of the people behind. Billy and his son had been adamant about coming with us, but Killian had put his foot down, stating that he needed them to oversee the prisoners. Though I wanted the strongest shifters with us, we couldn't risk losing the people we'd left behind.

Rosemary was flying to the coven while Eliza, Cyrus, and I rode with Alex and Ronnie. I hated to say it, but not having Sierra in the vehicle with us was a blessing. Everyone was on edge, and I was pretty sure Cyrus and Alex couldn't have handled her snark.

The reason it'd taken us so long to leave was our debate about whether we should allow Dave and Mila to come.

Mila was adamant that she wanted to help and that maybe she could connect with the women of the demon wolf pack since she understood the pain of losing a fated mate, which some of them might have endured. Not only that, but she wanted to take down the assholes who'd imprisoned her. Since she was finally coming around to our side, I'd talked Cyrus and Sterlyn into allowing her to come. We needed her to feel included, and if she wanted to fight with us, how could we say no?

After questioning Dave thoroughly, Cyrus and Sterlyn had decided he would come, too. He seemed sincere, and Cyrus and Dave had been close. My mate was inclined to trust him, and that was enough for me. We would have Ronnie stay near him during the fight in case he did something suspicious. He couldn't see her, and she could eliminate the threat, if it came to that.

Dave, Killian, Sierra, and Chad were riding with Sterlyn and Griffin. The other fourteen silver wolves and Mila had split up into an SUV and Ezra's van, while the twenty pack members from Killian's group drove in three additional large vehicles. The vampires followed in their cars.

We pulled off the exit, Eliza's leg bouncing.

She'd been a nervous wreck the entire way here, and I wasn't sure why. She'd already seen her daughter and the rest of the coven and made amends, for the most part. The only thing I could think of was that she was nervous about the impending attack.

I scooted closer to Cyrus to get a little distance from Eliza. I'd gotten stuck sitting in the middle, and when her leg jittered a lot, it smacked into mine.

Eliza leaned forward, over the center console, and pointed. "Take the right here."

Alex opened his mouth, then closed it and exhaled.

That was one of his most amazing qualities—he had respect for others, especially Eliza.

Turning her head toward him, Ronnie wrinkled her nose, giving him a playful glance.

"Thanks for telling me, but I do remember how to get there," Alex said slowly, measuring the sound and speed of his voice.

Eliza flopped back against her seat and bumped into my shoulder. It didn't hurt, but I had to bite my tongue.

Everyone's nerves were frayed.

The battle was looming, and even though the demon wolves would be weaker than the silver ones, they were still stronger than normal wolves, and there were more of them than us. Our biggest advantage was the help of the other supernaturals. At least Eliza knew they would fight alongside us.

Alex expertly took the roads that led to the coven, and when he turned onto the rough dirt one, he complained under his breath, just like last time. The coven neighborhood was remote, allowing them to live in peace.

"Slow down," Eliza said as we approached the hidden entrance.

Had we never been here before, I would've thought it was just dense trees we couldn't pass through.

The cars stopped behind us, but Eliza sat there with her eyes closed and her lips moving.

A door opened behind us, and a vampire climbed out of the car. "My king, what's going on?"

Eliza's eyes flew open, and she rasped, "Get him back in the car."

"What?" Ronnie glanced into the back seat. "Why?"

Three witches appeared at the tree line with Circe in the center. Her rich brown eyes focused on the vampire, and she frowned and raised her hands, which made her warm beige skin look pale in the moonlight.

Eliza opened the door. "Circe, wait."

Circe glanced at her mom. "What did you do? You brought all these people here after you shamed me into keeping our location secret?"

My heart dropped. Eliza hadn't told her daughter we were coming. I'd assumed she had.

"I had to. I knew that if I'd warned you, you'd have made it so I couldn't reach you." Eliza placed a hand on her heart. "Please listen to us. And if you decide not to help, we'll leave. No questions asked."

"This is a trick," Sybil said as her ocean-blue eyes stared Eliza down. "We need them to leave before they bring those damn demon wolves here." She wore all black, which matched her hair. Crimson stain coated her lips and contrasted with her porcelain skin. She didn't like outsiders, and we'd brought even more with us.

Herne's long ruby-red hair blew in the breeze as her onyx eyes examined Eliza and the vampire. "Maybe we should listen."

"Please, Circe." Eliza dropped her hand. "Don't make the same mistakes I did."

Circe's head tilted back as if she were searching for something in the sky.

Her decision would impact whether we won against the demon wolves or not. I scooted toward the door, and Cyrus took my hand and linked, *What are you doing?*

Giving us a chance. I stepped out and bowed my head as I tried to use the words I'd heard so many times. "We're trying to keep the balance of good and evil. If you don't listen, then saving me all those years ago will have been in vain."

Circe stared at me, and something unreadable crossed her face. She opened her mouth to speak, and I was afraid of what she might say.

CHAPTER TWENTY

CIRCE'S WORDS would finalize whether they would even consider fighting alongside us. I'd assumed Eliza would have warned them before bringing us here, but clearly, they weren't thrilled about us showing up.

Everybody, stay in the vehicles, Sterlyn linked with the pack. *I'll tell Killian and Griffin the same thing so we can get the word out.*

Good call. The more obvious it became how many people were with us, the worse this request for aid could go. We needed to do this in baby steps. *Cyrus, can you ask Alex to let the vampires know the same thing?*

On it, he replied, and I heard him softly relay the message to Alex.

"Before you decide," Eliza said, taking a few steps toward her daughter, "I want to say something. Our coven used to be part of the mundane world. Yes, we had security measures in place, but not like the fear I instilled in you. I lashed out at you over my own self-hatred. I never wanted to see you put into a horrible situation like I experienced, so I overprotected you all by encouraging you to cut yourselves off from the world, and that wasn't right."

Circe closed her mouth and tilted her head. She wanted to hear what her mother had to say.

"A witch's purpose is to help maintain balance in the world, and you did that by helping Annie." Eliza leaned toward her daughter. "You did the right thing by bringing Annie to me."

"You criticized me for not hiding our place and for using the same spell you did on the silver wolf twin," Circe scoffed and tugged her earth-brown shirt over her jeans. "And now you're conveniently changing your story and bringing a ton of people here? Is Annie that much more important to you than we ever were?"

Hope slipped away as the truth made my skin crawl. She was right. Eliza had voiced her displeasure about everything, and Circe was jealous that it had changed.

"I love Annie. I won't lie. I raised her since she was an infant, and she's my daughter as much as you are." Tendrils of Eliza's hair fell from her bun, framing her face. "But I'm not asking for your help because I love her more. This is about facing my mistakes and forgiveness. Between owning up to the things I've hated myself for and seeing the horrible drama unfolding around Shadow City, I realize I should've never left or forced you into hiding. That *you* were right all along. That's why I said don't make the same mistake as me. If the demon pack gets Annie back—which they are trying to do—and you don't help, you'll feel the same regret and pain I did twenty years ago."

A slight breeze swirled around us, filling the air with the scents of tiger lilies and rosemary. Even those soothing aromas didn't calm my racing heart.

Circe stared into her mother's eyes, searching for something. Maybe confirmation of what her mother had said, but I couldn't be sure.

"Don't listen to her." Sybil grunted, her face twisted in disgust. "She's playing you."

"There's one way to make sure that's not the case," Herne said as she stepped next to Circe and touched her shoulder. "We could perform a truth spell."

That was enough. "She's not lying. You'd smell it if she were," I reminded them.

"Not if she performed a spell to hide it," Circe murmured.

Eliza chuckled but frowned. "I have nothing to hide. Go ahead." She lifted her chin and set her feet shoulder-width apart.

What if they don't help us? Cyrus's tension rolled through me.

Sterlyn's steady, calm presence surged through our link. *Then we'll still win. It'll just be harder.*

Her confidence was what I'd needed, but I wondered how she could have such conviction. *How can you be so certain?*

No matter what, our group is strong together, and we're doing what's right. We didn't seek out the shifters we defeated today or the demon wolves—they found and attacked us. I have to believe in good prevailing and that we'll get justice for the slaughter of my pack and all the horrible things that have happened to the people I love.

My heart ached for her. She was always so strong and sure that I'd forgotten she had her own demons. Of course she believed in doing what was right and that we could win. Otherwise, why would she be fighting?

Sybil huffed. "I'm sure you don't."

Eliza's jaw clenched, but she remained silent. There were times when her restraint surprised me, and this was one of them. She was strong and spoke her mind, but occasionally, she kept her mouth shut, able to read the moment.

That would be a handy talent for me to pick up.

"Okay," Circe murmured as she examined her mother. I wasn't sure what she was looking for, but then she nodded and said, *"Veritatem dicere."*

Eliza's skin shimmered, and she kept her eyes locked on her daughter.

"Did you want to leave us?" Circe asked, her eyes darkening.

"Of course not—" Eliza dropped to her knees as a painful groan left her.

My blood chilled as I dropped down beside the woman who raised me. I jerked my head toward Circe, my voice lowering to a growl. "What are you doing to her?"

"See! I told you," Sybil exclaimed. "She didn't want to be with us."

The priestess's head dropped. "I didn't do anything to her. I cast a truth spell. She lied and paid the price."

"It's not like that." Eliza grimaced, wrapping her arms around her stomach.

Circe sliced the air. "I've heard enough. You, *your daughters*, and your friends can figure this out without our help."

"Wait, Circe," Herne said and squatted in front of Eliza. "We should give her a chance to explain."

"Why? So she can hurt us again?" Sybil spat.

Even though Circe didn't say anything, she remained in place.

"I wanted to leave because I wasn't a good role model for you or the coven. I love you, and I stayed even when I saw the signs that I wasn't making decisions that were best for the world after Sparrow died in that car wreck. When I traded an innocent life for my granddaughter, it was the wakeup call I'd needed. I was being selfish and causing harm—the very thing I'd vowed not to do." Eliza slowly stood and looked at her daughter.

Who's Sparrow? Cyrus asked.

Once again, something I didn't know. *I have no clue.*

Ronnie opened the door to the SUV, her brows furrowed. "I thought your parents died in the car crash."

"You assumed it, child, and I didn't correct you." Eliza glanced at Ronnie. "I told you that I'd lost the most important person in the world in a fiery car wreck, and you thought it was my parents."

"Then why did I assume two people, and who's Sparrow?" I didn't care about the misconceptions. I wanted the hard facts now.

Circe's brows lifted. "I thought you told them everything?"

I laughed. It was so inappropriate, but I couldn't help it. Circe thought Eliza treated us the way she wished her mom had treated her when that damn sure wasn't the case. "I didn't even know she was a witch until a month ago, right before Ronnie's wedding."

"And I only knew a few weeks longer because I'd gotten acclimated to my supernatural side and could sense and smell the witch in her." Ronnie gestured to Eliza as she kept her focus on Circe. "This woman hides things from us to protect us to a fault."

"Now, listen here"—Eliza lifted her chin—"I won't be lectured by the likes of you three. And I don't know why you assumed it was more than one person. Children have a way of hearing what they want. However, Sparrow was the love of my life, *my fated mate*. His death nearly killed me. Maybe I didn't make the best decisions, but I did what I thought was best to protect you. I didn't tell Annie because it was best she didn't know about the supernatural world. I *thought* it would keep all of this off her radar, but I've learned what I inherently knew all along: fated mate bonds trump everything. I didn't tell Ronnie because she was so scared of her demon side. It manifested as a shadow and terrified her, so I protected her from it. And I left the coven so you would have a chance to be led by the strongest, most ethical person I know—my daughter. I wasn't that person any longer because losing the love of my life had left me jaded, and I feared losing another person I loved so much that I caused two very good parents to think their child was dead. I inflicted on them the very thing I didn't want to experience."

My heart hurt for her. She'd experienced so much loss and pain, and she still wasn't making the right decisions, although she was beginning to realize that.

"She's telling the truth, Circe." Herne stood and laid a hand on her best friend's shoulder. "If she didn't think she was fit to lead, she did the right thing by leaving."

"I did." Eliza nodded and took a hesitant step toward her daughter. "It was so damn hard, and I know it hurt you. Though I didn't do it the right way, I *was* trying to do what was right. I should've told you why I was leaving instead of spewing my self-hatred out on you, and I shouldn't have vanished from your life. I wound up distancing myself from the very people I was terrified of losing, and I lost my relationship with you. I'm so very sorry. But Circe, you're a better person than me, and you know right from wrong."

Circe clenched her hands, and her bottom lip trembled. "How? I *begged* you to trade the silver wolf for my daughter, and I hid the coven after sending Annie to you. I'm no better than you."

"A mother's love knows no boundaries, and the thing is, if you had actually been the priestess in charge, I don't think you would've made the same choice I did. You would've gone to the silver wolves and told them what was going on, and you would've found a way to save them both. I was too scared to do it." Eliza touched her daughter's arm and sighed. "And you had to hide, not only to protect the coven but Annie, too. If her mother had found you, the other demon wolves would've been right behind. You weren't hiding from fear but to ensure you kept the balance between good and evil. That was why you hid her, after all—because the demon getting hold of her would have upset that balance."

"I—" Circe's gaze darted around, probably at the same speed her mind was processing the information. Her body sagged a little.

"I'm so proud of you. You've done everything I couldn't, and you're the strongest woman I've ever known," Eliza said softly. "Don't let jealousy turn you into someone you're not. Be stronger than me, and don't let anger and resentment fill your heart. You're so much better than that."

Her skin still shimmered, which meant the spell was in place. She was speaking the truth, and Circe couldn't rebut it.

Herne scanned our group. Everyone but Eliza, Ronnie, and I was inside the cars. At some point, the vampire had hurried back in under Alex's command.

I hated that everyone was witnessing this moment, but this reckoning had been long overdue. I wondered what had happened during those days Eliza had stayed behind while we'd gone back to Shadow Ridge. Obviously, the talk they'd needed to have hadn't taken place until now.

"What's your decision?" Herne asked.

"We'll let them inside, and they can stay the night." Circe flipped her wrist.

My mouth dried as my body grew lighter. They'd help us after all.

Eliza's skin returned to its normal shade, which meant Circe had released the spell.

"You can't be serious!" Sybil's mouth dropped. "All of that, and you're just going—"

"Enough," Circe said coldly, her irises turning almost the same onyx color as Herne's. "We will meet first thing in the morning, and I'll address the entire coven and hear what the others have to say. Once I get a feel for how the coven thinks, I'll make the final decision."

"May I be there and speak for my side?" Eliza asked as she dropped her hand from her daughter.

Awkwardness hung in the air. If I were Circe, I'd need time to process everything, too, so I couldn't blame her.

Finally, Circe nodded. "Of course. You're part of this coven."

At least there was that. She could've banned Eliza, but maybe things would work out after all...or maybe that was wishful thinking. It sounded like we'd find out soon enough.

"We'll spell the community building and bring blankets and pillows for the others." Circe straightened her shoulders and flicked her gaze toward me. "The same people can stay in the house, but everyone else needs to stay in the common area. A few witches will stay there with them. It's late, so let's get everyone settled and into bed."

Great, they were splitting us up. They trusted those of us who'd stayed here before, so I was guessing they wanted to keep an eye on everyone else. We *had* brought a lot of people.

She turned on her heel and walked past Herne and Sybil. Herne followed her priestess and best friend while Sybil snarled at us and glared. After making sure we knew she didn't want us there, she pivoted, refusing to be left behind.

"Get in the car, and let's go," Eliza said, and nudged me toward the vehicle.

I gritted my teeth and did as she'd asked. She'd just gone through an emotional meeting with her daughter. I climbed into the middle seat, moving with more force than necessary.

It's going to be okay. Cyrus took my hand. *I know she's being crotchety, but she got us in. I informed Sterlyn of the plan. She's communicating with Griffin and Killian now.*

I was glad he was handling the pack stuff, but I was still upset with Eliza. *Why didn't she tell them we were coming?*

Maybe because she knew they'd say no. Circe almost didn't let us in. Eliza had to grovel. Cyrus squeezed my hand.

Out of all the times, he decided to be rational now. He kissed my cheek as Eliza shut the door.

The witches walked through the perimeter, and the

neighborhood appeared. All the houses were the standard gothic style I'd seen in images of Salem, Virginia. I was learning that most supernatural neighborhoods had needed to be built quickly, and they'd stuck with a few basic house plans. The houses here had been built in the same gray stone and were all three stories high with a window at the very top center of each attic. Herbs grew in planters on the porches out front.

"Park at the community house," Eliza said.

Listening, Alex took us to the gigantic one-story house made of the same stone. He pulled into one of the spots, and we climbed out.

All the vehicles followed suit, and soon, everyone was unloading. Rosemary landed next to the Navigator, her black wings wide.

Circe walked over with Herne. My stomach dropped as I surveyed the area for Sybil. She was entering a house next to the community building, and I exhaled in relief. Maybe she would leave us alone.

Our SUV's trunk popped, and Alex and Cyrus walked back to get our bags.

Sterlyn headed over to the witches and smiled. "Thank you for letting us stay here."

"It's just for the night," Circe said sternly.

"We're grateful, nonetheless." Sterlyn turned to the building. "This is where you want everybody new?"

"Yes. A few witches will help monitor things, but you guys can go ahead and get settled where you stayed before." Circe gestured to the place two houses down in the middle of the neighborhood.

Bed.

That sounded too good to be true.

"Killian should stay with his pack, too. He wound up sleeping on the couch last time, so he said he might as well stay with the others, if that's okay with you." Sterlyn's chin lifted, suggesting she wasn't asking, but she wanted to be polite.

Circe shrugged. "If that's where he wants to sleep, who am I to say no?"

"Perfect." Sterlyn's eyes glowed faintly as she linked with him. Then her gaze settled back on me. "You have a huge day tomorrow. Why don't you and Cyrus go rest, and everyone else will be there momentarily."

I shook my head, but Cyrus cut me off. He linked to me, *You're going to fight your pack tomorrow. We all need our rest, but especially you. Though you hate Tate, he's still your father, and you have a connection with the pack.*

Ugh, I hated that he was right. Even though the demon wolf men were assholes and I wanted to hurt them, I didn't want to *kill* them. Just lock them up for eternity.

Realizing that Sterlyn was looking out for my well-being, I nodded. Cyrus had been shot with a tranq. He needed to sleep as much as I did.

"The door is unlocked," Herne said.

Are you sure— I started with Sterlyn, but she cut me off.

We won't be far behind. Take the same room as last time, if that works.

Sounds perfect, Cyrus linked, and tugged me toward the house.

Within seconds, we were stepping inside the familiar living room. The brown leather couch appeared untouched since the last time we were here, with the loveseat sitting directly in front of the red-brick fireplace. Behind the living room was a kitchen with gray cabinets, a firewood stove, and a refrigerator. Stairs in front of the door led to the second story and the bedroom we would be sleeping in.

The house was large. The second floor contained three bedrooms and two full bathrooms, and the attic at the top fit a full-sized bed. We had plenty of room. With Killian staying with his pack, Rosemary would take the couch.

We took the flight of stairs and walked into the first room on the right. The night sky was still dark, since it was nearing three in the morning, but with my wolf eyes, I could make out the same white walls and the full-sized bed. There was no other furniture.

Cyrus pulled out my pajamas, and as I changed, he stripped to his boxers.

I slid into bed, tossing the light yellow sheet over myself. Like last time, there was no comforter, and I laid my head on the small, worn, yellow-stained pillowcase. When Cyrus climbed in next to me, he pulled me against his chest and burrowed his face into the side of my head. He linked, *When this is over, I'm taking you out for a date. I'm thinking dinner and a run in the woods. Just the two of us. No matter how much Sierra pouts and throws a tantrum.*

That sounded so damn nice. We'd never done anything like that. The only times we'd had alone were in the bedroom, and though I wouldn't change that for the world, acting like a normal couple sounded like a dream. *Promise?*

I swear. I want to do things with you and make you happy. His hands slid under my shirt and came to rest on the small of my back.

My body warmed, and I breathed him in. Despite his chest being hard and muscular, it was my favorite spot to lie in the world. My face and back buzzed gently from the connection.

We needed sleep, but I yearned for something more as well.

I wrapped an arm around his waist and slipped my hands under his boxers on his bare ass. His body quivered from my touch, fueling my desire even more.

His hand moved to cup my breast. He kissed me as he gently rubbed my nipple.

I moaned softly, enjoying his taste and touch. Only he could make me feel like this, and after the long night, I needed him more than my next breath.

Your moans are so damn sexy. His tongue slipped into my mouth as he moved his hands underneath my bottoms and between my legs. As he circled my sensitive area, my eyes closed.

Following his lead, I stroked him, enjoying the feel of him.

He surrounded me, inundating every sense of mine—taste, touch, sound, and smell. These were the moments I lived for, when the world revolved around the two of us.

His breathing turned ragged, and pressure built inside me. I opened our link, wanting our souls to merge.

Damn it, Annie, he growled. He nipped my lips, and his hips quickened, picking up the pace. *You're driving me insane.*

My heart swelled as I relished the control I had over him. I released my hold on him, wanting to drive him over the edge.

In one quick move, he tossed me on my back, and his eyes glowed silver as his wolf surged forward. He removed my pants at damn-near vampire speed. My body warmed at his dominance and was ready for him.

He clutched my shirt, then gently removed it over my head. When I was naked, he sat back on his knees, ogling my body. *You are damn perfect.*

Same. I took the moment to stare at his bare chest and full lips. My chest heaved as my desire intensified. *Now remove those boxers, or this could get ugly.*

A sexy smirk spread across his face. *Maybe I want it ugly.*

He wasn't the only one who could be an alpha. I pounced on him and threw him on his back. His eyes widened, which empowered me. Like he'd done to me, I yanked off his boxers and took a moment to scan every inch of him before I straddled him.

Damn, that was hot. He groaned as I slipped him inside me.

He filled me, then scooted against the headboard so he sat upright. I rode him slowly, and his mouth lowered, capturing one nipple. His tongue flicked as his free hand caressed my other breast.

My head tilted back as sensations crashed over me. Before long, I quickened the pace.

Slow down a little, he linked, and I could feel him nearing the edge.

No. I wanted him to feel good, and my body wanted release.

Pulling back, he gripped my hips with both hands. He shook his head. *Too fast. I don't want it to be over yet.*

He felt my intent, so he rolled us over. He smacked my ass gently as he propped me on my knees. He moved between my legs and slid back inside me.

Him controlling our connection made my desire even stronger. I was surprised by how much I loved him handling me like that.

He chuckled. *I told you, not too fast.*

In this position, he went even deeper, and when he slipped his hand around my waist and back between my legs, all I wanted was more. Our pace didn't matter, as long as he didn't stop.

Using a slow, steady motion, he drove me closer to the edge. The friction intensified so much that I wasn't sure I would ever recover. Our bodies moved in sync, and I could feel that he was reaching the end, too. I moved my hips faster again, and he didn't object.

He thrust harder, driving me over the edge. An orgasm rippled through me, with his following seconds behind. Our pleasure intermingled, increasing our ecstasy. After a few seconds, he slowed and lay back on his side. He spread his arms apart, wanting me to crawl back into them.

There wasn't a moment's hesitation on my part.

We lay there in silence, enjoying our time together. It wasn't long before my eyes closed and I fell asleep.

THE FRONT DOOR SLAMMED, startling me awake. I blinked a few times and bolted upright, trying to get my bearings. The sun was in the sky, and it looked like it'd been up for a while. I had no clue what time it was.

Cyrus groaned and rubbed his head as Eliza yelled from downstairs, "A decision has been made. Get your asses down here."

A lump formed in my throat. She didn't sound happy.

CHAPTER TWENTY-ONE

MY STOMACH SOURED as Cyrus and I quickly dressed. I clutched my phone and saw it was close to eleven. We'd gotten nearly eight hours of sleep. I couldn't believe I'd slept for so long. It was a godsend, though. Had I known the coven was convening, I would've been beside myself with stress.

Now we only had to handle the terror of getting their final answer, and that was bad enough.

As we bounded down the stairs, the front door opened, and Ronnie, Alex, Sierra, Killian, Sterlyn, Griffin, and Rosemary filed in.

You've been up for a while? I linked with Sterlyn. I hadn't heard them enter last night or leave this morning. My breath caught. Was I losing my connection with my wolf?

Cyrus must have felt the same way because I felt his confusion flowing between us. "I didn't hear you, either."

Instead of responding through the pack link, Sterlyn said, "Eliza placed a soundproof spell on your room, knowing Cyrus needed to sleep off that tranq and you needed your rest for tonight."

My lungs began working again, and my body tensed, then relaxed. If they had come in while we'd been...*occupied*, they couldn't have heard our little sexcapade. I had been surprised that we hadn't heard them come in before we'd fallen asleep.

Sierra sashayed into the room and plopped down on the couch, waving a hand in front of her nose. "Which I'm glad about with the strong scent I smelled in the hallway heading up to the attic bedroom. I felt bad for Sterlyn, Griffin, Ronnie, and Alex having to walk through it, but I'm sure they added to it once they were alone."

Oh, my God. My face flushed red hot. I usually appreciated her commentary, but not when it was directed at me. Instead of stewing, I redirected that embarrassment elsewhere. "We're all going through the same stuff tonight. How come you didn't take extra time to rest?"

"Because they aren't facing down their father," Eliza replied bluntly.

Rosemary sighed as she pulled her wings into her back and leaned against the wall next to the windows. "Mortals have a hard time with their emotions, especially when dealing with their sire, even if they dislike them."

Even though angels seemed more rational than most

beings, I'd glimpsed a different side of Rosemary. "I've seen you upset before."

"I'm not saying I don't have emotions. I'm saying they're more subdued than those of other supernatural races." Rosemary touched her chest. "Tonight, you'll likely become very erratic."

My sister scowled at Rosemary and turned to me. She walked to the bottom of the stairs and took my hand, then pulled me down the rest of the way. She murmured, "When I killed Andis, it was hard. Killing, in general, isn't easy, but having to face the man who created me messed with my head."

"I didn't even kill my brother, and his death still haunts me." Alex's soft blue eyes darkened as he tugged on his button-down shirt.

Some of my emotions thawed. They were all being sincere, even if I disagreed with them.

Cyrus crossed his arms. "Still, we should've been included in that choice."

He wasn't used to people making decisions for him. At least now he knew how it felt. *It was done out of love, even if it was misguided. Don't worry. I have a lot of experience with this.*

Killian sat on the couch and ran a hand through his hair, disheveling it more. "We're all stressed, but we tried to do the best for everyone involved."

"I'm not going to break down." My blood pumped through my body. "I've already faced them. I killed some of them. Why do you keep expecting me to fall apart?"

"We don't think that," Eliza scoffed. "We just know what it's like to face your demons, both literally and figuratively. You've always struggled with your parents giving you up, and now you know why. This won't be easy. It wouldn't be easy for any of us."

They're right. Cyrus's anger cooled as he walked behind me and placed his hands on my shoulders. *It's hard facing down the men I used to train with, and this will go deeper than that. When I was in charge of trying to hand Sterlyn over to Dick, I felt a connection with her despite also hating her. Tate is part of your family, and don't think for one second he won't use Midnight against you. That will be the first thing he tries, and that's why everyone is worried.*

His words struck a chord deep inside me, and I closed my eyes, trying to push my rationalizations away. I'd gotten frustrated with Cyrus when he'd acted this way. I was trying to prove myself to everyone, but maybe this had nothing to do with Ronnie and Eliza and was more about me learning to love myself. Either way, I needed to act like an adult and focus on what was really important. "Okay, I'm sorry. Either way, it doesn't matter. What did the coven decide?"

Eliza blinked at me.

"Your tone has me on edge," Griffin said to Eliza, and stood next to his mate. "I think it's bad news."

Eliza exhaled. "It's not bad, but not great."

Blowing out a breath, Sierra rolled her eyes. "What is it with witches and being cryptic?"

"Very true." Ronnie glanced at me and arched a brow.

I couldn't agree more. I wished my foster mother would just spit it out.

Eliza scowled, and silence hung in the air.

Alex huffed. "What does that mean?"

"The coven listened to Sybil and me, and Circe asked for input from the others before making her decision." Eliza frowned and rubbed the back of her neck. If she'd had a coffee mug, she'd be wrapping her hands around it.

They weren't going to help us, but she'd said the news wasn't necessarily bad, so I was at a loss.

"What was their decision?" Rosemary tilted her head.

Eliza dropped her hands to her sides. "Circe decided she wouldn't force the coven to help, nor would she keep anyone from helping either. Each person will decide for themselves."

"So there's a chance that some will help." Sterlyn bit her lip. "It isn't a hard no."

Hand tightening on mine, Cyrus rasped, "But how many will actually care enough to help our cause?"

"More than you'd think. I tried to convey that part of this battle is about ensuring the balance of the world. That they helped save Annie from whatever demon she's promised to for that very reason. This is just a continuation of that decision because Tate knows she's alive and won't stop hunting her." Eliza paced in front of the window. "Sybil's concerns are more of a personal vendetta, so a few won't be swayed."

"How do we move forward?" Ronnie pursed her lips.

Sterlyn's eyes glowed. "As if we don't expect anyone to help. We should leave before dusk so we'll get to the demon wolf neighborhood right at twilight. They won't expect us to attack that early, and if we wait much longer and they're expecting Ezra, they could get nervous."

"I'll fly over now and see if I can get a view of anything." Rosemary headed to the door.

"Wait," Eliza snapped. "Your flying will take down the coven's barrier. Why don't you leave a little before we do, and we can meet somewhere to strategize if needed?"

"As long as it's not at the motel where we stayed before." Alex lifted his chin. "That's where the vehicles were when we escaped, so if they're watching for us, they'll have a guard keeping an eye out there."

Killian steepled his fingers. "Our best bet is to park a mile or so away and walk in."

Griffin nodded. "If there's a park or walking path close by, that would be ideal."

I was still missing an important piece of the puzzle. "How do we get the van to the neighborhood?"

"When I first flew over their land, I noticed a dirt road in. If I fly over again, I can get a better lay of the land and draw a map for Dave." Rosemary raised her brows and grinned. "Him knowing how to drive in there would lend credibility, too."

"But what if they *aren't* expecting Ezra?" We kept assuming the demon wolves were in on the plan, but something in my gut said they might not be.

Sterlyn shifted her weight. "It won't matter. If Dave

drives in like he knows the area, it'll catch them off guard. Whether we throw them off or they're expecting someone, it'll give us time to get into position."

"And put everyone in the van in danger." Killian exhaled and leaned back on the couch. "How do we know we can trust Dave? He could drive right into the pack and alert them about our entire plan."

There were so many variables...so many what-ifs. "What do you propose we do?" I asked.

"Wars are all about strategy." Sterlyn walked into a corner where she could see everyone. "There are never clear-cut answers, and things will always go wrong. Think about the attack on each pack neighborhood. Ezra didn't expect to lose. He didn't plan for it and had no backup when we confronted him. It's about risk calculation and which plan makes us most comfortable. But it's also about having a backup plan. Or three."

"If you're willing to listen to an old lady's opinion, I'll share some thoughts with you." Eliza stared at the floor.

I'd never seen her so uncertain before. My chest turned heavy, and I wished I could do something.

"Of course we want to hear it," Cyrus assured her. "You're part of the family and group."

Her head jerked up, and her irises darkened with emotion.

That was awfully big of you. My heart swelled with love for Cyrus. My feelings for him were so strong that they stole my breath. This woman had ripped him away from his family, resulting in him growing up without love or support, yet he stood here, reassuring her she was one of us. I never would've imagined being able to love him more, but each day, the emotion was becoming stronger and stronger.

I meant it. Cyrus pulled me into his side. *Yes, it sucks. She made a horrible decision, but you were protected. I might not have found you otherwise, and she's living with such remorse that she isolated herself from everyone. My uncle once told me that everyone deserves a second chance, and I'm finally in the right frame of mind to give her one.*

This man was completely amazing, and I had the honor of watching him transform into the strong, secure man he was becoming. *I love you.*

Not kinda? His eyes lightened to the almost-gray color that warmed my body.

I smiled, not able to hide it. *Most definitely not kinda. You have my heart and soul.*

"If I were making the call, I'd have Dave drive." Eliza rocked on her feet, her confidence slipping back into place. "He's not a wolf shifter, and that might throw the demon wolves off. I'd be in the back of the van so I could interfere if needed and help launch the initial attack. We'd need Annie in the back, too, pretending to be knocked out. I could cloak the rest of us until the moment came to attack."

"Absolutely not." Cyrus shook his head, his body rigid and his voice loud. "Annie *will not* be back there."

The love, which had been so overwhelming moments before, transformed into annoyance. I understood where he was coming from. I'd been in the same position when he'd been kidnapped. No plan was ideal, and I didn't like the way he was talking about me. "Tell me a better way. Because I will be in danger, no matter how we handle it. Tate is searching for *me*."

"That's a very good point." He lifted his chin. "Then you just won't go."

"Oh, man." Griffin exhaled. "I actually feel sorry for him right now."

"Annie hasn't trained him as well as Sterlyn and Ronnie have their mates." Sierra shrugged. "I'm not sure if I should be appalled that he's that slow or applaud his stupidity."

I ignored them and focused on Cyrus. "My absence would be idiotic. I should be in the back of the van unless you can think of a better alternative."

Cyrus turned to me, his jaw set. "You can't seriously think it's smart to be in the van. The whole point is to keep him from getting his hands on you, not give you to him!"

"It's a good plan." He had to see reason. Okay, maybe he didn't, but I had to get to him. "If Eliza cloaks everyone else in the back of the van and the demon wolves see me, they'll drop their guard, albeit temporarily. It could give us more of an advantage."

"Your life is more important than a temporary advantage!" Cyrus bellowed, silver fur sprouting across his arms.

Eliza clicked her tongue. "Boy, calm yourself down. You're about to shift, and she doesn't deserve to be talked to like that."

Her interference made my blood boil more. I could speak for myself. I didn't need help, especially when it came to him. My wolf surged forward, and my own skin tingled with a near-shift. "Cyrus, I love you and will always value your opinion, but I won't listen to you when you're being like this. You are *not* my alpha. You're my mate. Whether you like it or not, we are *equals*."

His breath hitched, and his expression crumpled. "I just meant—"

"Your intent doesn't matter. That's how it sounded, and I won't put up with it." I looked him straight in the eye. I might be short by wolf standards, but that didn't mean I wouldn't stand my ground. "Fewer people could get hurt if I'm in the back of the van. I'd like the same respect from you as I gave you the night you told me you had to try to save Mila and the others."

Grimacing, he exhaled as a mix of emotions rolled into me. Bottom line was that he wasn't helping, but neither was I. He could join the freaking club.

"I know it's tough, but I think it's the right call, too," Sterlyn said.

Griffin chuckled. "Dude, I've been there, and it sucks. When those dickheads were after Sterlyn, she made the same decisions that Annie is making now. It's hard, but we love them for their strength and heart."

"This is what I mean about getting too emotional." Rosemary shook her head and crossed her arms. "Eliza's suggestion is good. With our diverse group, we're set up well, and I don't think Annie will be harmed."

"I don't know—" Ronnie started.

I pivoted toward her. "Don't make me have the same conversation I just had with him with you!"

"Do any of you think I would allow something to happen to Annie?" Eliza placed a hand on her chest. "I would give up my life for hers. I swear to you, I will protect her until my last breath."

Alex placed his hands on his wife's shoulders. His eyes glowed faintly as he spoke privately to my sister. I hoped he was siding with us.

"It sounds like the plan is made." Killian stood from the couch and tugged his olive shirt over his jeans. "I'm starving, and we need to get the pack prepared. If we're done here, let's get ready."

I needed time to myself. Maybe they were right about tonight's fight messing with me. I understood where Cyrus was coming from, despite him not handling the situation well. Usually, I could find patience, but not right now.

Needing distance to clear my head, I marched out the door.

Dusk was upon us, and our group had congregated outside the community center. Circe stood with us, a scowl on her face. She hated being put in this situation, and I didn't blame her. Things were chaotic.

I'd avoided Cyrus as much as possible. Even though I wasn't angry with him, I couldn't overlook the way he'd spoken to me. I was tired of being treated like a child.

Ronnie stole glances at me. Shortly after I'd stormed out of the house, she'd found me and apologized. Cyrus still hadn't, and she knew me well enough to know how upset I was.

After that, Sierra kept popping up to check on me and making comments about how I should take mate-taming lessons from Sterlyn and Ronnie. Maybe I was missing an integral part of training. Was I giving him a reward when he was a good boy? At first, she'd annoyed me, but after a while, her persistence had made me smile.

Even Mila had come up to talk for a second. She'd mentioned that even when we were upset with our mates, we should always cherish our time together because we never knew when it might be the last time we'd see them.

Her words had made my stomach clench, but I couldn't bend to Cyrus. He'd continue to ignore my reasons.

So far, all the witches had stayed in their houses. They were avoiding us, and I wondered if that was on Circe's directive to ensure we didn't persuade them to help. Either way, I didn't have much hope for who might join us tonight. I hadn't even seen Aurora—Eliza's grand-daughter—or Lux, the two who had helped us before. I figured our group here was the final count.

Can I talk to you for a second? Cyrus linked.

I scanned the area and found him at the far end of the community house. *What's up?* My heart picked up its pace, betraying my brain.

He kicked the ground. *Please come here.*

Against my better judgment, my legs propelled me toward him.

"Hey, where are you going?" Ronnie asked as she shut the trunk of the Mercedes SUV. She'd been watching me like a hawk.

"Going to talk to Cyrus for a minute."

"We don't have time for makeup sex." Ronnie waggled her brows.

Sierra pushed her shoulder. "How else will she make him behave if she doesn't provide adequate rewards like you and Sterlyn do for your men?"

Yeah, there were some things I didn't want to talk to Ronnie about, and this was *definitely* one of them.

Ignoring them, I marched past the vampires and shifters congregating behind the vehicles and over to Cyrus. I followed him around the back of the community building.

I put my hands in my pockets, hating that I was awkward around him. He was my mate, but we'd never fought like this before. "You wanted to talk to me?"

He took my hand, and the buzz jolted between us. He sighed. "I'm sorry I was an ass."

Regret slammed into me. He must have been holding back his emotions from our link, which bothered me, but I understood. Sometimes, I wanted to process things on my own before having someone analyze them.

A corner of my mouth tipped upward. "You were one." I couldn't stay mad at him with the amount of guilt he felt.

"Thinking of you in danger..." He trailed off, looking skyward for answers. "It goes against my nature."

"I know." All my anger melted away as I stepped into him. My heart warmed. "But acting like that only makes things worse."

He booped my nose and murmured, "I know. I'm a jackass. But a jackass who loves you."

"No more being that way, though." I stood on my tiptoes and kissed his lips. "Promise?"

"I promise to do my very best, but if I act that way, call me out so I can grovel appropriately." He smiled against my lips. "And you always do what you think is best."

"That's a given." I wrapped my arms around him, burying my head in his chest.

Guys, if you two are done making up, we need to get rolling, Sterlyn linked. *Rosemary is itching to fly.*

And we needed her to fly so we could get the location of the road Dave needed to take.

This is pure torture, but I'm riding in the back with you, Cyrus linked as he pushed back a piece of my brown hair that had fallen out of my ponytail. *I have to be there in case something goes wrong.*

I wouldn't want it any other way. I hated that he was putting himself in danger, but it made sense for us to be side by side. We were stronger together.

No telling me I can't, he teased, and kissed me once more.

I closed my eyes, enjoying the moment. This was the

last bit of peace we'd have until the fight was over. *I'm not a jackass, unlike some people here.*

Touché. He winked as we headed to the front of the community building.

"Have you all lost your damn minds?" Sybil growled.

Something wasn't right. I turned the corner and couldn't believe my eyes.

CHAPTER TWENTY-TWO

I BLINKED IN SURPRISE.

Eight witches had joined our group: Sybil, Aurora, Herne, Lux, Cordelia, Aspen, Eliphas, and Kamila.

Sybil's deep-set scowl was almost comical, and her body quivered with rage. "You're going to help the group Eliza abandoned us for?"

"Grandmother didn't abandon us for *them*," Aurora scoffed, and flipped her dark bronze hair over her shoulder. Eliza's granddaughter squinted her chestnut eyes and placed her hands on her hips, wrinkling her sky-blue shirt. "We all know why she left—she's explained it many times. Her love for me started it all. I need to help them."

My heart tugged. Aurora felt responsible for Cyrus's hard life. When would we all stop blaming ourselves for things we couldn't control? Every one of us was guilty of doing that.

Cyrus took my hand and led me closer to the others. A tender emotion blew into me as he said with kindness to Aurora, "You don't owe us anything. If that's why you're helping, it's not needed. You were just an infant yourself."

"He's right, child." Eliza nodded. "You had nothing to do with the situation. It was all me."

That was when I'd had enough. "We have to stop blaming ourselves. Seriously." I spun around, looking at each member of our core group, then Circe and Aurora. "We have to move forward and stop holding on to the resentment and pain of the past. We've *all* made mistakes, and we have to stop beating ourselves up over them. If you want to help us take down the demon pack, we'll gladly take you up on the offer, but don't do it to prove something to yourself or anyone else."

Eyes sparkling, Sterlyn stood tall in front of the witches. "Annie is right. No one here owes us anything. We're thankful that you allowed us to stay and for saving Annie all those years ago."

Cordelia took two steps forward from the right end of the line. Despite being in her forties, she could've passed as twenty if her daughter, Kamila, who was close to my age, hadn't been standing right beside her. Her midnight-black curly hair was pulled into a ponytail, and her charcoal eyes glanced skyward as she bit her bottom lip. "That's all I needed to hear."

A weight landed on my chest. Even though I didn't want them to help if they didn't truly want to, I'd gotten excited for a minute, thinking we'd have more witch power on our side—another advantage the demon wolves wouldn't have.

"Thank goddess you're getting some sense knocked into you." Sybil's shoulders drooped, and she tugged the hem of her black tank top over her black jeans. "I got nervous for a second."

"I wasn't sure if I was going until now." Cordelia walked over to stand beside Eliza. "They aren't trying to force us into something, and they're fighting wolves who are connected to demons. How can I say no?"

Her daughter tilted her head, causing her loose, curly, dark brown hair to fall to one side. Her dark skin glowed magically as curiosity appeared in her ink-colored eyes. "Then who am I not to follow my mother's lead?"

Cordelia frowned. "Kamila, you can stay here with everyone else. You don't need to risk yourself."

Kamila stepped away from the others and crossed the invisible line that separated us from the witches. "No, you're right. The demons have taken more control than they should have in the past, causing wars. We can't let that happen again. The balance must be maintained."

That was news to me, but I wasn't shocked. Though I was more in the loop now, the witches wouldn't trust us with everything they knew.

A tall man with medium-brown skin rasped, "I can't let my wife and daughter go without me." He moved to Kamila's other side.

The lump in my throat swelled. We already had four times the number of witches we'd thought we'd have.

Sybil scowled at the tall man. "Eliphas, I expected you to talk sense into your wife and kid, not enable them."

"I can't believe the words that come out of your mouth." Herne *tsk*ed, reminding me of Eliza. "For being part of a coven led by a woman, you should know better. We women are just as capable of making decisions as men are."

Sybil glared. "You know I didn't mean it like that. I would've said the same thing to Cordelia if Eliphas and Kamila had made that decision first."

"I'm glad you feel that way, Mother." Lux batted her arctic-blue eyes. She straightened her shoulders and twirled a piece of her wine-colored hair around her finger. "Because I'm going with them."

"I figured you would, and I'll be right there beside you." Herne laughed and winked at her daughter.

Hands clenched, Sybil turned to Circe. "That's most of your strongest witches. Do something. You can't allow this to happen."

"I'm going to hurt her if she doesn't shut up," Sierra murmured beside me.

Circe lifted her brow. "I already made my decision. I will not force anyone to stay or go. We all make our own choice." She looked at her mother and blew out a breath before turning back to Sybil. "You and Aspen will need to take charge of the coven until I return."

"You can't be serious." Sybil pulled on the ends of her short hair.

"Actually, that duty will fall on you, Sybil." Aspen patted the angry witch's shoulder and smiled. He could have passed as a vampire with his very pale skin and long dark hair, but the herbal scent that surrounded him clearly revealed he was a witch. "I'll be going with my family to do what I think is right as well."

Sybil's face blanched, and she seemed speechless.

"Finally." Sierra pivoted on her heels. "I was ready for the witch to shut her trap."

"Listen here—" Sybil started, but Circe lowered her hand.

"We need to figure out who is riding with whom," Eliza said, and patted her daughter on the shoulder. A look of pride settled over her face, and her sea-green irises lightened even more.

I wasn't sure if Circe knew how much her actions meant to her mother. My heart got a little fuller at seeing Eliza like this.

"We're splitting into three groups," Griffin informed the witches. "One group will go in the van, and the other two groups will split up and move to separate sides of the wolf settlement. By doing that, we can encircle the area and hopefully trap them in."

Needing to be close to Cyrus, I stepped into him, our bodies touching.

"Who's going in the van?" Circe asked, her gaze on the vehicle.

"Annie, Cyrus, Eliza, and me," Ronnie answered a little too earnestly.

When Alex stilled, I realized why. He wanted her to include him.

She turned to him but didn't say anything out loud.

He closed his eyes and groaned, caving.

That was the thing with mates. We were protective

of each other, and thinking that our mate would be in harm's way without us there to help drove us insane. That was why Cyrus had acted the way he did earlier, and I was sure I'd feel that way again.

"I'd say our best bet is to split into equal numbers." Killian placed his hands in his pockets. "We won't know where most of the wolves will be located or whether they'll be evenly distributed throughout the pack lands."

"Do you have any insight?" Sterlyn asked, taking a step toward me.

I didn't. "My time there was limited, and they only let me see certain things. They watched me the entire time, even when we were walking from location to location, to see if I was taking notes."

"Which means they could've manipulated anything you saw so we'd guess wrong." Rosemary's dark wings exploded from her back. "I'll see what I can determine with my flyover, but we need to deal with the facts we have. They have at least a hundred pack members, and we have an idea of how the houses are organized."

Circe rubbed her chin. "That's a smart decision. We can take one of our vans and follow you there. Once Rosemary informs us of what she sees, we can break into groups."

"I'll get it now." Aspen ran off toward the houses.

I hadn't seen a vehicle here other than ours, but I assumed they had one for the rare times they ventured out to get items they couldn't grow or find here.

I hoped Rosemary could glean something new. "That does sound like the best plan." I turned to the witches.

"Do you know of a place we can meet a few miles away from the motel? We want to make sure they don't see us coming before we even get out of the car."

"There's a state park close by," Lux offered. "Some of the kids I went to high school with liked to go there. They thought they were so big and bad, sleeping outside." She rolled her eyes.

Rosemary held out her arms. "Do the rest of you know where it's located?"

"We've been there a few times over the years. It's nice to connect with the land that surrounds us," Circe answered.

"Will there be people there?" Ronnie glanced at the vampires standing next to their vehicles. "These vampires are used to being around humans, but we have weapons and don't want to raise an alarm."

"Hunters go there all the time." Eliphas frowned. "Our presence won't be a problem."

The angel's attention landed on Lux. "Do you mind flying with me so you can show me where to meet the others? We can take off now."

Lux beamed. "Uh, yeah. That was epic last time."

"Dear goddess, please take care of my baby." Herne rubbed her temple.

Cyrus assured Herne, "Remember when Rosemary was tired? She protected her even when she dropped from the sky."

"If that's settled, let's move. We'll follow your van." Alex rubbed his hands together and opened the driver's door to his vehicle. "We're already leaving later than we'd planned."

The sun dropped below the horizon, and the moon began its ascent. It wasn't completely dark, but it would be soon. The mid-September temperature cooled the air at night, making my wolf even more eager to run.

"We'll meet you once we've flown over." Rosemary picked up Lux and took to the sky.

I watched in awe as the angel carried the witch effortlessly. Lux was slender, but so was Rosemary. I wouldn't have guessed she carried any extra weight with how smoothly she flew.

Killian's eyes glowed as Cyrus linked with our pack, *Everyone, get in the car you came in. It's time to go.*

The rest of us split up, with Eliza rejoining Cyrus, Ronnie, Alex, and me in Alex's Mercedes. Once the five of us were ready, Alex pulled out and waited for Aspen to bring the van around to follow.

An engine started close by, and soon, an older passenger cargo van rumbled down the dirt road. Sybil stood close to the witches, waving her hands animatedly as she talked to them. I didn't need my wolf's hearing to know she was still trying to talk them out of leaving. I wasn't worried. Every person had decided on their own, and these were the type of people who seldom changed their minds.

Once the witches were loaded in the van, Sybil scowled, and she backed away as we passed by, leaving the coven grounds. I didn't bother glancing at her. It wouldn't accomplish anything.

None of us spoke the entire way to the state park. Instead, our nerves took over. Each one of us was stewing in our own anxiety, and my stomach became upset. The prospect of seeing Tate again bothered me more than I'd like to admit.

Hey, it's going to be okay. Cyrus wrapped an arm around my shoulders and pulled me into his side. *I swear I won't allow anything to happen to you.*

That's not what I'm worried about. I buried my face in his chest, breathing in his scent. *I'm more worried about you and the others, but something doesn't feel right.*

His arm tightened. *What do you mean?*

My heart rate increased, and my chest ached. I hadn't realized until this moment that something felt off. *When the demon found out that Tate was having a daughter, he gave him power, then took it away upon my supposed death. That last night we were there, Midnight helped us escape early because one of the princes of hell was willing to see him. What if he got the power boost back?*

Cyrus's fingers dug into my skin. *We'll warn everyone about the possibility, but we won't know for sure until we confront him. Maybe the power got taken away again when he couldn't deliver you. Either way, we have sixteen silver wolves fueled by a nearly full moon, a bear shifter, over twenty wolf shifters, and about as many vampires, an angel, and several witches. That has to count for more than a power-boosted wolf shifter.*

He was right. We had a mix of supernaturals fighting on our side. I was letting this man psych me out before I even saw him, which was unacceptable. *And we have guns.*

I doubt the demon wolves have them, let alone know how to use them. His fingers loosened, and he ran his fingertips over my skin. *They isolated themselves to control the women the way they do. We've got this. If I didn't think we would come out of this alive, I'd be fighting you about going there.*

His confidence eased some of the pressure in my chest. The demon pack was isolated, and the men were arrogant. I could tell that just from hearing them breathe. They belittled the pack women, and the one shifter who'd given me alone time with Cyrus had done so as a favor he'd owed my mother, Midnight.

Instead of stressing the entire way, I needed to cherish this time with Cyrus, as Mila had advised. I closed my eyes and focused on his scent, the sound of his breathing, and his touch.

"We're pulling into the park," Alex said, bringing me back to the present.

The little bit of serenity vanished as I sat up. Redbuds and cypresses surrounded us as we pulled into a gravel parking lot. "When she said *park*, I thought playground."

"That's because you grew up in a city." Eliza leaned forward, her body stiffening. "Down here, a park has a place to leave your vehicles and amenities for people who are camping and hunting."

The sky was fully dark. "Looks like we're the only ones here now."

"It's midweek, and summer break is over. Most people come out on the weekends," Eliza answered.

Alex pulled into the spot next to the van while the other vehicles parked nearby, and we all got out. Ronnie walked over to me, staying close as her breathing turned ragged. She was struggling with me being here, too.

Wings sounded, and I looked skyward in time to watch Rosemary descend.

Circe and the other witches climbed out of the car and joined us just as Sterlyn, Sierra, Griffin, and Killian reached us.

Upon landing, Rosemary released Lux and put her gently on the ground. Going straight to business, as usual, she said, "Several wolves are gathered in the middle of the pack settlement, but they don't seem anxious. I don't think they're expecting Annie."

"It's still our best plan," Sterlyn said, glancing at Cyrus. "If Dave drives up in a van and Eliza can hide everyone, they might not expect an attack. As long as Dave doesn't drive too fast, we can attack while they're distracted by you."

"Dave," Cyrus called out.

The bear shifter headed to the group, his expression neutral. "Yeah." His tone held an edge.

"It doesn't appear like they knew Ezra was bringing her. Did he have a plan?" Cyrus stepped in front of me as if Tate might appear to take me right then and there. *If Tate is clueless, I don't want you driving into the middle of the pack. They'll automatically be on the defensive, and we won't have a moment to get into position before they attack.*

I understood and appreciated that. I wanted to eliminate the risk however we could, but I didn't want to stupidly put any of us in danger.

Dave pulled at the collar of his black shirt. "He said something about learning the location from Andis and that they were handing Annie over as a sign of good faith. He didn't go into more detail than that, so I think I have enough information to make our ruse believable."

"Dear God." Ronnie groaned. "Are we sure this is the right decision?"

"No." Griffin shook his head. "But Sterlyn is right. It's our best plan. A van driving in will distract the guards. If anyone disagrees, now is the time to speak up."

Frowns were the only response.

"Follow me through the woods. When I fly up, keep going straight because you'll be close. I'll stay in the sky, and if things go awry, I'll be there in seconds." Rosemary fluttered her wings.

"Killian and Sterlyn, can you split up your pack while I split up the vampires?" Alex turned to Ronnie. He kissed her a little too passionately, and I had to avert my gaze.

"On that note, I'm going." Rosemary took off.

"Let's get into the van. I need time to set the spell before we move," Eliza said, and headed toward Ezra's vehicle.

"Mom, wait," Circe said as she caught Eliza's hand.

Eliza faced her. "Yes?"

"Be safe, please." Circe gave her a side hug. "I'd like to spend more time with you when this is done."

"I'd like that, too." Eliza smiled. Then her serious expression slipped back into place. "Let's go."

Obeying like good little soldiers, Ronnie, Cyrus, and I headed toward the van. Even though the back of the van was large, no one could touch me, so we had to rethink who would ride in the back with me. We settled on three people so I'd have enough room to lie near the double doors.

We climbed into the back of the van, with the three of them—Eliza, Ronnie, and Cyrus—against the wall that separated the front from the back. There wasn't even a window so we could talk to Dave. Eliza, though, planned to cast two spells: one so they could overhear what was being said outside the van, and a cloaking spell to hide the three of them.

Eliza murmured words, but my heart pounded too loudly for me to comprehend them. The back of the van was muggy, even with the cool temperature outside, and I was thankful we weren't stuck back here in the middle of summer.

All right, everyone has split up, and we're moving out, Sterlyn linked with Cyrus and me. *We have equal members on both sides to ensure we can stay in contact. Sierra and Darrell are staying in human form, as are Billy and Chad, so someone from each wolf pack can communicate with the other pack and the vampires.*

Sterlyn had covered all the bases, and some of my apprehension eased.

That was until the van rolled forward, and I wanted to reach out to Cyrus. But Eliza had put up the spell. Even when I looked where I knew they were, I couldn't see them. *Can you see me?*

Yeah, I can, Cyrus reassured me. *I'm right here. You're not alone.*

He said it, but I damn sure felt alone. I closed my eyes; I could feel his presence better that way, as if taking away my sight increased the power of our connection. I locked on to it and took slow, steady breaths, trying to remain calm.

I wasn't sure how long we drove. It could've been hours or minutes. All I knew was that the walls were closing in on me, and my body was slick with sweat. It was so damn hot back here.

When the van stopped, my heart took off.

We can hear your heart pounding. They'll know you aren't asleep. Cyrus pushed calm toward me, but I could feel the apprehension he tried to hide.

It didn't matter. He was right.

"Who the hell are you?" Tate's familiar voice growled.

Dave repeated what he'd told us back at the camp.

"Really? You expect us to believe you just brought the girl to us?" Tate laughed without humor. "Keep him restrained, and Echo, check out the back."

"Me?" Echo sounded surprised.

Tate growled, "Did I stutter? Don't make me make an example out of you."

Wow. Maybe Tate's golden boy wasn't so favored anymore.

Footsteps headed in my direction, and I took deep, muggy breaths, attempting to calm myself.

When the door opened, the overly sweet, musky smell almost gagged me.

"Tate," Echo said. "You need to come here now."

Oh, hell. Were the rest of us not hidden after all?

CHAPTER TWENTY-THREE

MY TERROR AMPLIFIED MY HEARING. I could hear the air filling Echo's lungs, and his maliciousness coated my skin. Even though I couldn't see him, I felt his gaze on me.

A shiver coursed through me, but I didn't move.

Loud footsteps pounded toward me, and I didn't have to guess who it was. A tidal wave of evil slammed into me. He felt more sinister than the last time I'd seen him, confirming my fear. *Cyrus, the demon did something to him.*

"If this is a ruse, I will kill the bear shifter and you for falling for it," Tate said.

I tried to keep my breathing steady, but it increased in pace.

Hey, I'm right here, Cyrus linked, and pushed his love toward me.

That didn't fix the problem. Having Cyrus close to

me made me feel stronger, but I was about to attack my biological father. All my life, I'd wanted to understand why my parents hadn't wanted me. Why they'd given me up. All I'd wanted was for them to love me, and that dream had been shattered. Yet I still wanted Tate to throw open those doors and pull me into his arms.

How sad was that?

Where is everyone? Cyrus linked with the pack. *They're about to take Annie.*

We're closing in, Sterlyn responded. *We'll be in position soon.*

Darrell linked, *Same for us. Some wolf shifters are heading our way. We should create a distraction so Sterlyn's group can get to you faster. Annie's father won't let her go once he gets his hands on her. We need them to reach you as quickly as possible.*

His plan was solid. They were the first group to stumble upon the demon wolves, and they would be discovered either way. Might as well use it to our advantage.

Fine, but if you need help— Sterlyn started.

We'll say so, Darrell cut her off. *We all need to make it home. We've lost enough of our own.*

What a true statement. The cold spot in my chest where Quinn had been was a void. I wondered if it would always be that way. No wonder Mila had been so broken.

Sweat dampened my armpits as footsteps reached the back, and it wasn't from the heat. I'd thought this was the best plan, but maybe we'd been wrong.

Tate rounded the corner, and his chuckle made my skin crawl. "Well, well. Look what we have here."

I wished Eliza had spelled me. I hadn't considered asking her to help me, and she hadn't offered, so I assumed there was a reason. Controlling my body was the hardest thing I'd ever done. My heart wanted to race, and air sawed through my lungs, but I powered through.

"Who sent you here with this gift?" Tate asked and sniffed, ensuring there was no one around except for Dave and me.

My head spun as panic sank its claws into me. *Can he smell you?*

I don't think so, Cyrus replied. *If he could, he would've attacked already. Didn't you say that the witches can also cloak our scents?*

That was right. Some tension left my body. I'd forgotten about that. The last time I was here, Tate had beaten me, and Sterlyn and the others had left the motel to come after me. Aurora and Lux had hidden their scents so Tate's sentries wouldn't know they were coming. By the time they'd reached the woods, the torture had stopped, and I'd convinced them to turn around.

Dave coughed, and my stomach dropped. He had no idea what to say. This was about to turn into a disaster.

"You don't know who told you to bring her here?" Tate growled.

Someone grabbed my ankles and dragged me out of the van. They weren't being careful, and they didn't pick me up gently. My upper body slid out of the back, and instinctively, I shot my arms out, catching myself before my head could hit the ground.

All hell broke loose.

A hand fisted my hair as Tate jerked my head back. My eyes fluttered open and watered from the sharp pain in my scalp. His electric blue eyes were cold, and his brown-black hair was longer than before. He also looked younger. Though he was in his early forties, he appeared no older than thirty. At least we didn't look alike.

Thank God.

A wolf howled in the distance, and Darrell linked, *We're attacking.*

Tate growled. "Did you really think you could trick me?" he spat. "You're going to pay for killing Nyko and Kevin and for hurting my mate. I will force you to watch everyone you love die before I take you to the demon you're promised to." His eyes glowed.

"Fuck that," Cyrus shouted. "Get your hands off her." Cyrus snarled as he, Ronnie, and Eliza materialized in the back of the van.

Tate's expression morphed into a smirk. "The mate, the demon, and the witch who helped hide my daughter. This is the best day I've had in a very long time. All this time, we thought we'd have to retrieve you, but you've delivered yourselves right to me." He didn't seem concerned about the wolves fighting our allies, which made my skin crawl. What kind of alpha was he?

The wolf shifters at the front of the van moved toward us. I guessed Tate wanted them to see the show.

We're close, Sterlyn linked. *Distract him so we can catch them off guard.*

"What do you want us to do with them?" Echo asked, his warm beige skin looking dull. He had a ginger-brown beard that was a little redder than his short, chestnut hair. He looked worse for wear, and I wondered where his twin brother was. The only way to tell them apart was that Troy was shorter, but not by much.

"Separate them and put them in the holds. Do *not* underestimate them, and make sure someone stays behind to watch them while the rest of you take care of the other shifters who came to help their *friends*." Tate jerked my head back more and ran a finger down my cheek. "This one stays with me. I need to take her somewhere."

Oh, hell, no. I knew exactly where he planned on taking me. I bucked against him, but he grasped my hair harder. My eyes burned as a few strands got yanked from my scalp.

"Let her go, now!" Cyrus bellowed, fur sprouting along his arms. "Or I'll make you."

Tate laughed, but it was affected. I hadn't spent much time with him, but his arrogant humor was lodged in my memory, and this sound was forced.

He was nervous.

I closed my eyes, trying to increase my hearing again. His heart was beating at a quicker pace than the others, confirming my assumption. He was trying to control his body like I had in the van, but you couldn't hide certain things if someone was looking for them. If he'd opened the trunk, he probably would've picked up on my anxiety.

Gunfire cracked, and a bullet whizzed toward us. One of the burly men closest to me crumbled to the ground, a bullet between his eyes.

Tate wrinkled his nose. "You brought guns? What kind of wolves prefer that over fighting in animal form?" His elitist tone spoke volumes, but no one was safe from a gun, not even an angel if you caught them off guard. That was how I'd escaped Ingram.

"*Conteram terram*," Eliza murmured.

"Someone, knock the witch out," Tate commanded.

Echo and another man rushed toward Eliza as the ground began to shake. They stumbled and fell to their knees.

"You're not getting loose again." Tate dragged me away from the van, keeping a firm hold on my hair. "You've been a pain in the ass since you were born, but you won't evade your destiny."

Bones cracked, and I could feel the tingle of the shift through my bond with Cyrus. He was shifting with every intention of coming to get me. *Just hold on*, he linked.

Refusing to give up, I dug my feet into the ground, slowing Tate's progress.

"Walk," Tate commanded, and lifted me off the ground by my hair.

"Get the silver wolf," a guy yelled, and I heard snarls, meaning my mate couldn't reach me yet.

The pain I'd experienced before was nothing compared to this moment. Agony from Tate's hold on me had my eyes so blurry I couldn't see, and tears dripped down my cheeks like a waterfall.

My wolf surged forward as the sound of wings flapping came toward me from the sky and Cyrus's snarls closed in. I assumed Eliza had remained behind to cast the spell to keep Tate's men from reaching us. Cyrus and Rosemary would be here in seconds, but I couldn't handle this torment much longer.

Letting my animal side guide me, I kicked, desperate to hit Tate anywhere. I connected with his knee, and he grunted as he stumbled.

When he regained his footing, Rosemary's floral smell filled my nose, and her feathers brushed by me as she slammed into Tate. His grip slackened on my hair enough for gravity to help out, and I landed on both feet.

Wolves darted in from the center of the pack neighborhood, coming to their alpha's aid. Rosemary spun around just as a wolf swiped at her with its claws. The nails cut into her shoulder, and the angel hissed, "I will get payback."

"Get the girl," Tate instructed, and climbed to his feet. "She's the most important thing."

Cyrus leaped in front of me, blocking the wolves from reaching me, but he couldn't hold them back for long. I scanned the area. More wolves were approaching and surrounding us. We needed to get out of this situation, and fast. I linked with the pack, *Where are you guys?*

Gunshots echoed, louder than they'd been a short time ago. They were getting closer; I just couldn't tell how quickly or where everyone was located.

Griffin and I and a few of the wolves have reached the van. Demon wolves are everywhere, though. Sterlyn's concern bled through the connection.

Yeah, we weren't in the best situation. *We knew there were many, and they know the area better than we do.*

Having a magical dagger like Ronnie's would have been a huge advantage. I had nothing with which to fight the wolves but my hands and feet.

I'd find a way to make it work.

The demon wolf that attacked Rosemary flew across the clearing and slammed into an evergreen. His head snapped back, and it looked like she'd knocked his ass out.

Three wolves descended on Cyrus. He was twice their size, revealing how much stronger his magic was with the near-full moon than the demon wolves, whose magic waned during this time.

The back of my neck tingled, and I spun as Tate grabbed my arm. His fingers dug into my skin as if to mark me.

I was so tired of him manhandling me. I punched Tate in the face, and his head jerked to the side, but his grip didn't slacken.

Rosemary's purple twilight eyes focused on me, and she headed in my direction, but one of the wolves fighting Cyrus pivoted and lunged for her.

I was on my own, but I'd prepared for this.

"Let's go." Tate yanked me toward the pack area. Most of the fighters were either in the woods or here. I had no clue why he wanted to take me deeper into the camp...unless the demon was waiting there. But how would the demon have known I'd be here today? They'd seemed surprised that we'd shown up.

Corrupt energy swirled around me, chafing my skin. It was similar to the weirdness I'd felt here last time, but stronger...more vile. It pulsed as if it had a heartbeat. *Something's here.*

I glanced over my shoulder as Sterlyn, Griffin, Dave, and the wolves charged into the area. Sterlyn's attention was on me, and she raised her knife. I needed to get a weapon to stash on me like she did; it would come in handy in situations like these. Despite not wanting to experience something like this again, I had a feeling it was inevitable, especially with all the corruption going on back home.

Tate almost jerked my arm off, desperate to get me away from the others. Ten more wolves ran into the mix, darting between us and the others.

Hell, no. They wouldn't separate me from everyone. My wolf rose, and I let her take over. I spun around, pretending I planned to kick him in the chest with my right foot. A sneer crossed his face as he caught my ankle, and then I jumped and kicked my left foot up. The bottom of my heel connected with his chin, and his eyes widened as his body lifted off the ground and fell back.

But he didn't release my arm. His grip tightened, catching me off guard. I fell onto him, and he rolled over on top of me. He smashed my hands to the ground, and his dark eyes took on a spooky glow. He rasped, "You will regret every bit of hell you've put me through."

I laughed, wanting to rile him up and make him irrational. "Oh, and how do you plan on doing that?"

"By killing your mate and mating you to the demon you were intended for," he snarled.

Mating.

I became nauseous. I knew I was promised to a demon, but I hadn't realized it was a sexual promise. I thought I'd be their slave. "Not happening."

"You will be his. But don't worry, he doesn't want you for babies, stupid girl." Tate laughed despite the fighting and chaos going on around us. "He wants you to mask his presence so he can visit Earth."

I had no clue what that meant, but it wouldn't happen. I was getting the hell out of this. I bucked against him. *Cyrus!*

I'm on my way. I just fought the last one off. Cyrus's fear and determination wafted into me.

Darrell linked, *We're trying to get there, but these wolves are stronger than I expected. They aren't much weaker than us.*

We're facing the same issue here, Sterlyn replied. *The moon is almost full. They should be pretty damn weak compared to us. None of this makes sense. Is Mila okay with you?*

Yes, she's by my side.

Panic flared through Cyrus and me as I heard paws padding directly behind Tate. Two wolves were there, ready to fight Cyrus.

My stomach dropped as I stared into my captor's eyes. I whispered, "You're stronger than you should be."

"I'm strong like I should have been all along," His eyes sparkled as he watched my face twist in horror.

Realization hit me. The demon wolves were pulling strength from their alpha, who had indeed been blessed with demonic power.

A shadow appeared next to Tate.

I wouldn't allow this to happen.

CHAPTER TWENTY-FOUR

I'D BEEN DETERMINED NOT to be captured, and here I lay, restrained by my biological father with a demon beside him.

The strangest part was that Tate didn't seem aware that a shadow was there, he was so fixated on me.

There was no way in hell I was going with that demon without putting up a fight. I bucked against Tate, and his eyes darkened while a sick smirk spread across his face. He loved that I was fighting, and he straddled me, pinning me to the ground. The rocks in the grass bit into my skin, but adrenaline pumped through me so hard I didn't feel anything but disgust. I wanted him off me *right now*.

The demon raised its arm, and I waited for it to turn toward me. The outline of a dagger materialized in its hand, reminding me of Ronnie. How many demons had that nifty ability? I'd have stabbed Tate and everyone else who got in my way *so* many times by now.

The demon's hand rose high above its head, so I closed my eyes. I didn't need to see it pivot and stab me. If Tate enjoyed hurting me, the demon would surely be enthralled with me thinking it would save me, only to torture me.

Annie! Cyrus linked, his concern wafting through me. *I'm trying to get to you.* He linked with the rest of the pack, *Can anyone reach Annie? She needs help.*

Ugh, I hated that I was in this situation, but even shifting into wolf form wouldn't help me. He'd still have me restrained in animal form.

He jerked my arms and grunted in pain. My eyes fluttered open as Tate released me. Warm liquid hit my arm, and the smell of copper attacked my nose. My breathing caught when I saw the demon dagger protruding from Tate's shoulder.

The demon must have gone for his neck, and Tate had realized it at the last second.

I blinked. Was I imagining things? Why would the demon help me, unless it was betraying Tate? That still didn't help my situation, but it served the twatwaffle right.

The demon turned its gaze on me, and my lungs started working again.

The eyes were a beautiful and, most important, familiar emerald.

Ronnie.

Tears filled my eyes as a weight lifted off me, both literally and figuratively.

My fear had overridden my senses, and I hadn't recognized my sister. That was insane.

We're trying, but they keep coming at us, Sterlyn connected. *We're overwhelmed even with Dave on our side.*

Darrell answered, *At least thirty are attacking us over here. We're fighting them the best we can, but the vampires are making the largest dent. These guys are just as strong as us, and we're outnumbered. The witches are in the back, casting spells so they don't have to worry about dodging bullets. We haven't lost anyone yet. The vampires are amazing shots, and we're holding our own.*

That was a blessing, but we needed to make more than a damn dent.

"What the hell?" Tate growled and turned his attention to my sister. "Who the fuck are you?" He reached for the dagger's handle, but when he touched it, he grimaced in pain.

"I think you called me 'the weird demon.'" Ronnie chuckled, her laugh furthering my relief. She clutched the dagger and lifted it up at an angle, making the wound worse.

He slapped his hand over the gash, but blood slid between his fingers and pooled at his feet. Ronnie had gotten him good. "You'll pay for that."

"I'd like to see you try." Ronnie lifted the dagger again, blood dripping from the shadow-tipped end.

I was still in awe that something like that could inflict so much damage in shadow form.

Tate clenched his teeth. "I know how to hurt a demon."

I wouldn't let this horrible person hurt my sister. I jumped to my feet and punched Tate in the face. I channeled all my hate and anger into the punch, despite my wolf whimpering in my mind.

His head barely moved, and my hand throbbed. I hadn't broken it, but how was he so solid?

He laughed maniacally despite the blood gushing from his shoulder. "I can't believe someone so stupid is my daughter."

His words stung, forcing my attention away from my hand. I tried to remain stoic, knowing the prick wanted to hurt me, but despite it all, it worked. I regretted every time I'd questioned how a child could remain loyal to an abusive parent. Maybe he hadn't hurt me as badly as he could have, but the way his opinion bothered me at all said more than I wanted to analyze.

"Go," Ronnie said, and lunged at him. "Help Cyrus."

She knew exactly what to say to get me to leave, but I knew her real motive. Alex's earlier words replayed in my mind. Despite not physically killing his brother, Alex had known that the outcome was very likely that night. Joshua, now one of his trusted guards, had killed the former king because Matthew had lost his humanity. Maybe Alex hadn't plunged the knife into his brother's heart himself, but he'd stood by and watched it happen. That day still haunted him just like this one would be forever seared into my memory.

I'd thought they were being a tad overcautious about

me struggling with the attack tonight, but they hadn't been. Though I hated Tate, my wolf recognized him as our father. It inherently went against my instincts to harm him, but he wasn't a good man. If we let him live, he'd never stop hunting me. He'd never stop wanting to hand me over to the demon so he could keep whatever misbegotten power it had given him.

Ronnie wanted me to leave so I wouldn't have to live with the regret of striking the final blow.

Instead of acting like a child, as I would have a week ago, I understood the situation for what it was. She knew I could fight my father, but that didn't mean I had to. I didn't want to be the one who killed him, and that was okay. Besides, Ronnie was a demonic vampire. If anyone could kick his ass, it'd be her, Rosemary, or Sterlyn.

A chuckle escaped me, cutting Tate's laughter short. Yeah, I probably sounded insane, but I loved the fact that a man who hated women so much would get his ass delivered to him by one. Karma was a bitch, and I was glad she was on our side.

Ronnie tensed. She must have thought I was laughing at her suggestion that I leave.

I nodded, wanting her to know that I'd listen. Now wasn't the time for regrets—that could come when all this was done.

Even in shadow form, I could see her shoulders relax. She'd expected me to give her a hard time.

I scanned the group, and my stomach churned. Three demon wolves fought Rosemary, three enemy wolves fought Sterlyn and Griffin, and everyone else had their hands full with a battle of their own. Finally, my attention landed on Cyrus. Two bulky wolves circled him so he couldn't keep an eye on both at once.

That problem was about to be solved. I rushed toward them just as the shorter of the two stood on his back legs, his claws extended. He swiped at Cyrus as my mate glanced at the taller one, who attempted to slash his back.

Letting my wolf brush my mind, I leaned on my left foot and swung my right leg around. The top of my foot hit the front of the wolf's stomach. He fell to his side, missing Cyrus's back by a few narrow inches.

If I'd been a few seconds slower, the outcome would've been greatly different. We needed the other group to meet up with us now.

You need to go! Cyrus linked, his silver irises turning granite. *I'll come find you, but get out of view. They're after you.*

A rather large part of me wanted to inform him that it was a good thing I'd gotten here in time, or he would've been bleeding and in pain.

I bit my tongue. He was scared and didn't want me hurt.

But I felt the same way. I added Sterlyn into the link: *I think they're after Cyrus, too. I was more than just promised to the demon. One of the princes of hell expects me to be his mate.*

What? Cyrus's rage plowed into me. *You're already mated!*

That's her point, Sterlyn replied. *They need you out of the picture so she won't be mated.*

The larger wolf charged Cyrus as if to prove my point. Cyrus hunkered down, ready to attack. His anger fueled him. *Go, Annie. I can handle this.*

I'm on my way, Sterlyn vowed. Snarling, she attacked her opponent more aggressively.

A tickle at the back of my neck warned we were being watched. I spun around as two more demon wolves appeared from between a couple of the nearest houses. Their eyes locked on me as if they'd known where I'd be.

Ronnie and Tate still fought, and I quickly looked around again. Each time Rosemary got rid of an opponent, another ran out to take its place. It was like that for each fighter, as if someone were coordinating the attacks from above.

No, surely not. That couldn't be.

As promised, Sterlyn fought off one of the wolves who was right on her and Griffin, but two more ran from the clearing.

That was it. Tate was focused on Ronnie, so someone else was pulling the strings. Echo and Troy had been part of his inner circle, and Troy hadn't been there earlier. It had to be him.

The two new wolves that approached us choked. Okay, it was probably laughter, but wolves weren't meant to laugh, and it came out like a gurgle.

Panic and fear slammed into me, telling me that Cyrus had figured out we were surrounded.

Damn it, he linked. *Are any of you getting closer?*

Instinctively, we faced away from each other, his furry butt touching my lower back. I'd wanted to stay in human form to communicate with Midnight and the other women, but that plan wasn't panning out. Maybe I should have shifted. It would be easier to fight that way.

I'll get there, Sterlyn replied. A loud growl came from her direction, followed by the sound of two bodies colliding. *They have to run out of replacements at some point.*

We're closing in, Darrell reassured us. *We should be there soon.*

The four demon wolves paced around us, tightening the circle slowly, probably to instill fear.

Ronnie fought Tate not ten feet away. He'd found a knife or had one stashed away. I couldn't understand why he was still in human form. Luckily, they seemed to be evenly matched, but that also worried me. Ronnie didn't have a ton of training in her demon form, and Tate wasn't above doing something shady.

Gunfire grew louder, which was promising, but the vampires were probably just at the van now. Even though it wasn't far away, all it would take was the demon wolves to get the advantage for everything to change.

This shit had to end. If something happened to Cyrus because I hadn't done enough, I could never live with myself. I let my wolf inch forward just as Circe appeared at the edge of the small clearing.

"*Fulmen inimicos meos ledo!*" she screamed, and raised her hands.

Thunder rumbled from the cloudless night sky, reminding me of the noise I'd heard the night that

Ronnie's demon father had attacked Shadow Terrace. Was this what had happened on the night Cyrus had taken me to safety? Ronnie didn't like to talk about it, and I hadn't pushed, but I knew Eliza had helped her defeat her father.

Now that the witches were here, I held back my wolf. I'd shift if things didn't get under control, but we had the extra help we needed.

Light streaked the sky, resembling the electric balls I used to love to touch as a child. The air around me chafed my skin as electricity charged around us.

Every battle paused as we looked upward. The demon wolves' fur stood on end all over their bodies, making it clear where the lightning would hit.

Concern washed over me, drying my throat. Circe had to be using a ton of her magic. Witches were capable of very strong magic, but when they cast spells independently, it drained them fast.

Aspen, Aurora, and Eliza rushed behind her.

"Oh, goddess," Eliza murmured, looking at Circe and everyone around us. She continued louder, "Aspen and Aurora, help Circe. I'm going to cast a different spell."

Obeying, Aspen and Aurora lifted their hands, joining Circe's chant. The lightning ball in the sky grew larger with three witches now casting the spell.

The demon wolves tensed and turned to leave the scene.

Oh, they were all talk until something horrible was about to happen.

"*Produc ventum!*" Eliza said, holding her hands in front of her.

A breeze churned the air. The wind whipped around faster and faster.

Guys, we're almost there, Darrell linked. *We see the van.*

That was good. They'd reach us soon. Maybe we had a chance at winning this.

As the enemy wolves tried to run away, they hit a barrier. The strong wind blew them back, keeping them in the clearing they were desperate to escape.

"Get out of the barrier as quickly as you can," Eliza shouted, her face turning red from strain.

I wasn't sure how the hell that would work since the demon wolves kept hitting the wall, but I would try. Eliza had never steered me wrong. I looked at Cyrus. *Let's go.*

We took off running toward the barrier. I closed my eyes, expecting to ricochet off, but I stepped through with just a rustling of my hair.

My skin eased as the electric charge left my body, and I turned to watch the rest of our group escape. Everyone scattered around the circular barricade Eliza had created.

Everyone except...

"Ronnie!" I lurched to go back for my sister, but Cyrus stepped in front of me. "*Ronnie!*" I shoved at my mate to get past him, but his huge wolf form blocked me. "If anything happens to her, I'll never forgive you." He was holding me back when my sister needed me.

I know, he said, then lightning hit the circle. *But she's a shadow, remember?*

The wind mixed with the lightning, creating a fire-like tornado. The strangest thing was that I didn't feel the temperature rise. It was contained in that area.

Sterlyn and several others rushed over to us, while the vampires, Dave, and everyone in the other group strode up and stopped behind the witches, watching in awe.

I saw Ronnie's shadow in the chaos contained in the circle. Tate had his arms wrapped around her, knowing he could get out by clinging to her. Once they escaped, he turned and ran toward the center of the pack neighborhood without pretending to care about the torture his men were enduring.

She crumbled to the ground, some of her hair whipping around her face.

"Ronnie!" I yelled again as I ran to her. I dropped to my knees, tears streaming down my face. I couldn't see much of anything, just the tornado-like electric thing still rolling.

Alex's syrupy smell appeared beside me, and I wiped the tears from my eyes to see his crumpled expression. He looked broken.

Oh, God, no. She couldn't be dead.

CHAPTER TWENTY-FIVE

I CLOSED MY EYES, shaking my head. I shouldn't have left her to fight Tate. Her death was my fault.

Pain engulfed my chest, and Cyrus came to stand beside me. He brushed my back, providing comfort, but it made me want to vomit. It wasn't fair for me to be feeling any comfort, fated mate or not. My sister was dying right in front of my eyes.

I collapsed and laid my head on her chest. It didn't move. I wasn't sure if she needed oxygen in her shadow form, but the lack of movement was so damn telling.

"Is that where she is?" Alex's voice broke as he stood over me. "I can't see her. All I can feel is our connection getting colder."

God, I hadn't considered how painful this would be for Alex. He was desperate to be near his soulmate, but he couldn't even see her.

She still has a heartbeat, Cyrus linked. *And she's a demon vampire. She might be able to heal herself.*

There were so many unknowns, but one thing was for sure—her heartbeat was slowing. Needing to be strong for Alex, I sat back on my calves and nodded. Sniffling, I wiped snot and tears from my face. "She is."

"Damn it, I need to see her." Alex clutched the roots of his hair and yelled, "Rosemary!"

My chest lightened. Rosemary could heal Ronnie, but where was she?

I looked toward the electric tornado. She'd been across the clearing from us, closer to the witches. I was certain she couldn't hear us. I linked with the pack, *Tell Rosemary to come here. Ronnie's hurt. We need her help.*

Uh...we can't talk to her, Darrell replied. My momentary relief evaporated.

Sterlyn interjected, *I'll link with Killian so he can.*

This was a good example of why it paid to have some wolves stay in human form.

She and Griffin moved behind Alex, facing the tree line in case anyone attacked while we were preoccupied. Sterlyn's concern and fear swirled through the bond, adding to mine and Cyrus's.

Ronnie's body flashed like a television trying to receive a transmission, drawing my attention back to her. Alex kneeled beside her as she slowly materialized back into her human form.

He bit his wrist and held it to her mouth. The blood trickled between her lips and oozed out the sides. He growled, "Drink it, love." With his free hand, he rubbed her throat, forcing her to swallow.

The sound of fluttering wings alerted us to Rosemary heading toward us. Ronnie's heart was barely beating, and I could only pray that Rosemary reached us in time.

My wolf whimpered, surprising me. She viewed Ronnie as a sister, too, which conflicted with her earlier emotions about Tate. I hated that it had taken this for her to realize that family wasn't necessarily blood.

Rosemary landed beside me, and her rose scent filled my nose, making my eyes burn again.

"This was what I was talking about earlier," Rosemary said, and smacked Alex's hand away. "Vampire blood heals non-vampires. She's mostly vampire and needs fresh human blood."

Crimson bled into Alex's irises. "I had to do something, and there aren't any humans here for me to bring to her."

My stomach sank. Ronnie could lose her humanity if she drank directly from a human. I was sure she'd rather die than risk losing that, but Alex was a desperate man trying to save his mate.

"Exactly. You've lost all sense of reason due to your overwhelming emotions." She lifted her hands, the white glow pulsing from her palms. "We both know she wouldn't want that. That's one reason I like her so much. She *knows* right from wrong."

I was about to scream at them to shut up, but Rosemary placed her hands on Ronnie's chest. Her lips pressed into a line as she pushed her magic inside my sister.

"And it's *right* if I *lose* my *mate*?" Alex growled, his

fangs extended. He was half vamped out, and his irrationality wouldn't do us any good.

"Stop distracting her." I stood and pushed him back a few feet. "Do you want her to heal Ronnie or not?" Though I knew Rosemary wouldn't let Ronnie die, we didn't need Alex harassing her while she worked a miracle. He wasn't used to people not bowing down to him since he'd grown up segregated from all the other supernaturals. He'd been raised as a royal, and every vampire had obeyed him...or they'd pretended to obey in front of his face.

Cyrus's huge wolf frame stepped between Alex and me. He hunkered down, facing the vampire, making it clear he would protect me. *If he tries anything, I don't give a damn that he's your brother-in-law.*

He's upset. We all were. As long as he didn't actually lash out, everything would be okay.

Alex's eyes hardened, and he glared at Cyrus and me, but he kept his mouth shut, likely due to the strong heartbeat that had started pounding in Ronnie's chest again.

Ronnie's eyes fluttered open, and Rosemary removed her hands from my sister's chest and got back to her feet.

"Alex? Annie?" Her brows furrowed as she scanned her surroundings. "Rosemary, why were you on top of me?"

"You were hurt—" Alex's voice broke.

Her eyes widened, and she flashed to her feet. "Tate —he's out there somewhere. When I raced for the barrier like Eliza instructed, he used my body as a shield. That's why it took me too long to get out."

He'd probably done it slowly on purpose. I couldn't believe his sperm had created me. I hoped to never be *anything* like him. "Probably because he got a demonic juice-up."

The lightning vanished from the middle of the clearing, but the wind still blew. I glanced over my shoulder and didn't see any of the wolves that had been there only moments ago. Thick ash blew in a tornado pattern, and the knot in my chest loosened. They'd essentially cremated the wolves, and I was thankful that Eliza was containing the ashes. I didn't want their particles up my nose.

"That took care of about thirty of them," Rosemary murmured, but more wolves were heading toward us.

"Guys, I think they have someone in a location up high or in an actual tree directing the attacks." This was the first time I'd gotten a chance to tell anyone my thoughts. "I noticed that they're timing the attacks perfectly to wear us down." Tate's words replayed in my head. He wanted me to watch my friends die, and I had a feeling that was exactly what the plan was: Wear everyone down until they could be slaughtered. And I'd be center stage, forced to watch it all.

"I'll go look around," Ronnie said, and her body began to flicker.

Alex's eyes turned completely crimson at the thought of her leaving, and his hands clenched into fists.

"No." Rosemary held up a hand. "Your mate was willing to do something stupid to save you. If you leave now, he'll go insane again. Stay here, and I'll let one of you know if I need help or see anything." Not waiting for us to argue, Rosemary took off, flying into the treetops.

Ten wolves ran from the neighborhood, but they stopped in their tracks at the two large evergreens as the wind tapered off.

Our group stepped forward, closing the distance between us. The vampires aimed their guns as Eliza turned her palm toward the sky. The ash became suspended in midair. She said, "Do you want to turn into cinders like your brethren?"

If this had been a movie, the theatrics would have been amazing. But real life? That was a whole different story. This even creeped my ass out, and she wasn't threatening me. Refusing to let Eliza take all the heat, I stepped in. "Your alpha ran, leaving thirty of your pack members to die. He won't think twice about leaving you, too. Are you sure you want to choose this battle?"

They glanced behind them, then back at us.

Are they really considering fighting us when they're clearly outnumbered and outclassed? Chad linked, his surprise evident.

Mila interjected, *They may not have a choice.*

She'd nailed it. If I hadn't seen how the pack operated, I'd have been confused, too. You would expect them to have a sense of self-preservation, but Tate would do whatever hideous things he could think of to hurt them before killing them cold. *If they fight us, Tate will respect them, and their deaths will be quick. If they don't, Tate will take his retribution out on their families.*

That's sick, Theo replied. *We need this to end.*

Don't hurt anyone who doesn't fight us, and try not to touch the women, Sterlyn reminded everyone. *We are not heartless like these people; it's what separates us from them. But be wary. Even the women could be misguided and afraid to go against their alpha. They might attack us to survive.*

She'd heard my stories of how the women here were treated. There were a few men I hadn't seen actively mistreat the women, but they didn't go out of their way to stop the mistreatment, either. I was on the fence about them, but when you grew up in an environment like this, what could you do? Tate had made everyone fear him, and he thrived on having that power over them.

The ten wolves charged us, and my heart broke. They clearly didn't feel like they had a choice. We likely outnumbered the demon wolves, but I didn't trust Tate to surrender. He had something up his sleeve.

I'm going to look for the women. I couldn't shake the feeling that the longer we stayed here, the longer Tate had to enact his final play. He had to know his pack wouldn't survive, especially with the spells the witches had carried out and the vampires with all their weapons. Not only that, but our entire group was intact.

We'll go together, Sterlyn linked. *Lead the way.*

That sounded promising.

Ronnie rolled her shoulders, limbering up for a fight. Alex stuck beside her like glue.

Move, Darrell linked. *The vampires will shoot their way in so the witches can recover.*

That was a very good idea. The vampires ran through

the center of the clearing, and the ashes of the demon wolves vanished from the air. Eliza dropped her hands, sweat coating her forehead, the wrinkles in her face again more prominent.

Within seconds, the vampires mowed down the ten wolves who had charged us. Not waiting for more to come, I took off toward the center of the village.

Don't leave my side, Cyrus linked as he caught up to me, running beside me. *You aren't in wolf form and have no weapons.*

Yeah, we should've thought that part through better. I needed something to use for defense, even if it was a rock, or hell, a thick branch. Anything would do.

Sterlyn, Griffin, Alex, and Ronnie caught up to us. We jogged in groups of two but stayed close together. The familiar log cabins appeared, and my horrible memories of my time here replayed. The one-story homes were quite basic but well maintained.

The sound of angel wings caused me to look skyward. Rosemary landed in front of me with Troy in her arms, her eyes tense. She said nothing as she dropped him to the ground.

His body hit with a solid thump, and he didn't even groan. Then I realized he didn't have a heartbeat, but he didn't look harmed. "How'd you kill him?"

"He was dead in the tree when I found him." Rosemary surveyed the area. "His heart just stopped beating, and there was an overly sweet, sulfuric stench in the air."

Demon.

Great, we hadn't planned for that. I definitely needed a weapon.

I spun around and marched toward the vampires, Dave, and Killian's wolves.

Annie, what are you doing? Cyrus asked, and shoved past the others, following close behind.

Getting a weapon. One of the vampires would surely have something I could use. "Do any of you have a knife, a saw, anything sharp?"

"A *saw*?" Sierra chuckled, her gray eyes lightening.

At least I could count on her to find humor in a moment like this. "Yeah, we may have a demon involved, and the only way to kill them is to cut off their heads." Ronnie had explained that it was due to the demon losing any trace of humanity and morality. Since they were literally heartless, decapitation was the only way to kill them.

"I brought an extra blade." Killian bent down and removed a holster with a knife. "Here—it should fit around your waist, since you're tiny."

Tiny. Another side effect of having my wolf shifter side repressed. I hadn't grown to the standard height that magic blessed shifters with when they were children.

As he said, it fit around my waist.

I don't like this, Cyrus growled. *I'm not leaving your side.*

You've said that before, and we got separated. I arched a brow at him. *You should be glad I have something to help protect myself.*

"Uh...has Ju—Cyrus trained you on how to use a weapon?" Dave's eyes tightened.

I didn't need yet another *man* telling me what to do. "I'll be just fine, thanks." I ran back in front. "Let's get this over with. I'm ready to go home."

Rosemary sighed. "I wished I shared your enthusiasm."

"Something is off." Ronnie lifted her hand, her dagger reappearing in her palm. "No more wolves are charging us."

Alex grimaced. "That could be because their scout is dead, or they want us to hunt them."

Almost like someone had flipped a light switch, pure evil laced the open air, charring my skin. I groaned and rubbed my arms.

The silver wolves whimpered, feeling the sensation as well.

Alex turned and glanced at everyone. "What's wrong?"

"Demon magic," Rosemary answered.

This had to be his big plan. We needed to end this before it got worse. "Let's go."

Rosemary stepped in front of me, cutting me off. "I'll take to the sky. Now's my best chance to go undetected. If the demon wolves get to you before I return, tell them I smelled a demon and took off. This might be the only advantage we can sustain over them."

My stomach dropped. She knew we were walking into a trap. Hell, we all knew. Maybe coming here had been a mistake, but it wasn't like they'd let us leave now.

Tell her that's a good idea, Cyrus linked with me, brushing his fur against my leg.

I repeated his message as Sterlyn filled in the other packs on what was going on and asked Killian to update the witches.

Footsteps pushed through the wolves as Eliza made her way to us. She first pulled Ronnie into a hug, then me, and said, "I'm not staying back there with you two up in front. I almost lost Ronnie and couldn't get to her because of those wolves. I'm staying with you two from here on out."

"That's fine with me." Alex patted her shoulder. "Your magic has saved us several times."

"Not to mention demons are involved, and it took your help to kill my father." Ronnie shivered, and I wasn't sure if it was from her nerves or the cooler temperature.

"He was a descendant of a prince of hell." Eliza *tsk*ed. "Those should be rare and few. The weaker ones should be easier to fight."

One could only hope. "Let's get going. Cyrus and I will take the lead." Trying not to overthink it, I hurried toward the horrible sensation. It would lead us wherever they wanted us to go, but we didn't have a choice. Tate wanted to weaken us, and he'd waited until we thought we had a chance to win, leading his pack to slaughter for the cause.

Of course we will, Cyrus grumbled, but he wisely grew quiet. Alex and Ronnie ran directly behind us, with Eliza next and Sterlyn and Griffin in the rear.

The large cafeteria-like building came into view, and screams came from the right, heading away from where the sensation was strongest. I wanted to continue on the path, but those were the cries of women.

"Please! Stop hurting us," Indra's silky voice pleaded. "We haven't done anything."

"You're a woman," an asshole's deep voice responded. "That's good enough for me."

That's where they're keeping the women, I linked to Cyrus and Sterlyn, not wanting to speak out loud.

Let's be careful. They'll suspect we're coming, so be as quiet as possible, Sterlyn replied.

Ugh, she had to remind me to use logic.

Cyrus ran closer to me, staying at my side. I could feel his concern. He knew how much saving these women meant to me, and he was afraid I'd do something irrational.

When we broke through the trees, the theater-like section with several benches circling an open area lay in front of us. Tate stood on a worn patch of grass in front of the largest tree at the center. This was where his pack listened to his speeches and threats.

The scene in front of us was worse than that. The thirty women of the demon wolf pack were in their human forms on the ground, and among them were three male children. A few had black eyes, others had fat lips, and worst of all was Midnight.

I gasped, and my heart stuttered. Midnight's long brown hair was covered in dried blood, and her honey-brown eyes were dark from pain. We could usually have passed for twins, but not right now, considering the cuts on her face from something I could only imagine. Tate held a knife to her throat, and the memory of what I'd done to Ronnie while under the control of a sick, demented vampire flitted through my mind. The two memories merged, and my breathing shallowed.

"There they are," Tate cooed. "It's about time. I'm not sure how much longer these women could handle this abuse. I almost thought you didn't care."

"Let them go," Ronnie said through clenched teeth. "This is your pack. Aren't you supposed to do what's best for them?"

Alex frowned. He wasn't thrilled that his mate had put the focus on herself, but Tate wanted all of us to die. It didn't make a difference.

"I *am* doing what's best for us because it's what's best for *me*." Tate's attention landed on me. "I'll give you one chance. Give me Annabel and leave. I'll forgive your transgressions for a little while so you can live relatively longer lives. If you don't, you die now."

The vampires filed in behind us, their guns pointed at Tate, with the witches lining up on one side. Our group fanned out the best we could in the small opening.

"We've got guns. Are you stupid?" Alex laughed. "Do you really think you have a chance?"

"Oh, I have more than that." He waggled his brows as ten demons appeared beside him. "I have backup."

The demons flew directly at the witches as random wolves who weren't part of his pack sprinted from the other end. They all ran in front of Tate, blocking us from having a clear shot at him.

We would have to fight the natural way. The random wolves looked desperate, charging at us in pure fear.

What is all this? Theo asked. *I thought you said we cut down their numbers.*

We did. There was only one thing Tate could've done. *He has leverage over these other packs.* Knowing him, he'd kidnapped people important to them, forcing them to do his bidding.

More wolves poured in, at least a hundred new ones.

That was why the asshole hadn't shifted earlier. He needed to coordinate with the shifters he didn't share a pack link with.

Try not to hurt them, but protect yourselves, Sterlyn commanded.

"You can injure the shifter girl in human form in front, but do not kill her!" Tate yelled.

"No!" Midnight cried, but Tate dug the knife into her throat. For a second, his face scrunched in pain, but he shook his head as he continued to abuse his fated mate.

Midnight had said there were some things you couldn't come back from, and this had to be one of them.

I had to get to my mother.

I had to save her.

CHAPTER TWENTY-SIX

MY THROAT CONSTRICTED as my heart hammered. The image of Midnight with a knife to her neck would forever be seared into my brain. Letting my wolf surge forward, I raced toward her.

I couldn't let her die. Not like this.

Annie! Cyrus linked. His paws hit the ground after me, desperate to remain by my side. *He's doing this on purpose.*

A wolf lunged at him, cutting him off.

I had no doubt the asshole was doing it on purpose. That was the problem. *I have to save my mother.* He would kill her if I didn't come to him. He was completely aware that I knew his intent and was using it to his advantage, but I couldn't stay back and watch her death unfold, not after everything she'd sacrificed for me.

The wolves avoided me, likely not wanting to chance Tate's wrath. I bet the demon wolf alpha was getting a high from seeing them scatter, knowing they didn't want to risk getting near me because of his threats.

A wolf slammed into me, taking me off guard. My knees hit the ground, and small branches cut into my skin. I rolled onto my back to get out of the way. It must have hit me by mistake. But when I got back onto my feet, it bared its teeth at me.

Okay, this gray wolf wanted to make a name for herself. My fingers itched to get the knife, but I didn't want to hurt her. Yes, she was attacking me, but I was sure she had a reason why. She lunged at me, and I spun. She narrowly missed my forearm.

She meant business.

Shit.

The wolf hit the ground so hard that it left a mark on her body. She jumped to her feet, her jade eyes full of rage. It was clear what she was seeking—vengeance.

Tate must have done something to set her off, but she needed to join the club. Unfortunately, she wasn't the only one he'd screwed over. "You're not being rational," I said, and grimaced.

Number one rule: never tell anyone they weren't being rational. It resulted in the opposite response you desired. That proved I'd been unemployed and not working with troubled kids for a while now. This kind of slip-up would've never happened a month ago, but being in a horrible situation made people all sorts of stupid.

Saliva pooled at the corners of her mouth as she growled, proving just how "rational" she was willing to be.

The image of a rabid dog flitted across my brain, and my wolf growled in protest, not liking the comparison. She'd have to get over being hurt.

"Look, I don't know what he's done to you, but let's work together." I clenched my hands at my sides, readying for her attack.

The desperate gleam in her eyes spoke of her pain.

My stomach soured. What if he'd killed her fated mate? Tate and his goons had done it before and taken the women as their chosen mates. Could that be his plan for this woman, too? Maybe Mila could reason with them.

She lunged, her mouth opening wide as she aimed for my neck. She wasn't playing games.

Not wanting to use my knife on her, I turned my body and punched her in the snout. Her head flew sideways, and her body flipped backward. She whimpered as she thudded to the ground, giving me a moment to check on Midnight.

Please, don't let her be dead.

I glanced in that direction to find that Midnight and Tate were gone.

No.

My chest stopped working as my body froze. Where the hell were they?

Annie, watch out! Cyrus linked as a snarl came from behind me.

Time sped up, and I turned back to the wolf determined to kill me. She had regained her feet and was inches from sinking her teeth into my leg. With the sound of all the fighting and my terror, I hadn't heard her move.

I'd reached for the knife, knowing I didn't have time, when my wolf tugged on my link with Cyrus. Magic exploded into me as if it were close to a new moon. With speed that should have been impossible, I kicked out my leg in time to prevent her from latching on. She snapped her teeth, expecting to hit her mark, then flew backward again.

Cyrus reached me and blocked me from her.

He would've been seconds late. I blinked, stunned at what had happened. I linked to Sterlyn and Cyrus, *Cyrus, did I hurt you?*

No. He crouched, ready to protect me, but two nearby wolves already had their attention locked on him.

I sniffed, waiting to smell rotten eggs—the signature smell of a lie—but it didn't come. *I pulled magic from you.*

I felt it, but it didn't hurt. Cyrus snarled as the two wolves approached us.

The girl wolf shook her head, but within seconds, her gaze locked on me again. No surprise there.

At least there's that. That had spared me an injury, but it would've been nice to know we could do it before now.

Sterlyn replied, *Ronnie's supernatural side pulled strength from Alex after they mated but before she was turned. Maybe since you're a wolf of demon descent, you two can share magic with each other.*

Demons were angels who'd fallen. If that was the case, and since our power was essentially the same, perhaps Cyrus and I could balance each other out between the full and new moon.

The two wolves charged, attacking Cyrus together. He fought them off easily, but he was distracted, leaving me exposed to the female gray wolf, which was fine. I wasn't useless even in human form.

Inching forward, the gray wolf stalked me. I had a feeling it was an attempt to intimidate, but it told me she was hesitant. She'd expected to land that last strike, and it had thrown her off when she hadn't. I knew the reason. She didn't.

"Please don't make me hurt you." That sounded arrogant, but even without accessing Cyrus's magic, I was stronger than she was. It wasn't a full moon, and though I was in human form, I'd already proven I could hold my own.

She leaped at me, and I narrowly dodged her, causing her to blow past me. She dug her feet into the ground, stopping her forward motion, and I jumped on her back. I clamped my legs around her middle and dropped to the side as I wrapped my arms around her neck. She fell on top of me, and I held her in place.

Thrashing her head, she tried to scratch and bite me, but she couldn't touch me in this form. I had to get through to her, or I'd have to knock her ass out. I went with the only strategy I had. "Did he hurt your mate?"

She went still and whimpered a heartbreaking cry.

My chest throbbed from that confirmation. I hated that she'd gone through this, and now that we'd lost Quinn, I had an inkling about how crazed a person would be from losing their fated mate. "The woman in human form over there," I said as I turned her head in their direction. "They did the same thing to her. And one of my packmates recently lost her mate." My eyes scanned the group I was referencing, and I found my mother's three closest friends huddling together. *Mila, I could use your help.* Luckily, Mila had stayed in human form.

Minx had been Troy's mate, and her honey-pecan hair spread across the ground as she lay almost lifeless on the ground. Ulta sat next to her, almost unrecognizable. Her warm beige skin looked several shades lighter, and her caramel blonde hair had been cut short, making her peridot eyes appear more sunken in. I'd hoped that since Nyko's death, she might have been given a reprieve, but it looked like she'd been worked harder, likely by Echo.

When Indra's smoky brown eyes latched on to mine, she stood. Her golden complexion had lost its luster, but she still appeared strong. She stepped in front of the two women like she wanted to come to me, but she stayed put.

I needed their help to convince this wolf to fight alongside us. Hell, I needed to convince all these women to fight.

Wanting the wolf to realize she wasn't in danger, I let her go. She rolled off me and dropped to the ground like she didn't have the strength to hold herself up. She was heartbroken and lost.

Standing, I ignored the chaos around me and walked past the wolf toward my mother's friends. The gray wolf snarled but didn't attack. Instead, she trotted after me, and I thought her curiosity had gotten the best of her.

Annie, what are you doing? Cyrus asked. Two more wolves attacked him. He was trying not to hurt any of them, but he was tired of this.

They were wearing us out, as Tate had planned. He knew we wouldn't want to harm any innocents.

Ending this. I marched over to the women, and although a few moved away, most didn't. They had seen me in action during those few days I'd been here. "We didn't come here to hurt you. If we had, you'd be dead by now." I grimaced. That had come out harsher than I'd intended, but I wanted to be honest. I wanted to be like Sterlyn—empathetic and strong.

"Instead of all this chaos, which is exactly what Tate wants, we should work together." I stretched out my arms and noticed that some of the fighting closest to me had stopped. My stomach fluttered. I hated being the center of attention, but these women were more likely to trust me than anyone else on our side. "These men treat you like you're nothing, and you are *so* much more than that." I turned to look some of the people who were fighting us in the eye. "And if you think Tate will follow through on his promises, you're delusional. He forced most of the women here to mate with his men, and he won't let any of you leave. Think about it. He wants power, and he wants to hand me over to a demon to get more. That will only corrupt him more."

"She's right." Ulta rose to her feet, her legs shaking.

"That's exactly what they did to me. They said if I came with them, they'd let my son go, but they killed him."

Every wolf paused, and I turned to the gray wolf who'd tried to kill me. "You should be after Tate, not me."

Cyrus trotted over to me, his body rigid as he waited for another attack. His attackers had halted.

Mila stood in front of the women. "I understand what it feels like to be broken."

"Annie, watch out!" Eliza cried.

I turned to look back at the group I'd come from. Three demons floated toward me in their shadowy forms.

Witches couldn't see demons, but they could feel their magical presence. She must have felt them move in my direction.

Her face twisted in pain as her lips moved. A blue flame left her hands and slammed into a demon, though two still barreled toward me.

Rosemary and Ronnie were fighting one on their own and couldn't help me. The other witches were engaged with the other five, Aspen and Eliphas helping their families.

The remaining demon wolves charged behind our group, attacking the vampires and wolves. Mass chaos erupted again. The vampires fired as Killian's pack fought the demon wolves who had broken through or gotten too close. Sterlyn and the other silver wolves charged forward, but we were too far away.

Dave shouted, "Go. I'll protect them."

Grabbing the knife from my side, I nodded and readied myself, linking with Cyrus, *If you get one, I'll get the other. Hold the demon down, and I'll cut off its head.*

One of the demons attacked Cyrus, while the third blew right past me, heading after Tate and Midnight.

I'm going after him. My gut screamed that this was their end game.

Cyrus growled, *No. Not without me.*

Fine. I wasn't stupid, but I didn't want to waste any more time, either. I spun around to find the demon on top of Cyrus. Its red eyes glowed with so much hatred as its shadowy hands grasped Cyrus's neck. Its whole focus was on my mate as if his presence offended it. It probably did, with him being a descendant of angels and all.

I rushed toward it, and the demon didn't even glance my way. Its intent was to inflict harm. I grabbed the knife and sliced into its neck. The blade went through like butter, and the head rolled off the body onto the ground.

I froze, stunned. Wow. I'd figured these would be weaker demons, but I hadn't thought that would equate to stupid.

Whatever. I'd take the small blessing.

Blue blood poured from its neck, coating Cyrus's beautiful silver coat. Cyrus blinked and tilted his head. *Uh. Thanks...I think.*

If you're going with me, let's go.

"More demon wolves are coming," Indra murmured.

Ugh, I needed to go but didn't want to leave them here unprotected. "Damn it. I thought this was all of them."

"It pretty much is, but twenty more are heading this

way. They informed the last few of Tate's favorites that the new wolves are refusing to fight." Indra chuckled. "They underestimated you."

I patted her arm. "No, they underestimated all of *you*."

Half the pack, stay here with the others while Griffin and I go with Cyrus and Annie, Sterlyn linked. *When you get in a good position, follow our scents and join us.*

Shouldn't we go with you? Chad asked.

I still don't trust that the demon wolves won't convince these other wolves to turn again. Sterlyn appeared beside me. *If they do, it could be a slaughter.*

Yeah, I wasn't certain, either. The demon wolves could be bringing family members or the alpha back out here to torture them. I wouldn't put anything past these guys.

"I'm going, too," Eliza huffed as she caught up to us. "Just...you'll have to move slower for me."

Tell her to get on my back, Cyrus linked.

That wouldn't go over well. "Cyrus wants you to get on his back so he can carry you."

Her lips mashed into a line.

"Fine." I shrugged, trying not to give too much attitude. "You'll have to catch up to us when you can. Tate has Midnight, and he'll kill her if I don't do what he wants." My stomach roiled.

Displeasure flowed from Cyrus. *We can't react.*

I swear I won't. But I have to save my biological mother. I stared into his darkening eyes. *Tate just has to think I'll sacrifice myself.*

You swear? Because Annie, I'll follow you wherever he takes you if you don't keep your word. Cyrus growled low like he was attempting to say the words out loud.

My heart constricted. I would be willing to sacrifice myself for Midnight, but not at the cost of whatever the demons wanted me for so desperately. *Yes. I swear.*

We'll be there to make sure she doesn't. Sterlyn's purple-silver eyes locked on mine, her message clear.

She'd alpha-will me if she had to.

Good. Relief washed over him as he hunkered down. He'd known his sister would do whatever it took to make sure my ass stayed here, too.

"This proves just how much I love you," Eliza grumbled as she hiked up her long skirt and straddled my mate. When Cyrus stood, she towered over me.

Ten more demon wolves charged in, and I counted thirty that were still fighting. The new wolves were no longer fighting against us, but they also weren't helping. I'd take it. With everyone we were leaving behind here, the demon wolves would be eliminated soon, but they were amped up from Tate. If we could kill Tate, that might end the fight faster.

Cyrus, Griffin, Sterlyn, Eliza, and I took off, following the scents of Tate and the demon.

We turned the corner of the last cabin, heading toward the log cabins, and the scent guided us back toward the ominous sensation. We moved at a fast jog, not wanting to get too winded before we arrived. We continued down the pathway that led to the garden where I'd worked with Midnight, Ulta, Indra, and

Minx. The evil sensation had been strongest here last time.

The large wooden privacy fence that surrounded the garden appeared. I wasn't surprised when we jogged past it and deeper into the camp. They'd never let me go this far.

I could hear our steady breathing, the only thing that was grounding me. I was glad I'd listened to Cyrus and waited for them to come with me. My skin crawled as we approached something sinister.

I'd expected to see more homes sprinkled throughout the woods like the rest of the settlement, but about fifty yards from the garden, there weren't any more houses. Instead, we entered the forest, and the evergreens gave way to the normal cypresses and redbuds.

Strange.

Where are we going? Cyrus asked. *Do you remember what was back here?*

There had to be a reason that I hadn't been past this point.

The forest was silent. Not even a breeze stirred. Something was *wrong*, and I had a feeling we were about to find out how Tate had gone to the demon world.

Sterlyn slowed. *I've never felt anything like this before.*

When we walked past a thick oak tree, my skin became raw, as if it were being peeled off. Sterlyn and Cyrus sagged, feeling the same thing.

Griffin jumped in front of his mate, but there was nothing to fight. It was just intense pain.

What is it? I wanted to vomit as sludge seemed to coat my skin.

We kept a steady pace despite the horrible sensation. Sterlyn answered, *Demon magic.*

A large underground cave with a huge, gaping opening came into view. The plants near it were dead, and no grass grew for at least forty yards around it.

The demon hovered in front of it, and he held his hand out, beckoning me.

Did Tate think that would actually work? That I would just run to him without a second thought? "I'll pass."

It laughed, making my skin crawl.

CHAPTER TWENTY-SEVEN

"I TOLD you she'd be difficult," Tate complained as he stepped from the cave. He still had the knife held to Midnight's throat, and he forced her forward.

She stumbled due to the awkward hold he had on her, and the blade nicked her skin. Blood trailed down her neck and onto her black cotton shirt.

Even with demon magic, Tate harming his mate should have gone against his wolf's nature. "She's your *fated mate*. How can you treat her like that?" I demanded.

His body shook with laughter, and the blade cut a little deeper. "Yeah, everyone *thinks* she is."

My throat constricted, and I couldn't swallow. I didn't understand what he meant, but my wolf did. She growled inside my head.

"What?" Midnight's voice hitched. "Why would you say that? You can't lie about our connection to make yourself feel better."

We all knew he couldn't; the air would out him if he didn't.

"We're not fated mates," he snarled. "You only think we are because of a spell Father had a witch cast on us."

The world tilted. If this information affected me like this, I could only imagine how Midnight felt. Her face paled.

The demon cocked its head, watching the show.

Why isn't he rushing us? I linked. The demon should have been desperate to bring me to Hell.

Sterlyn responded, *He's enjoying watching the pain and torture. Demons are patient. They're old, so what feels like a long time to us is nothing to them.*

If we keep Tate talking, the others might get here. I was sure I could drag this out longer. If Tate saw he could hurt us, he'd keep talking, wielding the power he thrived on.

Cyrus's chest heaved. *I don't know. Believe me, there are things we're better off not knowing. I grew up thinking my parents hated me and didn't want me. It was almost worse to hear that they thought I'd died and mourned me every day. It confirmed I'd missed out on the very thing I'd always wanted.*

Maybe he was right, but Tate and the demon were fifty yards away, near an entrance to Hell, with a knife to my biological mother's neck. I didn't have many options. *I know, but I can't lose her. If there's a chance we can save her...I can't live with not trying.*

We've almost defeated them, Darrell linked. *Ronnie, Rosemary, Circe, Aspen, Aurora, and Herne are on their way. They'll be there in a few minutes. We won't be far behind with the vampires and the remaining witches.*

The other wolves must not have fought against us again after all. I'd take that small victory.

Snot trickled from Midnight's nose. "Have you always known?"

"Not at first. I found out the day that Father and I visited Asmodeus, one of the princes of hell, to inform him I was having a daughter." His jaw twitched, and his eyes jerked to me as if he were reliving the memory. "He tried to take credit for it and *my* power."

He was insane. All this time, I'd thought he was a warped and horrible person, but it went beyond that. Something was wrong with him. "How could he try to do that?" My stomach roiled, but I held my voice steady; neither surprise nor disgust wafted through.

Annie, you don't have to do this. We can leave. Cyrus brushed against my leg.

But I had to. *You know leaving isn't an option. Not really.* Fighting him head-on was the best way, and I needed to understand why he had done what he had. Someone wasn't making it out of this alive. *I might regret the knowledge, but I'll regret not knowing just the same.*

Displeasure pulsed from him, but he didn't say another word. He remained beside me, and Sterlyn stepped closer on my other side.

"Because my father was so desperate for power, he gave my mother to a prince of hell in the hope that her living in Hell would influence fate to gift him a girl. As if fate would reward his sacrifice. The demon accepted, and my father went to retrieve my mother. He visited her in Hell regularly to breed."

We can see where this is going. Cyrus stepped closer to me. *And why he has so much rage.*

"But you're a man," I said without thinking. Clearly, we all knew that.

His soulless eyes landed on me. "Yes, my father was an idiot. In his quest for power, he did something stupid, thinking he could manipulate fate his way. When I was born, he brought me back here and searched for a witch who could find me the strongest mate possible and forge the illusion of a fated-mate connection."

"No," Midnight murmured, tears filling her eyes. "That can't be true."

Tears burned my eyes, too. Not only because of how hurt Midnight was but also from seeing how desperately these wolves had wanted a daughter, not to cherish her but to use her.

"Why would he do that?" Eliza asked, her forehead furrowed. "How would that help his situation?"

"He demanded to go with me to tell the demon about Annabelle, saying it was the alpha right." He chuckled humorlessly. "When we told the demon the news, Father informed the prince of lust that he deserved the reward for giving up his mate and forcing a witch to find a female wolf more likely to yield a daughter."

Midnight closed her eyes. "So you killed him?"

"No, though I wish I had." An evil smirk crossed his face. "The first time I saw my mother was when she slit my father's throat. Now, *she* is a woman of strength." His eyes sparkled. "The prince laughed. Fate bows to no one, and the power was rightfully blessed to me. That day changed me. When the prince gave me that power, it overrode the fake-mate bond on my side. When I came back and you still acted the same, I was surprised. I guess the stronger magic opened my eyes while you remained ignorant and bespelled like the woman you are."

If I hadn't been in this godawful situation, I would've vomited. The way he looked so proud of his mother and happy that his father had died was disgusting. "Is all this worth it?" I asked. "Most of the demon wolves are dead. The ones who survived are the young ones, so you'll essentially be alone."

What are you doing? Cyrus asked, bristling beside me. *You'll make him even less rational.*

That was my plan. We had to make him lose control. We'd come here hoping to surprise him, but he'd gained the upper hand. He must have had all these wolves here because he'd known an attack was imminent and that we would likely time it a few days before or after the full moon to have the maximum silver wolf strength.

"Those wolves you fought will become my new pack." Tate grinned. "Then I'll add more to my collection until I can take down your little city. Everyone will bow to me."

Power had made him worse. No wonder Midnight had been desperate for me to get away—he'd lost touch with reality.

"The angel is coming," the demon rasped. "Our time is up."

354   JEN L. GREY

A few seconds later, I heard the sound of her wings.

"Move your ass, or I'll kill her." Tate's jaw clenched as he dug the knife in a little more.

The trickle of blood thickened, and Midnight whimpered. She darted her eyes from side to side, telling me to say no.

She was too damn scared to talk, and I didn't blame her. Any movement could dig the blade in deeper.

I lifted my hands, and Cyrus growled beside me.

What the hell are you doing? He inched in front of me, attempting to block me from moving forward.

Buying us time. I prepared myself for the onslaught of emotions. His anger, frustration, and fear assaulted me through our connection. I pushed it all away, focusing on the plan. "If you want me to come, you have to prove you won't hurt her. Right now, I have no proof you won't kill her anyway."

Sterlyn's silver fur rose as she bared her teeth. *He's going to kill her, especially since she now knows they aren't fated mates. She has to pretend she'll cooperate.*

My lungs worked a little better since Sterlyn was siding with me. I glanced at Eliza, who rubbed her fingers, waiting for the perfect time to cast a spell. Between her, Ronnie, and Rosemary, hopefully, none of us would die.

"Fine." Tate relaxed his grip on the knife. "But I'm not removing it until you enter the cave with the demon."

"We don't have to concede anything to them," the demon murmured. He floated toward me. Everything screamed at me to get the knife, but if I did, Midnight would die.

The demon kicked Cyrus, tossing him back several feet, and grabbed my arms. He started dragging me toward the cave.

His hands chilled me to the bone, but the scary part was that the coldness wasn't unpleasant. The longer I was here, the more comfortable I became with the sensations. That must have been what had happened to my biological mother. Being around evil changes you fundamentally, and since I was part demon, part of me recognized the sensations as natural.

I refused to become one of their pawns like Tate. I linked with Cyrus, *Are you okay?*

No, I'm not, Annie. A snarl came from behind me. *A demon is trying to drag my mate to Hell.*

When he said it like that, it put the situation into a different perspective.

I was at a loss. Rosemary's wingbeats grew louder, and the demon lifted me into the sky, quickening his retreat.

Rosemary and Ronnie are here. Let's move, Sterlyn commanded.

Not sure what to do, I swung my legs like I'd done as a kid while hanging from the monkey bars. My body rocked, which slowed him down, but only marginally.

He hissed as we approached Tate and the entrance to the cave. I hadn't planned for this scenario. I figured I'd have to walk to them, but I should've known that another flying lesson was on the horizon.

356 JEN L. GREY

Why did anything that could fly keep picking my ass up?

Sterlyn's, Cyrus's, and Griffin's paws pounded the dirt as they raced after me. I couldn't see them, but there were three distinct sets of paw steps.

When we reached Tate, I kicked my legs to the right, knocking him in the head. He grunted as he and Midnight tumbled to the ground.

Eliza chanted, *"Fac eum tenaci sua stillabunt!"*

I closed my eyes, waiting for electricity, wind, or whatever she was calling. He was touching me, so if something got him, I'd probably go down, too. That would be better than visiting Hell.

Instead of pain, my hands slipped from his, and I tumbled onto the rocky cave floor. My knees stung, but I gritted my teeth and stood, ready to dodge and run.

"You stupid bitch! You're going into that damn portal," Tate growled. His body slammed into mine. The rocky floor bit into my skin.

Portal.

That was straight out of a story. But I should have known by now that those tales were woven from truth. Everything I'd read about as a child was real.

The demon shoved Tate off me and narrowed his red eyes. He warned, "You will pay for this when we get there."

He lifted me by my arms, digging his cold, shadowy hands into my cuts. I clenched my teeth, refusing to react.

I glanced back at Tate, who had a huge smile on his face as I was dragged deeper into the cave. A flash of silver was the last thing I saw before the light became very dim. My wolf surged forward, adjusting my eyes to the darkness.

A swirling, iridescent portal hung suspended in the air. It was square, unlike all the oval ones I'd seen in movies, but I knew it was a portal.

Holy *shit*. I had to get out of this situation. Not sure what else to do, I jabbed my fingers into the demon's wrists. I'd expected them to feel like air, but my nails scratched something akin to skin.

Inhaling sharply, the demon released his hold. I dropped to my feet and removed the knife at my waist. I'd caught him off guard, and I was pretty sure I wouldn't get free like this a third time. This was my chance.

Snarls from outside the cave indicated there was yet another battle with Tate.

"You're way more of a pain than you need to be," the demon said with a slight accent I couldn't place. "I can't wait until Belphegor gets a hold of you."

Ew. From what I could remember, Belphegor was the prince of sloth. All this trouble didn't seem very sloth-like.

The demon swung an arm toward me. I ducked, feeling his hand fly over my head.

Cyrus's bloodstained silver fur flashed in the corner of my vision. His teeth sank into the demon's arm.

I straightened and watched the demon strike Cyrus with his other arm. Cyrus's head snapped back, and his jaw released its hold. He flew across the cave and slammed against the wall.

Griffin leaped at the demon, who floated upward, and he landed hard on his stomach as the demon moved toward me, blood dripping down his injured arm.

"If you touch her, I'll kill you with my bare hands, scum," Rosemary warned as she appeared inside the cave. Ronnie hovered next to her in her own shadowy form.

"You think you can win?" The demon chuckled. "Just wait." He turned and flew into the portal.

What the hell? I had a bad feeling about this.

Eliza, Circe, Aurora, Aspen, and Herne joined us.

Eliza ran to the portal and examined it. "We should be able to close it before the demon comes back."

Circe ran a hand through her hair. "I've never done portal magic before."

"Neither have I, but I remember reading a spell for it in a grimoire." Eliza closed her eyes and swayed. "The words were *tu signatus in aeternum.*"

Herne agreed. "It won't hurt to try."

Circe waved her hands. "Move back, everyone."

I rushed to Cyrus. *Are you okay?*

I will be. Cyrus shook his head and nudged me with his head. *Let's move.*

Not fighting him, I felt my stomach drop as we headed toward the opening. "I need to check on Midnight."

As if I'd summoned her, Midnight stepped into the cave. She held a hand to her neck, putting pressure on the cut. Sterlyn walked beside her, her purple-silver eyes glowing and blood all over her snout.

"I'm fine, sweetheart," Midnight said, but her body

told a different story. She was slouched over like she was defeated.

"Tate—" I started.

I'm sorry, but I killed him. Sterlyn's remorse was so strong. *I didn't want to, but—*

You had to, I finished for her. We didn't have a choice but to kill. I was selfishly glad that I wasn't the one who'd killed him and that I hadn't had to watch.

As the witches chanted, Alex blurred into the cave. His gaze landed on where Ronnie hovered close to the portal, using their connection to locate her. He asked, "What's going on?"

"The demon went back through the portal, and they're trying to close—" Ronnie cut off as the portal began to flash.

"I really hope that's happening because of their spell," Midnight said.

That made two of us. Just as my lungs began working again, ten demons poured out of the portal, holding very solid knives. Their red eyes latched on to the witches, their intent clear.

"Keep chanting," Eliza commanded as she stepped in front of the others. She held her hands in front of her, palms facing the demons, and yelled, *"Respirare retro!"*

The demons snarled as their bodies were blown back to the portal. They hovered right outside of the opening.

A high-pitched groaning vibrated against the stone wall, and I covered my ears with my hands. The portal shrank, and Eliza walked closer to the demons as if she were trying to push them into the portal.

The wind picked up in the cave, reminding me of a tornado. The portal pulsed as it slowly collapsed.

"Eliza needs help!" I exclaimed as the woman who had raised me swayed.

A demon jerked forward to grab her. When that didn't work, it threw its knife...and the blade lodged in her chest.

I screamed as Eliza's eyes widened. She looked down at the knife protruding from her body but kept chanting with her hands lifted.

"No!" I cried, and ran toward her. I couldn't let her die, not after everything she'd done for me. Ronnie ran toward her, too. We had to make Eliza stop and let Rosemary heal her.

"No! Girls, stay back!" She glanced at us and saw the determination on our faces. "Ronnie could get sucked in with this spell."

The portal condensed and swirled, yet the demons were determined to get out. The surrounding breeze turned into a gale, pulling us toward the portal.

Cyrus and Alex ran after us. My feet slid on the rock as the wind surged and pushed me toward her.

Though Eliza was only ten feet away, it might as well have been miles. She swayed on her feet and yelled, "I love you all."

Then she crumpled to the ground. The wind picked up harder, pressing the demons into the portal...and Eliza along with them.

"*Eliza!*" I couldn't tell which of us had screamed that time. Maybe we all had.

Ronnie reached the portal just as it vanished. She extended her shadowy hand, but all she touched was normal air.

We'd missed her by milliseconds, and there was no way in hell she could survive that wound.

"Mom!" Circe screamed as tears poured down her cheeks. "No!"

I stood there in shock before reality crashed over me. My chest heaved, and I yelled to the witches, "Open it back up!"

"We...we can't," Herne whispered. "The spell we cast was to close the portal forever. We can't undo it." She began to sob.

Ronnie flickered back into view as she ran into Alex's arms. When Cyrus nudged my leg, I fell to my knees and wrapped my arms around him, not caring about the demon blood coating us.

Together, we mourned the loss of the woman we all loved.

THE NEXT WEEK passed in a blur. A numbness washed over me as I stood in the clearing where we trained in our new home—the Shadow Ridge pack neighborhood. Though we weren't combining packs, we'd all become family. We'd decided to stay here and help Killian protect Shadow City with the intent of bringing down the walls as soon as Sterlyn, Griffin, Ronnie, and Alex could make it happen.

Ezra had been removed from his spot on the council and was locked away in Shadow City Prison where he belonged. Sterlyn and Griffin had proved that he'd been responsible for, or part of, almost everything horrific that had happened to her and our allies since the slaughter of her pack, and now that he'd been caught, more and more shifters were stepping forward to speak the truth about his role.

Despite it all, Ezra refused to rat out Azbogah. No one knew why, but his reasons couldn't be good. There were things the angel had moving that we hadn't discovered yet, keeping Rosemary and her parents on edge.

We'd decided to tell the Shadow City council that the demon pack had been eliminated, but no one had mentioned the portal. We'd kept that information from the other vampires and Killian's pack, too, thinking it was best that it remained a secret. Sierra and Killian knew, but no one outside them. If we told the council that a coven of witches had closed a portal, it would raise questions, and Eliza had done everything she could to stay off Erin and her coven's radar, so we'd respect that decision. After all, she'd saved us.

The witches had gone home to mourn the loss of their priestess. We'd exchanged numbers, and we were going to keep in touch. First, though, we all needed time to process everything and mourn our dead.

As for the women and the three demon wolf boys of the demon pack, they went home to their original packs. Now that no one was threatening them, they were able to rejoin their families and loved ones. With the emotional and physical abuse they'd endured, it would take a long time for them to heal. Even in death, the demon wolves had left their mark, but at least the suffering hadn't been forever. The women agreed to meet with me during the next year to discuss their sons' futures. The demon wolves wouldn't die off, and we needed to make sure that from here on out, these children would be raised in a nurturing and loving environment. I was proof that demon wolves could choose their destiny—it didn't have to be what Tate and his family had turned it into.

Mila had left to go home and visit with Jewel and her family. She'd promised it wouldn't be permanent, but she needed space and time with her family. I couldn't blame her. She wanted to heal and finally mourn the love of her life.

As for Dave, he'd helped protect the women as promised and even stayed to clean up the aftermath. With threats no longer hovering over him, Dave had gone back to his family.

The other prisoners we had taken had been relieved that their dictators were dead. They hadn't expected us to take down Ezra, but we'd shown them we could. Now they were safe to return to their families with no more threats to their safety hovering over them.

Cyrus wrapped an arm around my waist and pulled me into his chest. I closed my eyes, enjoying the feel of the sunset on my face and the smell of my mate. It was now late September, and the leaves were turning into the beautiful fall colors the South was known for. He'd been my rock, and I wouldn't be standing here if it weren't for him.

The pinks, oranges, and purples filled the sky, and I inhaled, hoping that a deep breath would keep my tears at bay. *This was her favorite time of day. She said the transition from the sun to moon goddess was magical.*

And she's right. There's only one thing that rivals it, he linked, and looked at my face. *And dare I say, you easily have it beat.*

The corners of my mouth tipped upward despite the tear trailing down my cheek. God, I missed Eliza so much. *I love you.* He made me smile and feel human when I doubted it would ever be possible again.

And I might love you back. He booped my nose, a tender smile on his face.

My heart fluttered. Despite the horrible events, something amazing had happened. In truth, I was shocked he hadn't noticed. *I have something to tell you.*

His brows furrowed as he examined my face. *What's wrong?*

Our friends were behind us, talking and playing around. Killian and Griffin tossed a football back and forth while Alex watched with a puzzled expression. From what I'd gathered, Alex didn't understand how anyone could find that entertaining. Apparently, Alex hadn't played sports like that when he was a child in Shadow City.

Sierra was telling Ronnie and Sterlyn about something that had happened in the Shadow Ridge University coffee shop. She'd been working there to help out a shifter named Carter. She kept talking about some "bitch named Diessy," calling her annoying and undependable, and that was when I'd lost interest.

Nothing is wrong. Just hoping you'd figure something out. I smiled, even though the moment was bittersweet.

Figure what out? He scanned the area like he was expecting a threat to pop out.

I took his hand and placed it on my stomach. *Listen.*

What are you— His eyes bulged. *Wait. Is that...?*

The slight thumping of a second heartbeat was barely audible. I'd heard it this morning and thought I was imagining things.

His face paled, and my throat dried. Maybe he wasn't ready for...

A huge smile spread across his face as he stared at my stomach, and he widened his hand over it. *Are you serious? We're going to be a family? I'm going to be a dad?*

His happiness made my body relax. *You're going to be a dad.* Oh, how I wished Eliza were here to be part of this.

"Oh, gods, Cyrus." Sierra scoffed and placed her hands on her hips. "She doesn't have a food baby. What are you doing?"

But even Sierra didn't faze him. He picked me up and twirled me around. Then he grimaced and placed me gently on my feet. "Did I hurt her?"

"Her?" I was confused. "It's a girl?"

"I sure hope so. I want her to look just like her mother." His silver eyes were the light color he reserved only for me...and our baby. Somehow, that meant even more.

"Wait!" Ronnie shoved Sierra out of the way and ran over to me. "I'm going to be an aunt!"

My eyes burned as Sterlyn walked over more sedately and hugged her brother. Everyone was so happy. Even the guys were grinning.

"Uh...all I'm hearing is 'baby shower!'" Sierra squealed and clapped. "I've never planned one of those! Once Midnight gets here, we're going to plan! I'm thinking the 'what's in the diaper' game, 'how big is her waist' game, and oh, there are *so* many more!"

Rosemary stood there, staring at my stomach, a look of longing on her face. A rare grin peeked through, making the moment even better.

I laughed, embracing the joy coursing from Cyrus to me. Midnight would be here tonight, and I could share the news with her. She'd asked if she could join our pack, and of course, we couldn't say no. She'd wanted to see her parents first, since it had been so long, and they were all going to come down here for a visit. And Midnight would stay.

Despite the loss of Eliza, things were moving in a positive direction. And I couldn't wait to expand our family.

ABOUT THE AUTHOR

Jen L. Grey is a *USA Today* Bestselling Author who writes Paranormal Romance, Urban Fantasy, and Fantasy genres.

Jen lives in Tennessee with her husband, two daughters, and two miniature Australian Shepherds. Before she began writing, she was an avid reader and enjoyed being involved in the indie community. Her love for books eventually led her to writing. For more information, please visit her website and sign up for her newsletter.

Check out my future projects and book signing events at my website.

www.jenlgrey.com

ALSO BY JEN L. GREY

Shadow City: Silver Wolf Trilogy

Broken Mate

Rising Darkness

Silver Moon

Shadow City: Royal Vampire Trilogy

Cursed Mate

Shadow Bitten

Demon Blood

Shadow City: Demon Wolf Trilogy

Ruined Mate

Shattered Curse

Fated Souls

Shadow City: Dark Angel Trilogy

Fallen Mate

Demon Marked

Dark Prince

The Wolf Born Trilogy

Hidden Mate

Blood Secrets

Awakened Magic

The Hidden King Trilogy

Dragon Mate

Dragon Heir

Dragon Queen

The Marked Wolf Trilogy

Moon Kissed

Chosen Wolf

Broken Curse

Wolf Moon Academy Trilogy

Shadow Mate

Blood Legacy

Rising Fate

The Royal Heir Trilogy

Wolves' Queen

Wolf Unleashed

Wolf's Claim

Bloodshed Academy Trilogy

Year One

Year Two

Year Three

The Half-Breed Prison Duology (Same World As Bloodshed Academy)

Hunted

Cursed

The Artifact Reaper Series

Reaper: The Beginning

Reaper of Earth

Reaper of Wings

Reaper of Flames

Reaper of Water

Stones of Amaria (Shared World)

Kingdom of Storms

Kingdom of Shadows

Kingdom of Ruins

Kingdom of Fire

The Pearson Prophecy

Dawning Ascent

Enlightened Ascent

Reigning Ascent

Stand Alones

Death's Angel

Rising Alpha

Made in the USA
Las Vegas, NV
31 July 2022